I0788181

Let
BE ME
Your
Monster

IN TO HER

J A HUSS

INTO HER   HUSS

ABOUT THE BOOK

When AJ and Logan walked into Yvette Nightingale's bar they didn't expect to be there long. They certainly didn't expect to be dancing with her, or having sex with her, or spending the night with her.

Because they were sent there to kill her.
Not fall for her.
Not feel sorry for her.
Not want to take care of her, or protect her, or be in to her.

But sometimes people enter your life for a reason. Sometimes they even enter at the very moment you need them most. And Yvette Nightingale needs AJ and Logan.

She needs them even more than they need her.

CHAPTER ONE

YVETTE

The bell above the door jingles and a rush of wind blows the snow in. Two men come with it.

"Shit." I sigh under my breath. I was just getting ready to close. All the tourists from the nearby ski resort went home early this morning to beat the storm and the bar has been dead since lunch.

Apparently these two didn't get the memo.

"I'm just saying," the tall, rough one with the blond hair says. "It's just a fantasy."

The other one looks right at me and growls, "Would you shut the fuck up?" in a very low, very threatening whisper that makes my stomach clench for some reason.

He's talking to his friend, not me. So I don't know why I have that reaction.

But then again, I know why.

It irritates me though.

They both take a seat at the bar while I glance at my phone so I can pretend I've got some very important text conversation going. I even pretend to type.

Normally I'd be hospitable and welcoming but I'm not feeling very normal today. I've had too much to drink, too much time to think, and I'm tired.

The storm has been brewing just down the mountain for most of the day so I've got no cell service and no internet, but I'm nothing if not a pretender. My lies have been such a part of me for so long, this comes second nature.

I'm also pretty good at improvising.

My bar—the Snowbunny—is the only stop on the western side of the mountain until you get all the way down into Pagosa Springs. In the winter we are super busy Thursday afternoon through Sunday afternoon, especially when the snowpack at Wolf Creek Ski Area is this awesome.

Lots of locals come in during the week too. Plow guys, truckers, local cops, mail people—or mail person, since we only have one up here.

But it's Sunday evening now, the snow has been falling steadily for almost four straight days, and it's supposed to pick up as the final front comes through overnight. Anyone with sense has probably decided enough is enough and gone home.

So I've been bored, just counting down the minutes until I can close, and now I'm annoyed with the two strangers who just walked into my bar and ruined my plans.

At just under twelve thousand feet in elevation, people who live and work up here pretty much do whatever the fuck they want, whenever the fuck they want to do it, and I count myself one of them. That's the perk of living on the top of a mountain in the middle of a dangerous switchback pass.

There's no other reason why anyone would bother with all the inconveniences of living in such an isolated place.

Well, there are two other reasons, really.

One. They are ski bums. They live, breathe, and eat skiing. That's mostly who lives up here in the winter.

But the locals aren't ski bums. We're here for reason number two. We want to be left alone.

These two who just walked in are not locals. I know that for sure because I know everyone around here and they know me.

When I look up at them again they're having a tense, whispered conversation. I decide to move things along and say, "Can I get you something?"

The rough one drags his eyes off his friend to stare at me. His blue eyes are too blue. The kind of blue you see in photographs when someone's gone a little crazy with the Photoshop. The kind of blue that draws you in and makes you speechless. The kind of blue that puts you under a spell so you can't look away—and warns you not to look, all in the same moment.

"What?" I say. Because I don't fall for spells, I don't get lost in the eyes of strange men, and I take looks of warning very seriously.

He smiles and the spell evaporates.

Thought so, motherfucker.

He holds up two fingers in a v-sign and says, "Two Jacks, no ice."

I nod and turn away to grab glasses, put them on the bar, and pour them each two fingers of Jack.

Then I look at the other one—the suit guy—and slide the glasses over to them, keeping my distance. "Thirty bucks."

The suit guy glances up at the chalkboard above my head with the drink prices, then lifts an eyebrow at me. Like… *really?*

But I don't care. If I overcharge them, they'll get their shit together and leave. Get off this damn mountain while they still can and leave me alone.

Blue Eyes pulls a fifty out his wallet and throws it down. "Keep it all," he says, then tucks his wallet into his pants and turns away to whisper at his friend so I can't hear.

Whatever. I grab the fifty, shove it in my apron pocket, and walk around the other side of the bar so I can start stacking chairs on tables, dropping a not-so-subtle hint that they should drink their Jack and get the fuck out.

"We've done it before," I catch Blue Eyes saying. "What's the big deal?"

I glance over as I stack my chairs and find Suit Guy looking right at me. He says, "This is different. This is fucking business." And then, as he continues to stare at me, he downs his drink in one gulp and says, "Another."

I already don't like him and this is starting to piss me off.

But I have found that when people put on a power display like he's doing now, it's much easier to go along amicably. It gives people the opportunity to forget you. To move on. To take that attention you didn't mean to draw and focus it somewhere else.

So I smile. Nod. And walk behind the bar, grab the bottle, and meet his expectations.

"You as well?" I ask Blue Eyes.

He hasn't touched his drink. But he lifts it to his lips now, shoots me a wink, and then downs it like his friend. "Sure," he says, sliding his glass towards me.

I pour and slide it back.

"Just... come on, man," he says, looking at me. "It'll be fun."

And I'm thinking, *What?*

But he's not talking to me. He's talking to Suit Guy. "Not. Tonight," his friend growls.

Again, I get that feeling in my stomach that something is off. Something is happening here and I'm about to miss it.

That will not happen.

I don't miss anything.

So I say, "Listen, guys," in my most fake, most pleasant voice. "I'm about to close up and the snow's coming down pretty good now. You might want to get where you're going while you still can."

"The hours on the door say you close at nine," Suit Guy says.

"Well," I say, trying to keep that fake easiness going, "I've changed my mind about the hours on the door. And since I own this place, I can do that whenever I want."

Blue Eyes ignores this whole confrontation and says, "Come on, Logan. Relax." And then he gets up, walks over to the jukebox, slides in a bill, and starts picking songs.

I force myself to take a deep breath. Because this situation could go bad fast. I'm alone here. There's a blizzard brewing outside. No one is even out on the highway just past my parking lot, because for sure, it's been closed down for the storm by now. You can still travel on it if you have to. But go far enough down the mountain on either side and you're gonna end up at a road block. Which means there's no chance some random trucker will drop by and the locals aren't stupid enough to get stuck in this shit weather, so no one's coming through my door to break this little party up.

I look over at the bar where I have a gun stashed and wonder if I should just overreact and put an end to this now, or take the wait-and-see approach.

But just as I wonder that, *Ladies Love Country Boys* comes blaring through the speakers and Blue Eyes takes off his coat, throws it across a bar stool, and starts shuffling his way across the floor, thumbs hooked in the front pockets of his jeans.

Suit Guy groans loudly.

Logan, I correct myself, recalling his name.

"Come on," Blue Eyes says. "Have a little fun with it."

Is that what they were arguing about? Line dancing?

Logan shakes his head and looks back at his drink.

Blue Eyes says, "How about you?"

I look at him, find him grinning, and realize… he's handsome. And now that I take a moment to really study him, he does have that rough, cowboy look going. Maybe he is local and this other guy is just a visiting friend. He doesn't have a cowboy hat or anything like that. But he's got a barely-there shadow on his angular square jaw, dark-blond scruffy hair, and the body of a man who works for a living. He's wearing faded blue jeans, a tight, long-sleeved white thermal that shows all the muscles it's trying to hide underneath, and well-worn cowboy boots on his feet.

"Take a spin with me?" he asks, shooting me with his fingers and spinning in the middle of the dance floor. "Since my friend here is shy?"

I relax a little.

Dancing. They were arguing about dancing.

I allow myself a smile and decide, *Fuck it. Why not?* and walk out from behind the bar, shuffling my way towards him.

As soon as I'm within arm's reach he grabs my hand and pulls me into a country version of the West Coast swing.

I laugh, unexpectedly, and forget about the warning bells in my stomach. Forget all about my plans for tonight and just… have a little fun for once.

And he's good at this. Like really good at this. He leads me like a pro. Twirling me and spinning me back to him with grace and confidence.

We break apart for a second, shuffling and stepping. I start doing a few of my favorite moves— because I am also one hell of a line dancer. Country night on Fridays has always been my favorite thing about this bar.

So I do something I don't normally do. Especially in the company of strangers.

I let go.

I forget who I am and why I'm here.

I erase my past and live in the present.

I let this man take me away from all that.

And then, just as we're really finding our rhythm and getting into it, he twirls me away from him, lets his fingertips slide past mine, and I bump into the chest of Logan.

I look up at him and find him frowning down at me. He took off his coat too and underneath he's wearing a charcoal-gray suit that matches his dark gray eyes. No cowboy boots on his feet. No shadow on his jaw. No blond hair. He is as different from Blue Eyes as you can get.

How did they become friends? I wonder.

He takes my hand, leading me—just as well as his blue-eyed friend—and takes over.

And just like that we become a trio.

The song ends, but another one begins immediately. And we don't break the beat or stop. They pass me back and forth like we've done this millions of times. Pulling me into their chest, then pushing me away so the other can claim me and do the same.

It's sexy, I realize.

Maybe too sexy.

I find myself thinking about them. Who they are and why there're here. But mostly, I find myself wondering how many times they've done this together? How many girls have they seduced in an empty bar this way? Because some of this feels very *planned.*

"What's your name?" Blue Eyes asks in a low, rough voice just loud enough to be heard over the music.

"Yvette," I say.

He tips an imaginary hat and says, "I'm AJ," he says. "And this is Logan. Pleased to make your acquaintance." But he doesn't have that Southern boy drawl. If anything he comes off like a wolf. A predator. One of those guys who will do unspeakable things to men and unforgettable things to women.

I should put a stop to this. But just as I think that, Logan twirls me into his chest and the song changes, turning slow.

Logan holds me close, one hand firmly gripping mine as he rests it between our shoulders while his arm circles my waist. We dance like that, no space between us, and I hold my breath, waiting for—no, anticipating—what might happen next.

I find out soon enough. Because AJ has come up behind me. He places his hands on my hips. Low on my hips. And then reaches around my body, caressing my lower belly as he bends his knees and grinds against my ass. Slow-dancing with us as his cock becomes hard and lets me know what's really happening here.

I don't want to look up into Logan's eyes. I really don't. Because I know what I'll see there. I know all the silent questions he's gonna ask. And I don't have an answer ready.

But I can't help myself. I can't stop myself from looking. I tilt my head up, find his eyes, see his question, and then…

He kisses me and I give him my answer.

"Yes," I whisper into his mouth. "Yes."

Why not, that inner voice says. *Let's put this day to rest with a bang.*

CHAPTER TWO

We didn't plan this.

It's a moment you can't plan. There's no way to line up all the variables and come out the other end with *this*.

Believe me, we've tried.

I lean my head to the side so I can watch them kiss. Logan's mouth meets hers like he's hungry for her, even though five minutes ago he was the one who wanted to skip the dance.

Logan opens his mouth, and Yvette opens her mouth, whispering something to him. And then I catch a glimpse of tongues touching.

I'm already hard and I don't even bother trying to pretend what's coming next isn't coming.

We've done this before. Couple dozen times probably. But all those times feel different. They never felt like a sure thing and there was always the possibility that wires would get crossed or minds would think twice.

It doesn't feel like that with Yvette.

Everything about tonight feels different. Everything about her *is* different.

She's wearing tight jeans tucked into high boots. The jeans are dark and the boots are brown suede with laces that start at her toes and go all the way up to her knees. Her top is covered by a black apron that has the name Snowbunny embroidered just under her left shoulder.

I have an urge to see her top so I drag my hands around to her hips with fingers splayed so I can touch as much of her as possible, and untie the apron string around her middle.

She sucks in a breath.

Now would the time to stop me. Right now. Before I go any further.

But she just leans into Logan and kisses him harder as he threads his hands into her long, blonde hair and picks it up, exposing her neck and the hidden strap of fabric that's holding her apron on.

I slip it over her head and they break apart just long enough for me to remove the apron and throw it on the floor.

Her light-brown shirt matches her boots. The front is cropped at her waist, embroidered darts that pull the fabric into a tight, slim fit, accentuating how tiny she is. There's a tail of cream-colored lace that falls over her ass like a peekaboo curtain.

I grind my hips into the curve of her ass just above her thighs, but lean my chest back just enough to take in this view.

Logan catches my eye as I do this and he's gone.

There's no stopping him once he gets started. We both know this. So the look in his eyes is defeat, and acceptance, and hunger all in one glance.

Oh, yeah, I think. *This is gonna be fun.*

It's been a while since we tag-teamed a girl. We used to do it a lot back when we worked together more often, but that was before he got promoted.

I've missed him and from what I can tell, he's missed me too. He just hides it better.

A laugh escapes my mouth and I just grin like a man who got lucky while he wasn't looking.

Logan is unbuttoning her shirt. And there is a shit-ton of buttons so it takes forever. But I just watch them as they continue to kiss—their tongues hungry, their lips glistening with each other's saliva—and picture what her mouth will look like when it slides over the tip of his cock.

Finally he opens her shirt and it's my turn. I drag my hands up the curve of her hourglass shape, reach around, and fondle her breasts. Squeezing hard, then easing up, then squeezing hard again.

They stop kissing and Logan takes a step back so he can watch. It's like we've been doing this forever and didn't drift apart over the last couple years. Every move choreographed. Every reaction anticipated.

I grind harder on her, my cock swelling bigger, and bigger. And I'm not gonna pretend that Logan has nothing to do with that. I'm tired of pretending.

So I lean forward again, taking my lips to Yvette's neck, and kiss her while I watch my friend watch me.

She moans, whispers something like, "No, no, no…"

"If you say that," I hiss, "you better mean it. Because we'll walk away right now."

I don't get a reply, but Logan's eyes dart downward, meeting her gaze. And he grins a little, so I guess I don't really need an answer.

I let go of one of her breasts and reach for him. Hook my hand around his neck, and pull him towards her mouth.

He doesn't fight me. Just kisses her passionately.

I lean forward a little more, allowing myself to stand fully erect, and get in on this action.

My lips touch the corner of her mouth and she turns her head to meet me, her tongue swiping over my lip.

And then Logan's mouth touches mine too and this… this is the part that sends me over the edge.

He kisses me and her at the same time.

The best part of fucking girls with your best friend is sharing.

I grip his hair hard, forcing the kiss to become urgent. Yvette's breathing becomes erratic as I continue to grind against the small of her back. She's shorter than me by several inches, but when I look down she's on her tiptoes, the thick, high heels of her boots in the air so she can reach us both.

What must she be thinking?

I don't care.

I've wanted her for a long, long time. Long before we found her up in these mountains two weeks ago. Long before we put this plan together. And I always knew Logan would meet me halfway if we ever got this far.

We've had so much fun together. There's no way, once we started, that he'd pass up this second chance.

And she's the perfect girl too.

One night. *Wham, bam, never gonna see you again, lights out, thank you, ma'am* kinda night.

One night. That's all we get. One night to fuck her brains out together.

And then put it all behind us.

So you can damn well bet I'm not gonna waste a second of this.

I reach for Logan's pants, undo the buckle, then the button, and unzip him. I take her hand off his waist, where it's been passive for too long, and slip it down in his pants. She squeezes him from the inside as I squeeze him from the outside.

"AJ," he cautions me.

"Fuck you," I say. Because I lied. It's too late to say no. For either of them.

This shit is a done deal.

I pull the front of his pants down, giving her more access, and then, without me even telling her, she pulls his cock out and begins to slowly jerk him back and forth.

My attention is on step two now. *Her* pants. There's no way to get those boots off her legs without a major time-out, so fuck that. This chick is getting the half-dressed fuck whether she likes it or not.

The music changes again, this time to a faster, upbeat, country tune, and our bodies respond in kind.

Her cock-jerking becomes more urgent and my desire to get my dick inside her takes over. I walk her backwards, popping the button on her jeans and dragging her zipper down as I go, and stop when I've backed into a table.

Her jeans are tight, so it takes me a good thirty seconds to work them down over her hips to the middle of her thighs.

I'm gonna fuck her on that table. But not yet.

Logan is lagging a few steps behind, coming along because she never let go of his dick.

I know he's having second thoughts. I know he's thinking, *Do I want to do this again? Do I really want to start this shit up again?*

But I just don't care. He will do it. I know how to make him do it.

The palm of my hand finds the top of her head and I push down, urging her to kneel.

She does it, protesting slightly. "I don't know, I don't know…"

But it's too late.

That time has passed. And she must realize this because she looks up at Logan, two-fisting his cock now, and leans forward.

This is one of my favorite moments when Logan and I tag-team. The look on the girl's face when she gives in—or maybe just gives up—and decides she's gonna suck him off. She's gonna turn into my little slut. She's gonna do everything I tell her. She's gonna become my little toy and there's nothing she can do to stop it now.

Logan presses forward like he's on autopilot. And I think to myself, *Do I know this guy, or what?*

I lean to the side a little, not wanting to miss the moment, and catch a glimpse of her just in time. Just as she opens her mouth and places it over him. Over the center of his cock. She lifts her chin, ducking underneath his dick a little, and drags her wet lips down the front of his shaft.

Logan closes his eyes, his jaw clenching. Because she did it perfectly. She did it just the way he likes it.

"Good," I say. "Very nice." Encouraging her with words as I begin to rock her head back and forth, dragging her mouth up and over the tip of his cock, then back down the front of his thick, long shaft.

Her hands have stopped, momentarily forgetting what she was doing. But I help her. I reach for him, wrap my hand over hers, and we jerk him off together. Slowly at first, as she finds the rhythm, and then faster. I step fully to the side now, willing to put my own needs second as we take care of Logan first, and use my other hand to grip her hair tight.

She knows what's coming because she takes a deep breath, opens her mouth wide, and lets me shove him down her throat.

I force her until she gags, but instead of easing up, I whisper, "Shhhh… just relax. Just follow my lead." And because I'm a good guy and I like to help, I start counting. "One," I say. "Two," I say. "Three…" And when I get to five, I yank her off him.

She gasps for breath, choking as saliva drips over her plump, pink lips and lands on her chin.

Logan groans, reaching for her again. And I know that I've won. I know he won't turn back now.

But I'm nothing if not considerate. I'm nothing if not a helper. So I do it again. Only this time I force her to the count of ten.

She almost throws up when I lift her off Logan's cock, but holds it together. Her eyes are watering, her make-up starting to smear down her face.

Logan is almost beside himself. He looks at me like… *Dude…*

Because even though when it comes down to which one of us is the bigger threat here, it's hands-down *him*—I am a force in my own right. In my own way.

So I look at him and just smile as I push her head back down and force her to the count of twelve.

She pulls off this time, gagging and choking, saliva dripping down the front of her chest until it disappears into her bra.

Such a little slut.

But I already knew that before we walked in.

I saw it all in my head. I saw the drinks, I saw the look of fear flash before her eyes, even though it was fleeting. I saw the dance, and the way she joined in. I saw Logan, meeting me halfway. I saw her on her knees. I saw his cock in her mouth. I saw the choking and gagging.

I saw it all.

And I knew she'd be up for this. I *knew*.

Because even though I might be a stranger to Yvette Nightingale…. she's no stranger to me.

I know a lot about this woman.

That's why we're here.

What she knows of us, what she thinks of us, what she feels for us—won't matter in a few hours.

Because she'll be dead.

CHAPTER THREE

LOGAN

AJ and I have been stalking Yvette Nightingale for two weeks under the direct supervision of our boss, Damon Dell'Ariccia. And regardless of how good we are at our job, sometimes it sucks.

Not because we're going to kill her after we're done fucking tonight, but because I hate the fucking mountains.

I get it. Some people like nature. Some people like mountains, and snow, and the great outdoors. I like that shit too. Sometimes. But not here. It took me three days to get past the altitude sickness. Fucking headaches, fucking heavy breathing, fucking dizziness. And that whole time I had binoculars pressed to my face watching from afar. Or I was hiking up the goddamned hillside out back of this bar. Or AJ was making me ski with him like we were on vacation and not out on a hit.

And now this fucking snow.

I don't know how people live up here. It's a goddamned nightmare.

Damon called earlier today and gave us the go—since it's now abundantly clear that this Yvette chick isn't hiding the thing we thought she was hiding, so her usefulness in our little operation is over.

I just wanted to sit outside in the truck, wait for the tourists to go home, and then maybe—*maybe*—have a drink before we pulled the trigger.

And now where am I?

Yvette fucking Nightingale has my cock down her throat.

AJ lets her know that he doesn't like quitters while I'm musing on how we got here.

"Give it another go," he says.

And she does.

Maybe willingly. Maybe not. Maybe she sees the trap she fell blindly into. Dancing. I actually roll my eyes. He hasn't used that one in a long time.

At least I don't think so. This is the first hit we've been on together in almost two years. So who knows, maybe he's the country boogie king of dive mountain bars. I have no clue.

But even if she doesn't yet realize our steel trap just clamped down on her ankle, she's well on her way to scared. I can see it in her eyes as she looks up at him.

Will we rape her?

That's her question.

The answer is no, of course. She's going to agree to all of it. AJ will make sure of that.

"Good," AJ says, when she keeps my cock deep in her throat for the count of fifteen.

Practice makes perfect.

I actually laugh a little at that.

"Bored?" AJ asks.

"No, I'm good," I say.

He leans in, wraps his hand around the back of my neck, pulls me closer to him, and then puts his mouth right up to mine.

I let him. Not because he's the one who calls the shots in this little partnership, just because I want to.

Hey, if this Yvette wants to go out sucking cock, who am I to object? I might as well enjoy the part I have to play.

We're gonna leave here tonight with her body, dump it over the side of a ravine we scouted out last week, and clean up any evidence with the help of my friend Manny—no thanks to Damon. Fucker insisted we didn't need a clean-up team, this was too simple. But I dot all my i's and cross all my t's, so I called up Manny myself and have him on standby anyway.

After that's all done, I'll go back to the real world again.

I can't wait.

But AJ is fun. We've been friends for a long time and this is our last job together because he's next on my hit list.

We're gonna look over the side of that ravine, watch Yvette's body tumble down like a sack of flesh, and then I'm gonna back up, pull out my gun, and shoot him in the back.

Hopefully he pops over the side all by himself, but if not. Whatever. I'll just push him.

It occurs to me that I might be evil.

I kiss AJ harder because I'm gonna miss him. I slip him a little tongue and think about all the good times we've had over the years. All the girls we fucked just like this. All the times we got drunk, and danced, and didn't kill the girl once we were done.

Sometimes we even stayed the night with them. Once we played house for a whole weekend. Woke up and made breakfast, took her shopping, had a nice dinner, and fucked her brains out for another night before we left.

Good times.

But Damon doesn't have the same fond memories as me.

My eyes open and my gaze wanders around the bar. It's got a mountain retreat look to it. Exposed beams running the length of the flat, ten-foot ceiling. Unfinished pine tables and chairs. And a few of those seating areas with strategically placed mismatched furniture you see in city coffeeshops.

I wonder what'll happen to this bar when she's gone?

"Dude." AJ laughs as we continue to kiss.

"What?"

"Come back here, man. Just… stop fucking thinking."

I wonder how he'd act if I was his hit instead of the other way around?

Nah. That's so stupid.

AJ is loyal to a fault. He'd kill Damon before he ever killed me. That's why he has to go. Well, that and the half a million dollars that went missing six months ago.

But he's a true friend, as they say.

"Stand up now, darlin'," AJ says, pulling Yvette up from her knees by her hair.

She's breathing hard, her face is a mess of streaked black mascara, and she's looking all over the room. Anywhere but at AJ or me.

Oh, yeah. She knows. She realizes her mistake.

Been on the run for a very long time. She made it pretty far too. Took Damon years to finally catch up with her. She was good. Careful. Probably suspicious of everyone for good long time.

And yet… tonight… she just falls for AJ.

Why, Yvette?

I'm so curious about that.

Why now? Why him? Why us? Why are you standing here in front of me, half naked, your own spit dripping down your chest because you took my cock deeper than you ever took a cock before?

Why?

I'm gonna ask her, I decide. Get the reason before we off her. I just need to know. Because even though AJ has always been a charmer, he's not any better than me. He's not better looking than me, he's not nicer than me, that's for sure.

So he's loyal?

That's not the reason. She doesn't know he's the kind of guy who'd mow down a whole crowd of people if it was the only way to save a friend's life.

So why, Yvette? Why did you take his hand and dance with him?

You should know better.

Why did you let him do this to you when you've been so very, very careful in the past?

I bet she's wondering the very same thing right about now.

AJ looks at me. "Let's give you something else to think about, OK?"

I smile at him. Because even though AJ hasn't been a good friend to Damon, he *has* been a good friend to me, and thinking about how he's not gonna be around after tonight is a little bit sad.

He turns Yvette slowly. She's wobbly and it's clear she's not OK. "Are you drunk?" I ask her.

But instead of answering, she leans up on her tiptoes and kisses AJ on the mouth.

He grins through it, kissing her back, his hands wandering down to her ass. And when they break apart he says, "Bend over," in that growly, seductive voice he likes to use during sex. "Logan wants you to show him your pussy."

Yvette shoots me a look over her shoulder, grins crookedly and licks her lips.

She is drunk. Totally drunk. How did I miss that earlier?

But she follows directions. Kinda like she's on autopilot. And there's no chance I don't glance down and look at her pussy lips peeking out from the bottom of her ass. It's sexy. Both the way she bends over and the way the waistband of her tight jeans cuts into her thighs as she tries to spread her legs.

I raise my eyebrows. Because while not all girls have a pretty pussy, this one does.

I reach down with my fingers and slide them back and forth across her wet folds.

This makes her moan.

AJ is leaning against a table, fisting her hair as he slowly lowers her mouth down over his cock. "Try a little harder now, OK?" he says, holding her face against his stomach, practically suffocating her.

She struggles, trying to pull back. But I begin playing with her clit to take her mind off the war waging in her throat.

AJ reaches some predetermined threshold and lifts her up off his cock. She comes up gasping for breath. Inhaling deeply.

He likes this part. I remember that much. He likes it when he's got them a little bit scared. Ready to say, *No more*. He wants to hear that, actually. He likes it when they protest.

And then he'll stop, like he is now. And wait. Like he's patient, when he's not. It's all just part of his plan.

"Done?" he asks her.

Which is my cue, I realize. And I almost miss it. My cue to shove my cock in her pussy so she'll want more. So she'll say yes.

He wants to hear a no but the win is when he gets a yes instead.

"Should we stop?" he asks her.

I fully expect her to say yes. Because everything she's doing right now—everything she's allowing us to do—this isn't her. Maybe the her she used to be, but definitely not the her I've seen over the past two weeks, that's for sure.

"Is she drunk?" I ask him.

"Yvette," AJ says, shaking her head a little by her hair. "Give us an answer."

"Keep going," she says. Then dives back down on his cock.

I thrust my dick inside her in that same moment and she squeals. I can only imagine how her vocal cords are vibrating against AJ's thick shaft.

"Fuck her hard," AJ says. "Give her what she wants."

I pull back. Far back. Until her wet, pink pussy flaps are hugging the tip of my cock. And then I thrust forward so hard, AJ's cock slips out of her mouth and her head bangs against his stomach.

AJ grins and laughs. "Yeah," he says. "Do it again."

So I do. Again, and again, and again. And somehow he gets his cock back in her throat. And she's making noises that drive us both wild. And she's trying hard too. Trying hard to do what he's asking.

I reach forward, grab her long, blonde hair, pull her back. AJ's eyes dart up to mine, surprised, but not in a bad way. Because he shakes his head and smiles. Like... *You do you, bro.*

My hand wraps around her neck, my palm flat against her throat, and I lean in to whisper in her ear.

I don't even know what I say. I'm watching AJ jerk himself off, his hand pumping up and down his dick with furious abandon.

I know he's close and so am I. I know this is the last time we'll ever do this together and I want it to be good. I want to keep him happy. So I say... "Join me?"

His loud chuckle startles Yvette because her whole body jerks a little.

But I'm holding her tight now. Her back is pressed up hard against my chest. AJ reaches down behind her knees and he picks her up. Her jeans are in the way, so he can't spread her legs wide. But we know how to get around that.

I grab the back of her calves and hike her knees up to her chest on either side of her ample tits, and her pussy magically becomes accessible for AJ.

He wastes no time. Just slips his cock up to mine. His fingers stretching her open so he can fit. There's a moment when she struggles, like he's puling too hard on her sensitive skin, but my mouth is right up next to her ear and I say, "Shhhh. Just relax and let it happen, Yvette."

It doesn't help much. There's no denying that two cocks inside one pussy is not something that just happens without effort. So there's a lot of, "Shit, oh, shit!" and "Oh my God," as he forces his way inside, sliding along my shaft until I have to pull out just a little so we can both fit.

But we do fit. We knew this. Done it plenty of times before.

Done this exact scenario enough times to understand our limits.

We slow down after that. He wraps his hands under her thighs as I hold her calves, and find our rhythm.

In and out, back and forth. One at a time we do this. We fuck her like pros.

I'm gonna miss him. Really fucking miss him.

His face contorts a little. Eyes closing and I know he's about ready to explode.

Just thinking that gets me there too and a moment later we're filling her with hot, shooting come.

I get lost here. Close my eyes and just enjoy this last day with my friend. Enjoy this girl I had absolutely no intention of fucking when we walked in.

And I decide it's a gift.

One I give him. One he gives me.

And hell, why not. One we both give Yvette Nightingale too.

We're considerate like that.

CHAPTER FOUR

YVETTE

I don't know how I got here.

Well, that's a lie.

I started drinking just past noon so I've got a decent buzz going right now. And it's been months since I lost myself in sexual pleasure with a stranger.

Owning a bar has perks like that. There are always men coming and going. Maybe they didn't find what they were looking for out there on the slopes. So they hang out here on Saturday night to get a second chance at getting laid.

And there I am. Like a little golden goddess. Ready and willing to hand over the bartending duties to someone else and take them upstairs to my apartment and give what they need.

What I need too.

Why not? I never see them again. Not once has one ever come back and tried to have a relationship with me.

Which is just fine. Just the way I like it.

And it takes my mind off things. All the bad things better left forgotten.

I wasn't planning on doing this today, but hey, getting two of them at once like this? Hell, it's like a little bonus.

Having both of them inside me feels incredible. And I'm just about there—just about to let loose and come all over their dicks—when I feel them come first.

"What the hell?" I whisper.

But it's too late. They are moaning and groaning. Grinding into me. Into each other as their hot, sticky semen leaks out of my pussy and coats my ass.

Logan lets go of my calves and they drop forward onto AJ's shoulders. But he pushes them aside and then my boots clank on the floor.

We are officially done.

What the fuck? I didn't get to come?

AJ is sitting on the table looking down at his huge cock as it rests alongside his lower stomach. Laughing.

Did they leave me hanging on purpose?

I look over at Logan, who is already reaching for a napkin on the nearby table. He wipes off his dick like this is just another thing that needs to be taken care of, then tucks himself away, fastens his pants and buckles his belt and says, to AJ, not me, "I'll be right back. I gotta go get something from the truck."

With that said, he grabs his coat, heads for the door, and disappears through it as the bells jingle his exit.

I just turn away, wondering what the hell is happening. I'm not that buzzed. Jesus. What did I just do?

I pull up my pants, leaving them open so I can start buttoning my shirt. Which is a huge task since it's one of those fancy costume-y shirts with a million tiny buttons that go all the way from my cleavage to my waist.

"Come here," AJ says.

I look over my shoulder at him. He's wiping his dick off too. Like I played no part in this little tryst at all. It was just about them.

I turn away, go back to my shirt buttons.

"Hey," he says, hand on my shoulder so he can turn me around. "Let me help you." His fingers swat mine away and he starts buttoning me up. "That was fun."

"Uh… yeah," I say.

How are men so clueless? I mean did they really think stuffing their cocks down my throat and double-teaming me was enough?

Maybe they just don't care?

I slap AJ's hand away from my shirt.

"What?" He laughs.

"You missed one," I say. "You're fucking up my buttons. I don't need your help."

"Someone's unhappy."

"Yeah, well. That happens when expectations aren't met."

"What? What are you talking about?"

"Just… I'm closing. Can you please go so I can lock up?"

He opens his mouth to say something, but in that same moment the bells jingle above the door and Logan appears.

"We have a problem," he says.

AJ turns around and looks at him. "What kind of problem?"

Logan nods his head to the door. "We can't get out of here."

"What? No," I say, shaking my head. Please don't tell me…

I walk over to the door, pull it open, walk through the little vestibule, and pull the outer door open too.

A mound of snow falls in and outside, under the dim parking-lot lights, I see what I feared.

Snow is falling in thick sheets. If you've never seen that, it's hard to imagine. But it's literally so thick, coming down so fast, I can barely see the lamp post at the edge of my property where it meets the highway. Almost a foot of snow blankets the entire parking lot and there's a two-foot drift blowing up against the back of their truck.

"Well, shit." AJ laughs.

"It's not funny," I say. "You two need to leave. I'm closing up. So whatever that takes, shoveling… whatever… just *do it*."

Logan pushes me back away from the door, and closes it up. "Sorry to ruin your night, but we're not going anywhere."

"Oh, for fuck's sake," I mutter. That's what I get for giving into my urges. This is totally what I get. I should've just stuck to the plan. Just made them leave before they sat down. At least they'd be stuck on the highway and not in here with me, fucking up my night.

Logan taps AJ on the shoulder and points to the bar. "We need to talk," he says, disappearing through the door.

I look at AJ, wondering what this is all about. But he just shoots me with his finger and says, "Your lucky day, Yvette," and then follows his friend inside.

Back inside I find them having a heated whisper-fight in the far corner. But I don't care about their problems. I go behind the bar, grab my phone, and pray for service.

"Come on, come on, come on," I mutter, holding my phone up as I walk around the bar and go over to the door. "Please."

I have a local snowplow guy who would not be happy to come out on a night like this and clear my parking lot, but he'll do it for the right price. If I can just get a signal...

"Hey."

I turn around, startled that Logan has walked up right behind me and I didn't notice.

I need to get my shit together. Drowning my sorrows in alcohol this afternoon was not a good idea. This is a serious situation. If I had known these two inconsiderate jerks would be stuck with me all night, I'd have never—

"Who you trying to call?"

And for some reason it comes out like a threat. Like I'm doing something wrong.

Every one of my inhibited instincts fire off like crazy. Red flags, danger warnings, and flashing lights come to mind.

"The snowplow guy," I say. "Maybe I can—"

But he snatches my phone right out of my hand and looks at the screen. "No signal," he says, huffing out some air. As if in relief. "OK. So... we gotta deal."

"We have a...? We don't have a deal."

"No. I mean we *have to* deal. With this situation. Looks like we're spending the night."

I look around. This cannot be happening. It's like the worst morning-after-a-one-night-stand that could ever happen, only upped a million times.

I sigh. Realize there's nothing I can do. They're not going to leave. Even if I could manage to get them out the door and lock up, they're stuck in my parking lot.

"Well," I say, resigned to this fate, "I guess you can sleep on the pool table."

Logan actually guffaws. Loudly. "We know you live upstairs, Yvette. We'll be sleeping up there with you. You're not leaving our sight."

I look at them. First Logan, because he's right in front of me. Then AJ, who is standing on the other side of the room with his eyebrows raised, like he's waiting for me to explode.

"How do you know—"

"It doesn't matter," Logan says. "We just do. So…" He rubs his hands together. Like he's eager for something, and not like he's trying to get warm. "Lead the way. I'm kinda hungry. I've worked up an appetite."

"Hold on," AJ says, walking towards me. "I think I know what you mean."

"What?" I say, confused.

He comes right up next to me, takes the unbuttoned edges of my shirt—because, I realize now, I never finished buttoning it up—and swings me side to side a little. Like he's being playful.

I slap his hands away. "Oh, no, buddy," I say. "Sorry. Show's over. Shit just got real and I'm not—"

"She didn't get off," AJ says, looking at Logan.

"What?" he says, with some confusion.

"She's pissed because we came without her."

"No. Look," I say, pushing AJ away with two firm hands on his chest. He takes a step back, but just a little one. "I'm fine, OK? I'm good. You guys can sleep down here and—"

"No," AJ says, grabbing the edges of my partially buttoned shirt again. "We gotta make things right."

"Really," I say, trying to be firm. "You do not."

But now Logan has come up behind me. "Oh," he says, his tone somewhat softer than it was just a few seconds ago. "Shit. Well."

"Seriously," I start. But Logan is already reaching around my waist to slip his hands in my still-unbuttoned jeans.

"Relax," he says, leaning his face into my neck. "It's the least we can do."

I close my eyes when his fingers slip between the lips of my still slick pussy.

AJ leans in and kisses me on the mouth. And even though every fiber of my being is telling me to put a stop to this—make them stop *right now* before it goes any further...

I can't.

I just can't.

I was so worked up a few minutes ago, so ready for the explosion that never happened, that my body reacts the exact opposite way my mind is telling it to.

I stop talking. I stop protesting. I kiss AJ back. I lean in to Logan's chest to give his fingers better access.

"See," Logan whispers into my ear. "Feels good, doesn't it?"

I don't reply, but my answer is yes.

Which is so fucked up.

So fucked up.

AJ's fingers are busy unbuttoning my shirt. But he gets frustrated halfway through and just—

"No!"

—rips it open.

He laughs into our kiss. "Sorry, but I don't like those buttons." And then he grabs the top edge of my bra and yanks it down, freeing my breasts so he can play with them. "You won't be needing it after today, anyway."

OK. Weird. But…

Well… maybe…

Fine.

I'm in. This wasn't *at all* what I wanted before they came into the bar. And for sure, it's bizarre. Everything about this encounter is fucked up and strange.

But I'm here. And they're here. And we're…

Yeah.

We are doing this.

Again.

So I say, "OK."

And they… holy shit. Everything the last time wasn't, this time *is*.

Logan begins strumming my clit while AJ kisses me softly. So different than the way we just kissed before. So tender, and caring. So attentive. His tongue swirls against mine so slowly, his lips moving just the right way as his hand continues to play with my breast. Only it's not rough and hard.

It's a caress, I realize.

He brushes the pad of his thumb over my nipple, making it become bunched up and hard until it's peaked to maximum height, and chills run through my entire body.

Logan eases my tight jeans over my hips. Slowly, like AJ's kiss. Being careful not to pinch or burn my skin this time. He gets them down to about mid-thigh and stops, his fingers returning to the wetness between my legs.

One finger pushes up inside me. Almost lazily. No urgency now. No desperation or lust.

It's like… it's like we know each other. Which is stupid. But that's how it feels. Like a lover who is familiar with all the sweet spots on my body and knows just what to do to make me feel good.

Not make *himself* feel good.

Me.

Am I hallucinating? What is happening? Did I fall into some half-buzzed dream state where strange men who fucked me hard just a few minutes ago, with only their own desires in mind, are now attentive and thoughtful?

But as soon as that thought materializes in my head, AJ's finger is pushing inside me too.

Two fingers. Two men.

Like last time with their cocks… only better.

Because it is better. There's no way for me to pretend this is anything but good.

"Oh, my God," I say.

Which was exactly what I said last time. But it means something totally different now.

"Like that?" Logan asks.

"Yes," I say, when he and AJ begin to fuck me with their fingers. One pulling out while the other pushes in. A perfect rhythm.

They've done this before. No doubt. And the silly teenager inside me, who almost never makes an appearance these days, feels slightly jealous that I'm not their first.

What the hell is wrong with me?

No time to think more about that, because AJ lowers himself to one knee, spreading the lips of my pussy apart, and begins to lick me while still they fuck me with their fingers.

I look down, because I can't not watch, and place my hands on AJ's head, threading my fingers into his hair.

He looks up at me, tongue still swirling, and grins. His eyes bright and sparkling with mischief.

And I come.

All over their fingers.

AJ pulls his finger out, reaches up and smears my own heat and desire all over my lips.

I lick it hungrily as my body spasms and goes limp.

But the last thing I remember before the climax fully hits me is AJ sticking his finger in Logan's mouth so he can taste me too.

CHAPTER FIVE

I want to fuck her again immediately. And when I look up into Logan's eyes, I see he does too.

He smiles at me, sucking on my finger like it's my cock.

He's never sucked my cock before but I have a feeling about tonight. I have a feeling the three of us are about to do a whole lot of things we've never done.

This snowstorm might be the best thing that ever happened to Logan and me.

Hell, Yvette too, from the looks of it.

She goes completely limp and I take mental notes for later. She's dirty, for sure. She'll let us use her any way we want. But when we're done we give her all the things she never gets. All the attention. All the orgasms. All the sweet, sweet sex she craves and wants so desperately.

Deal, I decide. And then I grin just as Logan stops supporting her body and she slumps to the floor in front of me, a pile of satisfied ecstasy.

I pick her up, place her on the table behind me, and say, "We need to get rid of these boots."

She laughs, lazily. Says nothing. Just watches me as I untie the first one and then begin unlacing them.

"These fuckers are a huge commitment."

I look over my shoulder at Logan and find him staring at us with a frown. "What?" I ask.

He shakes his head but says nothing. Just grabs at his dick, which is hard again, I can't help but notice, and repositions it so it's not so obvious.

"Don't worry," I say, still looking up at him. "We'll do it again. Won't we, Yvette?"

Her eyes are still half mast. Still drowsy. She was drinking earlier. It's very apparent now.

"Logan, get us all a drink, will ya? It's on the house."

He just lets out a long breath of air, like he's got something on his mind. Which, I assume, is the fact that we were supposed to kill this girl, dump her body over a ravine, and be back on our way.

And none of that is happening tonight.

We're stuck here. There is no point in killing her when we can't even leave. That's just bad execution. No pun intended.

"Relax," I say. "We're still good."

He nods, then walks off behind the bar and starts pouring another round of Jack, this time for everyone.

I finish unlacing the first boot and push Yvette back a little so she has to prop herself up with both hands flat on the table behind her. Then I tug off the boot, which, even unlaced, takes some effort. "Jesus," I joke with her. "Who were you expecting today that you had to dress up in these flashy boots? And don't get me started on that top. Your whole outfit is like a costume."

She frowns, which makes her nose wrinkle a little.

"What?" I laugh. Because she's a very cute girl. Not like one of those sophisticated high-society women or anything. Not the model type, either. Just… damn cute. And this costume makes her look like… I dunno. Like she was dressing for a sexy Renaissance fair or something.

"It is kind of a costume, I guess," she finally says, once I'm unlacing her second boot.

"Yeah? What part were you playing?"

"Sad girl with nothing to live for. But she wants to look sexy when she dies." And then she laughs.

But I don't. I just stop what I'm doing and look at her for a second. "What?" I say.

Logan appears with the drinks, distracting her away from my question. She takes one, he sets the other down on the table next to me, and then retreats back to the bar to get his.

By the time I look back at Yvette, her grin is gone. She downs her drink in one gulp, then calls out to Logan, "Hell, just bring the bottle."

But her comment—*wants to look sexy when she dies*—what the fuck was that? Does she know who we are? Why we're here?

The lights flicker. Three or four times, but don't go out.

"Shit," Yvette says. Then she sighs. "This day, man. I fucking hate this day." All her words run together and some of her vowels are missing.

I don't know how things just went from sexy-great weird to dark-bizarre weird, but they did.

"The power will go out," she tries to explain. "They flicker like that during a storm. Then… *poof!*" She laughs.

"Hmm," I say.

"Another?" Logan asks, already tipping the bottle of Jack to her glass.

"Fuck yeah," she slurs. She downs that in one gulp too.

"So the power," Logan says, refilling her glass again, picking up on our conversation. "You got a generator or a wood stove or something?"

Leave it to him to be practical.

"I do have a generator. But it's in the building out back." She looks over her shoulder to what I can only assume is where the back door is hiding behind hallways and walls, then says, with some difficulty, "But I've never run it. I don't even know how to turn it on. I have a wood stove upstairs too. We can just use that."

The lights flicker again.

"Fuck that," Logan says. "If we're gonna be stuck here for the night, we're gonna do it in style. AJ can start the generator. He's handy like that. Right, Aje?"

Aje. Damn. He hasn't called me that in years. Not since we first met. Before all this life-of-crime bullshit changed us into these two guys we are now.

I grin at him just as I start tugging on Yvette's second boot.

Why was I so insistent on getting her boots off again?

Oh, yeah. Sex. Her tits are still popping out over the underwire of her bra, her shirt ripped open, her pants halfway down her thighs.

The whole thing is something out of a bad Seventies porn flick.

I stand up, pull Yvette to her feet—which she does reluctantly—twirl her around so she's in my lap, and say, "Take her pants off, Logan. I want her naked."

He grabs her pants at the ankles and pulls. Would've been a smooth move if he got them off in one swoop, but he doesn't. They're skinny jeans. So he chuckles a little and then goes about working them over her ankles, finishing big as he tosses her pants over his shoulder.

We just stare at her.

She's oblivious. Too busy pouring herself another drink, because somehow she has downed that last one too.

"Anyone else think this has gotten weird?" I ask.

Logan huffs some air.

Yvette says, "Who cares?" and tips the glass back to down it in one go.

But I grab it from her hand before she gets more than a sip. "How about we take it easy on the Jack, huh?"

She looks at Logan to see if he agrees. "Whatever," he says, noncommittal.

"OK, geniuses," Yvette says. "How am I supposed to show AJ the generator if I have no pants on?"

I look at Logan and shrug. "Lights aren't out yet."

He grins back. "How about we take a break and get something in Yvette's stomach first?"

"Kitchen's closed," she slurs. "I'm not opening it up. It's closed for good."

"Huh?" I ask. "Are you… going out of business or something?"

"You could say that."

Logan looks at her and frowns. Then he says, "Let's go upstairs, shall we?"

I take her hand and pull her to her feet, but she wobbles. So Logan positions himself on one side of her, and I get on the other, and together lead her over to the doorway she points to.

"Up there," she says.

It takes more effort than I figured to get her up the steps. And once inside the apartment, she doesn't even flip the lights on, just stumbles forward into the darkness and collapses onto a couch, sighing. "I figured this day would be boring and uneventful until midnight. But I was wrong."

"What the hell is she talking about? I ask.

"No clue," Logan says, finding a light switch. The room illuminates with a soft glow from a single lamp in the far corner. "But listen. Yvette," he says, redirecting his words to her. "You relax here on the couch while Aje and I have a little private chat."

She mumbles something I don't catch and turns her back to us.

What a wreck this chick is. Tits hanging out of her bra, no pants on, and her underwear is riding up her ass crack.

Which I sorta like, so I'm not complaining.

"Come here," Logan says, directing me to the hallway that leads to the bedroom.

I follow him to the end of the hall and say, "What's up?"

"Well… this isn't exactly going as planned."

"No shit."

"So we're in agreement?"

"About what?"

"Fucking her until the snow stops."

I smile. Because he left something out. "You mean fucking *each other* until the snow stops? Because she's wasted."

Logan stares at me for a long second. "Do you think—"

But before he can finish the lights flicker three times… and go out.

CHAPTER SIX

LOGAN

"Shit," AJ and I both say at the same time.

It is dark as fuck up here without lights. Especially in the hallway. But there's just enough light from the glow of snow through a window for us to make our way back to the living room without much issue.

"Yvette," I say, walking over to the couch. "Do you have flashlights?"

"Of course she has flashlights," AJ says. "Mountain people with generators have all kinds of cool end-of-the-world shit like that."

He turns towards the kitchen, feeling around the countertops until he finds drawers to search.

Yvette is asleep. She doesn't even move.

If the roads were clear and we weren't stuck here, now would be the perfect time to just stuff a pillow over her face and get the job done.

But it would be very stupid for us to kill her and then be stuck here with her decaying body. Risky as well.

People must care about her up here. From what I can gather she's been running this bar for a couple years. Long enough for people to know her. Long enough for her to make friends. So there's also a chance that some nosey, well-intentioned, trigger-happy local will drive a tractor, or a snowcat—or a fucking sleigh pulled by moose, for all I know—over here to make sure she's OK.

Yvette Nightingale isn't her real name.

Her real name is Glori Dell'Ariccia.

Yes. Related. She's Damon's runaway wife.

Which he wouldn't care so much about except she took something very valuable with her when she left and he wants it back.

The problem is… she no longer has that something. Since we started watching her two weeks ago there has been no evidence that she even knows where that something is.

This is why Damon's done with her and wants her dead.

"Found some," AJ calls from the kitchen. He comes back into the living room shining a powerful beam of light and says, "Catch."

Fucking flashlight almost hits me in the head, but I snatch it out of the air just in time.

He shines his light in my face and says, "Just keepin' you on your toes."

"Fuck you," I mutter, turning the flashlight on, then say, "Go find that generator. I'm not in the mood to be stuck here all night in the freezing-ass cold with no heat."

AJ pans the beam of light around the room and stops on the fireplace, which is really a massive stone hearth with a wood stove sitting inside a wide stone alcove with a pipe reaching up through the chimney. "There's that," he says, panning the light over to a stack of wood and thin branches. "Have at it. I'm guessing this generator is gonna take a while to get started. That's if she even has fuel to run it."

This was not how I was planning on spending my Sunday evening. I was hoping to be back in Durango before midnight and on the jet back to the city by daybreak tomorrow. And it's already too cold up here. There's no way I'm gonna huddle to stay warm and wait for a goddamned rescue.

"Fine," I say. "I'll start a fire. But you need to get that generator started."

"I'll do my best," AJ says, walking over to the still-open door and disappearing through it. His boots clomp on the stairs and then a few seconds later I hear a door slam.

I go over to the wood, and start stacking kindling inside the stove. There's a little wire basket off to the side filled with long kitchen matches and bits of wood shavings. Not the kind of shavings you buy for rodent pets, but the kind you whittle off a stick with a knife.

Fucking rustic. I hate everything about it.

But it's a good thing it's here because making a fire is extremely simple. And a few minutes later I'm stacking logs and heat is pouring out in waves.

I crouch in front of the stove for a few minutes, letting it warm me up, then stand up, flash my light around the room, and take it in.

It's a cozy place, that's for sure. Small. Just one big open room with a kitchen on the far end and a makeshift dining area. But the ceilings have impressive wood beams. Not simple beams either, but trusses. Specifically, hammer beam trusses.

I'm impressed with myself for knowing this, but Damon built a house several years back and used this design. And this one isn't even angular—like his was—but arched.

Custom, I decide.

And then I remember that they fought over this exact design element in the new house just before she took off.

Looks like she got her way after all.

The floors are wide-planked pine and look old and worn. There's a large sheepskin rug that covers almost the entire living area and once I take a closer look, I decide the couch is very pale yellow velvet.

Oh, man. If Damon saw this he'd lose his mind. This whole time she's been gone he's made a big deal about how she left with no money. How she was broke, living in some hovel. How she was probably starving. Probably waitressing to make ends meet because she had no skills or education. Hell, she never even finished high school.

He wasn't that far off. She's a bartender, not a waitress. And she owns this place, so not starving. But she is most definitely not living in a hovel and she is decidedly not broke.

The kitchen is modern and looks brand new. Dark soapstone countertops, rustic pine cabinets that climb too far up the wall to be practical, large stainless-steel farm sink, and matching appliances.

Oh, he'd be livid if he saw this.

Maybe I should burn the place down when I leave? So he never has to see it?

I turn back to the living area and look at her. Glori. Yvette. Whatever she's called.

"Yvette?" I say.

No response. Not even a mumble or a slight change in position. She's out.

So I wander back down the hallway to the bedroom. There's only one and it's massive. Almost as big as the entire living area.

In it is an equally massive canopy bed. I pan my flashlight over the top to get a better look because— fuck me—that shit has to be custom too. This is not the cheap white-frame canopy of a little girl's bedroom. It's got the same matching wood as the trusses in the living room. And the ceiling treatment continues in here, but they're not trusses, just long, thick beams that span the width of the room.

There's fabric hanging from the bed frame. And I can't help myself, I reach out and touch it. Because it's the same soft, pale yellow velvet as the couch. And there's another room-sized sheepskin rug underfoot.

Jesus. This whole place is custom.

Oh, yeah. Damon cannot see this.

This apartment is not just cozy and quaint. It's fucking luxurious.

Where did she get this kind of money? I mean, OK. I could *maybe* see her scraping enough cash together to buy the bar. It's not quite a dive, but on the outside it looks like any other hundred-year-old rectangle building you see on the side of a secluded mountain highway.

So maybe—I dunno—she stole the money somehow? Maybe from Damon and he didn't know it? I could come to terms with that.

But none of it makes much sense.

We've watched the bar long enough to know she does a good business on the weekends. But it opens late and closes early Monday through Wednesday because the place is mostly dead. There's no way four days of ski tourists a week can fund these kind of improvements. And how does she make money in the summer when the lifts are closed? There just cannot be that many people traveling along the highway through Wolf Creek Pass to fund this type of lifestyle.

"You have secrets," I say out loud. "And I want to know what they are."

Not that I'd ever tell Damon. And not because I want to spare his feelings and make him feel good. I give no fucks about Damon. He's a means to an end just like every other person I've ever met in my life.

I just like to know shit.

So I walk over to the bedside table—rustic pine, just like the floors—and pull open the top drawer. And what do I immediately find but a whole slew of sex toys?

Bright pink vibrator. Longer, thicker teal-green one too. A clit pump—which makes me smile because I've never actually used one but have always wanted to. Maybe Yvette will wake up and I'll get my chance? There's also anal beads… who is putting those inside her? And—I have to stop and laugh—a bottle of deep throat-numbing spray and an oral sex essentials kit.

Yvette, you are a kinky little miracle.

No wonder Damon was pissed when you took off.

I didn't know Yvette before she left. I knew *of* her, but I was just one face among many back then. Just a guy who did stupid tasks like collect money and beat the shit out of people who didn't pay.

I still beat the shit out of people sometimes, but AJ mostly does that now. I still collect money too, but at the organizational level, not the street level. AJ runs those guys too. I clean the money now.

But Aje and I have been with Damon since we were all kids. Back when Damon's father ran shit. Yvette—Glori—was Damon's girl once he started moving up in the org. She was still in high school and I always wondered what he saw in her. So fucking young, ya know?

She was pretty enough, for sure. I saw pictures of her. Damon kept one in his office of the two of them and I can recall many times sitting in the chair in front of his desk, listening to him berate some no-good worker about whatever bullshit he was pissed off about, and staring at their picture as I came up with a plan on how to kill said no-good worker in front of Damon so there'd be minimal mess afterward.

It was typically choking. Sometimes with my bare hands, other times with a garrote wire, but usually bare hands.

I even went to their wedding. AJ didn't. None of the street killers were invited. It was classy like that and classy isn't a word I'd ever use to describe AJ.

I didn't mingle at the wedding because I was working, so I never actually got introduced to Yvette-slash-Glori. I was busy with security.

So I guess that's why he sent AJ and me. We worked together in the past. We did our jobs. And I suppose this job was just too personal to trust some other team to take care of it.

Which I understand and that's why I said yes. Besides, once I knew I'd be offing AJ as well, I wanted to spend a little goodbye time with him.

And that's working out pretty well.

I like AJ. Have always liked AJ. He's a very sexual man. And we've done lots of sexual shit together. I missed him, maybe.

So am I sad that I have to kill him before I go home?

Sure. A little bit. Maybe not sad, though. Maybe just… disappointed.

But I'm not loyal to anyone but myself. I learned that lesson the hard way when I was a kid. You can't count on anyone to save your ass. Ever.

My motto is every man for himself.

Besides, that money did go missing on AJ's watch. I got heat for that too because AJ and I are both responsible for the money on the highest level.

So fuck it. Damon told me to kill him and I'm gonna see it through. I'm not done using Damon just yet so I follow orders. It's just that simple.

Besides, it's just business. And if AJ had been told to kill me, instead of the other way around, he'd probably do it too.

Gotta survive, ya know?

Except… he's not really that kinda guy. We have a lot in common—we like to fuck, sometimes together, we both work for Damon, and we've both killed our share of people.

But we're different in lots of ways too.

I close the kink drawer back up and visualize all the ways I can make use of it before this job ends, then walk around the other side of the bed to open the other bedside table drawer.

This one has a book.

No, I decide, picking it up. A journal.

Nice find, Logan.

I open it up and shine a light on the first page.

My True Confession, it says.

Jackpot.

I turn the page and start reading, then stop. Because there's a single piece of paper stuffed into the middle of the book. I open to that page and I'm just about to pull it out and see what it is when I hear a muffled laugh.

"AJ?" I say, closing the journal and dropping it back into the drawer. "That you?"

Better not be. Because the fucking lights are still off.

"AJ?" I say, walking out of the bedroom and entering the living room.

Nothing.

I shine the light on the couch and find it empty.

"Shit. Yvette?" I call, louder now. No answer. "Yvette!"

I shine my flashlight all around the room and catch a glimpse of movement outside a large sliding door.

"Yvette!" I call again. Because she's outside on the terrace in this freezing-ass blizzard in her fucking underwear.

I jog over to the door, pull it wide open and say, "What the fuck are you doing?"

She's got her back to me, her skin already bright pink from the cold. How long has she been out here?

"What the hell?" I say. "Get back inside. You'll freeze to death."

Which is stupid, I realize. Because she's not gonna live long anyway.

Maybe I should just let her stay out here? Fall asleep drunk and freeze to death?

That would be a nice way to go. Both for her and for me. No mess. No questions. No body disposal. I think I might do that—for both my targets, actually.

But then she drops something over the side of the railing and leans over—far over—to look at it.

I walk up behind her and look over too. "What was that?"

I can't see, even when I shine my light down, because whatever it was, it's disappeared into a tall snow drift.

"My end," she says.

"What?" I laugh. What the hell is she talking about? "Come on," I say, grabbing her shoulders and turning her around. Her fucking tits are still hanging out of her bra. *What is your deal, chick?* She cannot be that drunk.

"Let's go back inside," I say.

Because we still have a drawer filled with kink to explore before I let you die of hypothermia.

CHAPTER SEVEN

The building out back is massive and this chick is full of surprises.

Inside Yvette has a beat-up old Corolla, a beat-up old Jeep, a snowcat, a tractor, an empty chicken coop, two horse stalls—also empty—and a gym.

It's a pretty nice gym, and even though there's no power and it's about ten degrees inside this place, for a moment I consider taking a turn on the bag hanging from the ceiling.

Generator, I remind the squirrel inside me. *Gotta find the generator.*

It's in a little room in the front of the building with a big window looking out at the house. There's also a fully-stocked workshop. I'm talking shit I'd have in my outbuilding workshop if I ever manage to acquire an outbuilding workshop. There's even a floor lift for a car.

I just shake my head.

But then I wonder… does she have a boyfriend?

We didn't see a boyfriend since we've been watching her. But that doesn't mean much. He could be in the military. Or one of those oil rig workers who live on rigs in the ocean. Or a scientist down in Antarctica.

But none of that is likely.

So what is the deal with this place? It doesn't make sense.

She doesn't make sense either.

I get who she is to Damon and why he wants her dead. She ran away and took something valuable. So this secret mission to get rid of her makes some sense. But not a lot.

I didn't know Yvette before Logan and I got this job. Never even met her. I just know Damon married her while she was in high school.

Which is pretty weird, but then again, not so weird when you're in a crime family, I guess.

Still, I don't get it. Why not just leave her alone? So she took something. Maybe money, maybe information, a car? I dunno what she took. Logan's in charge of the recovery mission.

The only way this makes sense is that Damon's a jealous asshole. He's one of those guys who figures, *If I can't have her, no one can.* Because the dude's got plenty of dirty money. She can't know too much about his business or he'd already be in jail. She's been gone for almost three years, so even if she did know too much, she's not sharing that with anyone. And no one loves a beat-up old Corolla or a beat-up old Jeep that much, right?

"Not your job, AJ. So who gives a fuck?"

On to the generator. She says she's never turned it on but that makes no sense either. Surely this place loses power enough that she'd want to do that. And it's one of those generators that has a fucking switch, for Christ's sake. There is no rolling a dolly out and hooking it up to the electrical box. It's a massive, whole-house generator, firmly affixed to a concrete pad, that requires two seconds to turn on.

And she has fuel. Not only is there fuel *in it*, but bright-blue barrels of diesel sit off to the side. Like whoever set this up was preparing for Armageddon.

So again, I have to ask myself, who is this chick and why is she so important?

Damon has known where she's been. I don't know how long he's known, but we didn't have to go hunt her down. Dude gave us an address. Said, "Go watch her." Which we did. And then yesterday he calls up, Logan gives him a report, and then he says, "End it."

So we are.

But I'm starting to maybe not like this idea so much. Too many weird things not adding up now that I've seen this building.

This is not her place, I decide. This is an outbuilding a man owns. And there is no man here now and no man returning, of that I'm certain.

I shine my flashlight on the generator, find the switch, and I'm just about to turn it on when I hear a laugh outside.

Turning my head to the large window overlooking the house, I see Yvette standing out on the terrace in the thick falling snow, wearing only her underwear.

Her tits are still hanging out of her bra and it's clear she's cold, because her whole body is bright pink.

I walk over to the window, about to tap it and see if I can get her attention, when Logan comes out behind her. He says something and then… she drops something into the snow.

It disappears into a snow drift. But I don't look at that for more than a moment. Because Logan is turning her around and leading her back inside.

What the hell is going on in there?

I go back to the generator, flip the switch, wait for the machinery to come to life, and then the lights go on outside.

Satisfied I've done my job, I feel an urgency to get back inside. So I leave the building and I'm retracing my steps in the snow—which are already refilling, it's coming down so hard—and I'm just about to pull the back door open when I see the place under the terrace where the object she dropped disappeared.

I force my way through the high snow drift and stick my already freezing-cold fingers down into the snow until I grab something and pull it out.

It's a pill bottle.

The label is a little bit smeared from the snow, but when I open the cap, sure enough, there's pills in there. Big ones, too.

I shove it in my coat pocket, make my way back to the door, and go inside, stomping my feet off on the mat.

Music is playing in the bar, the jukebox still bellowing out the songs I picked from earlier. But I ignore all that and just go back upstairs.

So here's the next odd thing I notice when I pull open the apartment door. Something I didn't really notice when we dragged her ass up the steps twenty minutes ago.

This place is the opposite of that shop down there.

So apparently feminine, it's clear that regardless of how that shop looks, no man lives here with her.

What the fuck?

"Good job," Logan says.

"Thanks," I say, taking off my coat and hanging it on a chair. "What the fuck was she doing outside? I saw her on the terrace."

Yvette is sitting on the couch with a throw blanket wrapped around her shoulders, shivering like crazy. She's got her head tilted back against the cushions and her eyes are closed.

"I have no clue, man. She just walked out there."

"Where the fuck were you?"

"Checking the place out."

I nod. "She dropped something out in the snow."

"I know. I saw it."

I reach into my pocket and pull out the bottle of pills. "She dropped this."

"What is it?" Logan asks, walking over to me. He takes the bottle from my hands, swipes the melted snow off it, and squints at the label. "Fentanyl," he says.

"What the fuck is she doing with fentanyl?"

"How should I know?"

I snatch the bottle back and try to read the label. See who the prescription was written for. But the name isn't legible. "Yvette," I say, walking over to her. "Are these yours?"

She inhales deeply, then opens her eyes and stares at the bottle in my hand. She laughs, closes her eyes again, and shakes her head.

"Whatever," Logan says. "Doesn't matter. What matters is that the power's back on. I'm hungry. You hungry, Aje?"

"Sure," I say. But I'm not convinced it doesn't matter. "That building out there is weird."

"Weird how?" Logan asks, opening and closing drawers and cupboards in the kitchen.

"It's got a lot of shit in there. There's a snowcat," I say.

He stops his drawer-banging to look at me. Raises an eyebrow. "That right?"

I nod.

"So we're not stuck here."

"What do you think we're gonna do?" I laugh "Ride that fucker all the way into Durango?"

He shoots me a look that says, *Don't be an idiot.* "It's just good to know we're not really stuck."

"Sure," I say. But everything about this job is suddenly feeling way off. It seemed so simple. Just come in after all the tourists left, kill her, dump her body over the ravine, and then head out.

That plan is decidedly off the rails now. I don't care how much diesel is in those barrels, that snowcat can only hold so much. It's probably not even enough to get us to the ski resort. And what good is that anyway? Our rental truck is sitting in her goddamned parking lot. We didn't use our real names, but for sure, that's a loose end we can't afford to leave hanging.

Also… Logan is being weird. I don't know how to describe it exactly, I just feel it.

The sex was good. He felt normal then. But ever since he got off the phone with Damon this morning he's been different. I just can't place my finger on it.

"She's got a whole drawer filled with sex toys in there," Logan says, nodding his head down the hallway.

It's my turn to raise my eyebrow.

"So why don't you go get those and we can figure out what to do with them?"

My cock jumps a little at the suggestion. Because this is normal Logan.

No, we haven't spent a lot of time together lately. But all the times in the past have come with lots of good sex.

I forget about my burgeoning conspiracy theory and go into the bedroom to check it out. "Where?" I call.

"Bedside table," Logan calls back.

I like her place, I decide. Not that it matters. But it's sorta romantic, I guess. Lots of texture. Velvet and sheepskin. Like the outfit she was wearing earlier, the bedroom feels dressed up for something.

Her bed is made. That's the first thing I notice. She's got a ton of decorative pillows near the headboard, artfully arranged in a pattern of fuzzy cream-colored fur, vintage-looking cotton, and of course... velvet. Only the velvet isn't yellow like her couch or the hanging drapes that surround the frame of her bed. It's dark gray.

I've never really understood the purpose of pillows like that. Every woman I've ever known just throws them on the floor when they go to sleep. So what's the point?

Just decorations.

I go over to the closest bedside table and pull the drawer open.

"Oh, fuck yeah." I pick up the huge teal-green vibrator and fist it in my palm. It's thick, and long, and has a bulbous head. Then I pick up the other one. Pink, this time. Smaller and more slender than the teal one. I turn them both on and try out the different speeds.

"What the fuck are you doing?"

I turn around and hold up both the toys to Logan. "Quality," I say. "Is she awake? Because I want to use these on her right now."

He shrugs. "She's sitting up. But her eyes are still closed. Did you see the other stuff?" He gives me a crooked smile so I drop the vibrators down on the bed and reach for the clear plastic zipper bag that says Oral Sex Essentials kit, but I drop it just as quick and pick up a cock sleeve with nubby ridges down the length of it. I wiggle it at Logan. "No wonder she's so hot for us. She dates little guys."

Logan smirks, but slaps it away from his face and picks up a clear plastic box with a set of couples toys. "I didn't see this earlier." He opens the box and take out the cock ring. "I'm definitely gonna try it," he says, switching on the attached bullet vibrator. "And look, it's got a toy for her too."

"And a remote," I say, lifting up the little control mechanism. "Oh, we could have some fun with this, for sure."

"Oh, shit, what's this?" He lifts out another toy and holds it up.

I snatch it away and nod my head, smiling. "Oh, yeah. I've used one of these before. Goes around your cock and this part," I say, pointing to the thick end, "vibrates along your balls so you can tickle her ass while you fuck her."

"What are you doing?"

We both turn and find Yvette standing in the doorway naked, her bra and panties discarded while we've been in here snooping.

"Making plans for tonight," Logan says.

She leans her lithe, toned body against the doorjamb seductively. Her hair is a little bit wet from being outside in the snow, just enough to make her look like she just got out of the shower. And even though I have a ton of questions for her about that little trip out onto the terrace, I can't stop looking at her fucking tits.

They are so erect, her nipples practically point to the ceiling. And they are round and firm. So beautiful, in fact, for a moment I wonder if they're fake.

But they're not. I fondled them enough earlier to know.

"Come over and find out," I add to Logan's weak invitation. "We'd like to take all your dirty little toys for a spin."

"What makes you think I want you to?"

"Well, you are standing in the doorway naked. So… you know. We might be men, Yvette, but we're not dumb."

She just stares at Logan with furrowed eyebrows. I laugh a little because he's so serious. And he never was good at the whole foreplay stuff. That was always me. So I decide to take over now. "You got a favorite?" I ask her. "Come show me."

She turns her head to the side and lowers her chin, somehow looking uninterested and totally interested in the same moment. "I'm not really up to teaching you how to pleasure me with toys," she finally whispers.

Right. She's still drunk. And the pills. Did she take any?

Nah, I decide. I'm not into drugs but I got plenty of friends who are. And I know what fentanyl does. Even in small doses. If she took just one of those, especially with alcohol, she would not be able to walk.

"Who says we need lessons?" Logan asks.

She huffs out a very small laugh. "Oooooo, what's this?" she says, mimicking Logan. "It's a cock ring, boys. The latest Swedish version."

"Yeah?" I say. "You got some kind of sexy toy fetish?"

"What do you think?"

"I think that's a yes." Logan laughs, picking up the two vibrators off the bed. "So come on. Let's do this."

I roll my eyes. *Let's do this? Come on, dude. Up your game a little. I get it, she's buzzed and willing, but a little game goes a long way.*

So I walk over to her, unbuckling my pants with one hand as I hold the new and improved vibrating cock ring in the other, and by the time I stand in front of her, looking down as she looks up, I'm jerking off.

She glances down, then back up at me, does that little head-tilt look-away thing that I'm starting to like, and says, "So put it on." But then she smiles. "Better yet," she says, nodding at Logan, "you put it on him."

Oh, hell yeah.

"Yeah, Logan. Come over here and show us your mad sex toy skills."

CHAPTER EIGHT

YVETTE

My head is foggy, my legs are shaky, and I just had a really amazing orgasm about an hour ago. But fuck it. These men are my gift and I'm going to spend every last hour of this day doing whatever the hell I want.

The sex toys used to be a joke. Back when jokes were a thing in my world. They were fun back when I was happy. And I've used them a little in the time since they stopped being a joke. A few times, with a few random men. But nothing serious.

But there is an inevitable conclusion coming at the end of this night. One that can't be stopped. And I've got several thousand dollars in sex toys in that drawer that have mostly been ignored.

So… why not?

I'm still drunk enough that I don't have the energy to think too hard about this. And hell, these two men are big, and muscular, and sexy. And it doesn't hurt that they both have huge cocks.

I do one of those come-here motions with my finger as I look at Logan. I get these two now. AJ is the muscle but he's also the charmer. He's one of those upbeat guys even when he's stressed.

Which is perfect because Logan is the uptight one. Literally, the suit. He's all business. He's got scars on his knuckles, just like AJ. So he's a fighter too, but he does something else now. Like maybe once upon a time he was just a street thug but he's since moved up.

I have a feeling AJ can fix cars, and dishwashers, and turn on generators, while Logan can sign the fuck out of a check, or get you out of some jail time, or fix the fucked-up accounting in your books.

Which makes me laugh. Because nobody's fooling anyone today. I know who these guys are.

"Come here," I whisper, when Logan just looks at me. "AJ needs help." I take the cock ring from AJ and hold it up like exhibit A. The exact evidence Logan needs to be convinced.

He doesn't take a single step.

But he does unknot his tie. Slowly. Carefully. Looking me in the eyes while he slips it out of his collar and throws it on the bed, like maybe he's gonna use it to tie my wrists together later.

He takes off his suit coat and drapes it over a chair, then starts unbuttoning his shirt.

I let out a breath when he exposes the well-defined muscles of his chest and my fingertips have an almost uncontrollable urge to touch him.

He takes off a pair of cufflinks, places them on the bedside table, and then slips his shirt down his arms, letting it hang there, half on, half off, so I can get a good look.

He grins. "Like what you see?"

I swallow and nod, then look at AJ, who has the same hungry look on his face as me.

"Should I keep going?" Logan asks us. "Or do you want me to keep the clothes on?"

"Off," AJ says. "Take everything off."

I have no idea if these guys are like… partners. Or if they're just friends who dabble. But I can tell they have a certain level of comfort with each other. I can tell they like each other. I can tell they're turning themselves on right now.

Logan unbuckles his belt. It jingles in a very sexy way when it falls open. His fingers deftly undo his pants and pull out his thick, long cock. His shirt is still hanging off his arms so he's the perfect picture of a man who is about to fuck you into oblivion.

He looks like a model with his dark hair, and chiseled jaw, and intense gray eyes.

He jerks on his dick a few times as we watch. Then he grins and kicks off his shoes. "I'll tell you what," he says. "AJ can come over here and finish. And then you, Yvette, can undress him for me while I watch and enjoy. And then… we can talk about who's gonna put a cock ring where."

AJ looks at me like we're the partners in this room and not the two of them. He smiles, silently asking what I think of the new deal. I don't say anything but my answer is yes, and AJ understands this.

He hands me the cock ring and walks over to his friend. His large hands land on the round, muscular flesh of Logan's shoulders, hesitating for a moment, like it feels good. Which I imagine it does. I want to touch Logan so bad right now, my fingers are tingling.

AJ slowly slips his hands down Logan's shoulders, dragging the white button-down shirt off as he goes. It drops to the floor at Logan's feet like a discarded cape. And then there's one moment of hesitation. Less than a moment, maybe. And AJ reaches for Logan's fully erect cock and begins to jerk him with one hand while the other one reaches up around his neck and he leans in for a kiss.

They kissed earlier so I know Logan's OK with it. But for some reason I expect him to back away.

He doesn't.

He opens his mouth, reaches for his friend with his tongue, and kisses him full on without regrets.

AJ mumbles something sexy. Something that might just be a moan or might be more, I'm not sure.

And Logan replies with, "Keep going. She's patiently waiting for her turn."

Which makes me hold my breath and AJ chuckle.

He backs away from the kiss and looks down at his hand, still jerking on Logan's dick. Then he bends down and I step forward a few paces to get a better look as he places his mouth on Logan's lower stomach and drags his scratchy face down the soft, sensitive skin.

Logan grabs AJ's hair, holding him still for a moment while he closes his eyes and looks up at the ceiling.

I take a few more steps towards them.

I want AJ to suck him off so bad. A warm, tingly feeling builds between my legs as I get wet for them.

But AJ just slips Logan's pants and boxer briefs down his legs until he steps out. He takes each of his socks off, one at a time. And then Logan is bare.

Naked for us. Looking like the god Adonis with his perfectly muscled body in the soft glowing light of my bedroom.

AJ stands up and turns around, his hand outstretched, and says, "Now me."

I walk forward on autopilot. Even if I wanted to say no to this, I wouldn't be able to. I want to see what's under that white thermal shirt he's wearing. I want to feel the muscles of his arms. I want to see them both naked. Standing next to each other like Greek gods incarnate.

I take AJ's hand and let him pull me close. Logan puts his hands around my neck and squeezes just enough to make my body flood with adrenaline. With fear, too.

But Logan's grip loosens as he leans forward. He kisses me. Not the urgent, all-accepting way he did Logan just moments earlier, but tentatively. Like we're new at this. And he whispers, "Get AJ naked," into my mouth.

I exhale, my fingers reaching for AJ's shirt. But I break away from the kiss so I can watch. So I can look. So I can get that first peek of what this well-built man is hiding underneath his clothes.

I find the hem. It's ragged with rips and undone seams. Well-worn and familiar, and maybe old and overused, but in a good way. And that's kinda how I feel right now. Like all my seams have come loose and are about to unravel. Like I'm old and tired, but still— there is this one night left for me. This one last chance to be part of something.

I lift up, anticipating the washboard abs, and I'm not disappointed. He is even more cut than his friend.

Even harder with muscle, if that's possible. I look up at AJ's face as he lifts his arms. But I'm not tall enough to take the shirt completely over his head so Logan helps me.

And then there he is. His whole naked chest. Tattoos and scars. Rough and perfect. I trace the outline of a large angel on his chest. A woman with long, flowing hair and outstretched wings.

Not an angel. A valkyrie. A goddess killing one man with a sword while she saves his brother-in-battle to fight another day.

"Keep going," AJ urges.

I drop to my knees, my legs spread open wide to give them a peek at my pussy, and lift up the hem of his faded and ripped jeans so I can get his boot off. Then do the same thing for the other foot as Logan bends down and begins to finger my pussy.

I have to stop and close my eyes for a second

But again, AJ is there, hand gripping my hair, urging me on with a, "Keep going."

I unbutton and unzip his pants, pulling them down his hips. Logan helps me now. Just one hand because the other one is entering me with his thick fingers.

AJ steps out of his pants and pulls me up to a standing position by my hair.

Logan rises with me, his fingers still inside my pussy. Still pumping in and out.

And there we are.

The warrior angel between two men.

Only the best part is—I don't have to choose who lives and dies.

I get them both.

CHAPTER NINE

LOGAN

Maybe it's the lighting. It could just be the lighting. But the three of us look like a trio of beautiful supernatural beings.

Yvette, with her long, blonde hair and perfect tits. Her pussy so wet from my fingers and her nipples erect and pointed.

AJ with his hard, muscled body. His broad shoulders and eight-inch cock poking Yvette in the stomach.

And me. Behind him, my cock flattened up against his ass like I'm about to enter him.

There is so much sex in this room I want to come right now.

But the cock ring is on the floor at Yvette's feet. Dropped there and forgotten until I see it. I crouch, dragging my tongue down the back of AJ's leg, grab it, and lick my way back up, stopping briefly to take the skin at his waist between my teeth and nip him until he says, "Stop that, you fucker."

Which makes me smile and let go.

I stand up holding the black cock ring, and say, "You still want me to put this on? Because your dick is hard and it's gonna grip it tight."

"Fuck yeah," AJ says, always willing to take one for the team.

I turn to the drawer of sex toys and grab a tube of lubricant. I smear a little over the cock ring, which is not a regular cock ring, but more like a vibrator with a curve at one end that will wrap around his shaft as the vibrator lies in front of his balls.

AJ and Yvette begin to kiss while I bend down and take his massive dick in my hand. I can't help myself, I pump him a few times, making him moan into her mouth.

But I'm anxious to get this on him so I spread the curved part of the ring open wide enough to force it over his shaft, and then I let go of the tension until it grips tightly around his skin.

AJ moans, his fingers threading through my hair, and then he fists it tight when I position the vibrator next to his balls.

I stand up and admire him.

"There's a remote too," Yvette says, breathing heavy as she points to the drawer.

I nod, find the matching black remote, and place it on the nightstand for later.

Because we're not done exploring here. No way is AJ the only one having toy fun. Yvette has enough for everyone.

Inside her secret sex-toy treasure chest is another remote-controlled vibrator. Much like the one AJ's wearing, except it's bright purple instead of black. I hold it up and smile. "Your turn, Yvette."

She sucks in a deep breath. Like maybe she's nervous. Or *maybe*... she can't believe her dumb luck.

AJ takes it from my hand and studies it. Like it's perplexing. It's a vibrator, but not just a vibrator. Just like that cock ring he's wearing isn't just a cock ring. It's got a curve at the end, like his, but hers is flat and will line up with her clit.

"Lie down on the bed and spread your legs," I tell her. "AJ's gonna do the honors this time."

Yvette bites her lip. But not in hesitation. Because the skin on her arms prickles up, making the tiny hairs stand on end, and her nipples bunch together even tighter, if that's possible. She bites her lip with anticipation.

"Come on," AJ says, taking her hand and leading her the few paces over to the bed. "I can't wait to figure this out."

She lets out a nervous laugh, but crawls onto the bed until she's right in the middle, and then turns over on her back. AJ doesn't wait for her to open her legs. He slips in between her knees and spreads them wide himself.

He looks over at the lube in the open drawer, reaches for it, but I place my hand on his and say, "Believe me. She doesn't need it."

He slips two fingers between her legs and presses them up inside her to check, then says, "You naughty little slut," when he pulls them out coated with her juices.

She giggles at the insult. Because it wasn't an insult. I like a girl who knows the difference.

He leans down to suck on the thin folds of her labia. AJ is nothing if not an attentive lover. And even though he knows she's ready, he plays with her clit for a minute. Licking and twirling his tongue until she's squinting her eyes tight and clenching her teeth together as she grabs his head with both hands.

AJ laughs a little and pulls back, positioning himself so he has easy access. And then he spreads her pussy lips apart and pushes the tip of the vibrator up inside her.

She sighs as he continues to push, until the only visible part is the flat clit stimulator.

I take the matching purple remote out of the drawer, place it on the table next to the black one meant for AJ, and then remove the final toy meant for me.

OK. So maybe I've saved the best for last and maybe that makes me a little bit selfish.

But I've never pretended to be anything but selfish, so I give no fucks that the final toy is the king of all men's pleasure paraphernalia.

The prostate stimulator.

AJ has obviously never used one of these because he just looks at the teal-green toy in confusion.

"Don't worry," I say. "Yvette gets to put this one in and I'm confident she know what she's doing."

"Oh, shit," Yvette says, realizing what we've set up here.

Three people with three very different, very erotic, remote-controlled sex toys.

"Move over, baby," I say, slapping her thigh. "And be generous with the lube."

AJ sits back near the end of the bed as Yvette sits up on her knees and takes the tube of lube and the vibrator that will go in my ass. But it's not just a vibrator. I know. I've used this before many times and the moment I spied it in the drawer earlier, I knew this girl was gonna blow my mind. Because this is yet another example of two toys in one. While one end sits in my ass, pressed up against my prostate, the other end slides right up behind my balls to stimulate the perineum.

I pump my cock a few times as I bend my knees and open them up, giving her the access she needs by lifting my hips slightly off the mattress.

AJ gets up, grabs the purple remote from the table, and begins to experiment by pressing buttons.

"Holy mother of—" Yvette exclaims.

AJ just grins as he walks over to the other side of the bed and lies down next to me. I look at him for a moment, wondering if this is getting weird. But he leans over, kisses me, and says, "Thank you."

Which makes me laugh. Until I realize Yvette has lubed up her fingers and is massaging the entrance to my ass. And that makes me groan. It's been a long time since I did any ass play and I'm ready for this.

"Want me to jerk you off while she puts it in?" AJ asks.

"No. I'll come immediately if you do and I want to enjoy this for as long as possible."

AJ nods, like this is serious shit, and begins to play with Yvette's remote. She moans as she continues to massage my tight hole until it relaxes enough for her to stick her finger inside me.

I close my eyes and just… float in the sensations. It feels so damn good.

She doesn't ask me if I'm ready, just slowly, and at the same time, slips her finger out and begins to press the vibrator into my ass.

AJ stops playing for a moment to grip both my knees and tilt me up a little higher, giving her more access.

I have to wonder for a moment. Just wonder what it would be like to keep these two.

To not do my job when this is all over.

To let them live.

To live with them and have erotic, mind-blowing sex with them forever.

But it's a stupid fantasy. One that's easily forgotten when the vibrator is snug up inside me and the perfectly shaped and positioned nubs are pressing in all the right areas.

AJ lets go of my knees and lies back. Yvette grabs the other two remote controls off the table, handing the black one to me, so I can control AJ, and keeping the teal one for herself, so she can control me.

Then she climbs in between us, filling all the empty space.

She and I turn ours on at the same time and as the room fills with the soft sound of vibrating sex toys we are all suddenly… *equal*.

I lose my mind in that moment. Just… float into nothingness.

Except that's not true. I float into ecstasy.

AJ begins to moan as I remember to tilt my little remote. These are high-quality toys, so each remote has motion sensor technology. Tilt it a little, the toy it links to vibrates a little. But tilt it a lot and…

"Fuck, yeah," AJ moans.

The sound of vibration increases and Yvette begins to breathe hard. She lifts her knees up and stretches her arms out, one hand on my chest, lightly dragging her fingers up and down my stomach, but careful not to grab my cock. I will explode uncontrollably if she does that.

And I don't want to explode yet. We just got started. So I whisper, "Thank you."

"I want more," she moans.

"Climb on top of me," AJ says.

"No," I say. "Wait. We can… we can all do this together."

It's a complicated puzzle but I know it can be done. I force my mind to refocus. Make myself figure it out.

Then I say, "Get on top of me, Yvette. And let AJ fuck you from behind."

The two of them are in motion. Slowly repositioning themselves until Yvette is straddling my stomach, my cock lying flat out in front of her.

I do not need to fuck her to get off. AJ probably doesn't either.

But what's wrong with a little torture to go with our pleasure?

AJ gets it immediately. Because he's already behind her, pressing his cock up against her pussy.

She will be very full once he's inside her.

And her clit vibrator is already pressed up against the base of my shaft. That, along with the internal prostate stimulation and the perineum vibrations, has me about undone. But I force myself to remain calm. I let the motion of AJ inserting his giant cock inside her pussy take over.

And then, once we are all settled—once we are nothing but a tangled mound of vibrating sex organs attached to over-excited bodies—we begin to move.

We fuck each other like some kind of alien being. All one.

My hand tilting the control, making AJ groan and grunt as he slowly fucks her from behind.

AJ tilting his control until Yvette's vibrator is thrumming along like an old muscle car.

And Yvette… Yvette takes it all to the next level when she tilts her control up to maximum.

I can feel *all* of this. Every single vibration. My ass. My balls. My lower stomach where Yvette's clit stimulator is pressed. AJ's balls, trembling from the cock ring, transferring the waves of motion to mine as he slowly pushes forward until they touch mine, then pulling back, making sure I miss him desperately when they're not.

Coming for me isn't like a regular ejaculation. It's a stream of liquid pouring out the tip of my cock. Sliding back and forth between Yvette's stomach and mine.

AJ grunts, leaning back to slap Yvette's ass as he explodes inside her.

And Yvette… Yvette lifts her upper body off my chest, places both hands palm down on my pecs, arches her back so she's looking at the ceiling and…

Screams.

With pleasure.

As her fingernails dig into my skin and draw blood.

Evidence of her orgasm in sticky red.

CHAPTER TEN

"I don't know what that was," I say, rolling off Yvette and taking her with me.

She moans and squeals as I lie on my back and draw her on top of me.

"Turn it off." She laughs. "Turn it off!"

"Oh, shit. Sorry," I say, unable to stop my own chuckle. I do not remember ever having this much fun during sex. Or feeling this good.

Logan is silent.

I turn my head to find him perfectly still, eyes closed. Yvette's remote tossed to the side and still.

"Dude? You OK?"

"Shhh," he says. "Don't talk to me. I'm still coming."

I look down at his cock. Which isn't coming. There's a sticky hot mess of semen smeared over his entire chest and stomach. "What the—"

"Just let me burn this moment into my brain. Because I'm pretty sure I will never have sex like this again and I want to enjoy it a little longer."

"It lasts a long time," Yvette says, panting. She's lying on top of me, her back pressed up against my chest. And I wish there were mirrors on the top of her canopy, because I want to see her pussy like this. Filled with the vibrator and little streams of white, milky come dripping out from her lips.

If she were going to live longer than a day, I'd have been more careful about that. Be a little worried that I put a baby AJ inside her.

But she won't. Live, that is. So I don't worry about it.

After a few more long silent moments Logan finally says, "Fuuuuuuuuuck."

"Done now?" I ask.

"Hold on," he says, stretching his head back and opening his mouth. "OK. I think I'm done."

I might have to give the butt vibrator a go before we kill Yvette. Or hell, who knows? Maybe Logan and I will become a thing? Do this more often once we get back home.

Could happen.

Logan sits up a little, his abs tightening into rows upon rows of muscle, as he looks down at his chest. "Jesus. What happened here?"

"You're a dumbass, you know that?"

"I need a shower," he says, sitting all the way up and swinging his legs over the side of the bed. And then he walks off towards the en suite bathroom, teal-green butt vibrator sticking out of his ass.

"For fuck's sake!" I yell. "I can't unsee that, you dick."

He stops in the doorway to look over his shoulder. "You two coming or what?"

"He's so romantic." Yvette laughs. But she sits up, swings her legs over the side, and follows him.

I just lie there for a few more seconds, looking up at the ceiling with a stupid grin on my face. There are worse ways to spend a Sunday night stuck in a blizzard, that's for sure.

The shower starts and steam puffs out from the open door to the bathroom. I sigh and look over at the window. There are heavy golden-yellow velvet drapes pouring down the edge of the frame and outside there's enough light to see that the snow is still coming down in sheets of white.

I look over at the other bedside table and see a drawer partially open. Turning over to reach for it, I open it up and see a book. Or a journal.

Or a diary. Hmmm. Bet there's some good reading in there. This Yvette is a total sexy freak.

"You coming or what?" Logan calls.

"Yeah, I'm coming."

I get out of bed and the cock-ring vibrator loosens since I'm no longer hard. I take it off as I walk, then toss it into the sink where the other two toys are already waiting.

Yvette and Logan are in the shower, Logan standing off to one side as secondary jets spray his back, Yvette standing under the circle pouring down from the rain shower above. She's got her arms lifted up, working the water into her long, blonde hair, and this makes her tits look delicious.

I meet Logan's eyes as I open the glass door and step inside.

We grin together.

Because we know. We know what we're gonna do next.

The tag-team fuck cannot end until there's been a double penetration.

Sex toys don't count.

But first we wash each other. I grab the sweet-smelling bottle of soap and squirt some onto my palm as Yvette and Logan trade places. I step towards her, massaging the bubbles onto her breasts. She gives me a quirky smile and I wonder... how did Damon let her get away?

Or maybe the question is... why did he make her want to run?

She seems cool. Nice. Open to new experiences. Interested in Logan and me equally. Kinda chill, actually. Which is a welcome change to the women I've dated in the past who were all psycho.

Because that's how this goes. Psycho comes along for the ride. You want kinky girls who are up for anything? You got it. Just deal with this unstable personality while you enjoy your vibrating cock ring and prostate stimulator.

But Yvette seems calm. Almost Zen. Like she knows her place in this world and she's satisfied with it.

I like that.

I might even like *her*.

She has soap in her hands too. And when she places them on my shoulders and begins to rub up and down my arms I feel myself relax. A warm rush of easiness fills me.

I want to talk to her. I want us all to talk for some reason. It feels like we should have things to say.

About our day. Or what some asshole did in the car behind us on our way home from work. Or some jerk person we were forced to interact with at a drive-through while we got lunch. Small talk, I realize. It feels like we should have some small talk.

Which most people might think is meaningless, but I don't. Small talk says you know each other. You have little things on your mind you'd like to get over. And this person you small-talk with is the one who erases the tension or the leftover bad feelings about an argument, and makes everything better.

Just makes things better. Life richer. Shit like that.

Logan and I trade places. I stand under the rain shower and rinse off while he shampoos her hair.

It feels like such an intimate gesture. Feels almost… wrong. Because even though we all just fucked and blew each other's minds, we are not connected. Not even a little bit.

Logan and I are here to kill this girl. *Kill her.*

We have a plan. We have body disposal figured out.

And yet he shampoos her hair.

I step away from them, trying to figure this all out. Trying to make all these jagged pieces fit together into something that makes sense.

Yvette steps under the water and he helps her rinse out the suds so he can apply the conditioner.

I just watch them. Take a seat on the stone bench on the far side of the shower, some random shower head down by my feet blasting hot water onto my lower legs, and become an observer. A voyeur.

We say nothing because there's nothing to say. We literally have nothing to talk about. And that sucks.

After Logan rinses the conditioner out of her hair I stretch out my hand. Because I know what comes next. I want there to be more to this. I want there to be a connection, but there isn't. It's not there. And it's not gonna magically appear.

This is just… sex.

Yvette accepts my offer and takes my hand. I pull her towards me. She straddles my legs without being told. Because she knows it too. She feels it.

This encounter has no meaning at all.

It's just sex.

I frown. And Logan says, "What?"

Logan has positioned himself behind Yvette. Her long, wet hair sticks to her breasts, winding down and over her nipples. He wraps his fingers around it from behind and pulls it into a ponytail before arranging it down her back. I look up at him and have no explanation for the expression he's reading on my face.

So I just shrug and say, "Nothin'."

Does he accept my answer?

Yeah. He does. Because even though we were close once, it was a while back now. We were pretty tight then but now… all the connections are still there, but they're loose. Some of them lost, maybe.

I look at Yvette, trying to figure her out. But she's got a blank face. There's nothing to see there. Nothing to read.

Logan massages her shoulders, his long fingers and strong thumbs kneading the tight muscles to either side of her neck. Yvette closes her eyes and smiles.

But it's not a smile of, *Thank you. I appreciate you. I really need this today.*

It's a smile of, *I know what comes next.*

So do I.

Logan's hands slowly begin to explore, dipping down to the top of her breasts, then back up to her shoulders. He does this several times before he actually cups both breasts and begins to massage them instead.

It's a classic move every guy learns to do. *Would you like a massage? Let me take that tension away. Oh, did I just grab your tits? Did I just take my shoulder massage down to your pussy?*

Classic, no-brainer move.

And even though Yvette—and pretty much every other woman on the receiving end of one of those *let-me-help-you-with-that-tension-ma'am* massages—appreciates it, and thinks it feels good, it doesn't change anything.

It's just sex.

"AJ," Logan says. "What is your problem?"

This breaks the spell still-half-drunk Yvette is under and she opens her eyes.

Now I have two people looking at me for an explanation. Because I'm thinking when I shouldn't be.

"Nothin'," I say. "I'm fucking great, actually."

I throw out one of my charming smiles. The kind people expect from me now. The kind that says, *Sure, I'm a six-foot-three meaty monster of a man and I can kill you seventeen different ways—none of which have anything to do with the gun in my hand pointed at your head—but don't worry.*

I have this good-natured personality and smirky smile to put you at ease.

"AJ," Logan says, kinda laughing. "What the fuck are you thinking about?"

"More sex," I say. "With you two." Because that's the correct answer. And it's stupid, anyway. To think about this shit when nothing will ever come out the other end.

So I place my hands on Yvette's hips and lift her up a little.

My cock is hard again. Even though my mind isn't. So she understands what I'm asking and obliges me by sitting up, reaching between her legs to grab me, and placing me at the entrance to her pussy.

This pacifies Logan, because he's grinning down at me like, *OK, yeah. You're normal again.* He steps to the side of Yvette's head just as she sinks down onto my cock with a moan. His also-hard cock aimed right for the invitation her open mouth implies.

Her hand goes to my shoulder to steady herself, while the other one takes his cock and guides him forward until her lips seal around the tip of Logan's dick.

Logan grips her head, bunching her hair up in his fist, and pushes her into it a little further.

I watch as his shaft begins to disappear inside her throat.

It's slow, at least. Maybe even a little bit careful. And this makes me relax against the cold, tiled wall.

I sigh. Because being inside her feels good. And watching her devour Logan's cock feels erotic. So I let go of all that stupid connection bullshit. Let go of my desire for small talk and just... enjoy it while it lasts.

Tomorrow this storm will be over, the roads will be clear, and Yvette Nightingale's body will be wrapped in a tarp at the bottom of a ravine. Waiting to be found when some hiker happens upon it in some future spring.

CHAPTER ELEVEN

YVETTE

I don't really understand how this day went from how I planned it to mind-blowing sex with two strangers… but I'm not sure it matters.

It feels good.

They feel good.

And I deserve this night with them.

That's what I keep telling myself.

I deserve this. I earned it.

But I didn't earn anything. My life is a series of bad choices and unfortunate circumstances. It's just luck, I guess.

Whatever it is, I like it. Feels good. So I erase all the stupid thoughts in my head about how I'm now behind schedule and just live a little.

I take Logan's cock as deep as I can. Deep enough to trigger my gag reflex when the tip of his head bumps up against the back of my throat.

But Logan is there to pet my wet hair and murmur encouragements. Things like, "You got this." And "Yeah, I like that."

And AJ fucks me slow. Or rather, lets *me* fuck *him* slow. Lets me find my own rhythm and set the pace. Lets me rise and fall on my own good time. Lets me lead.

So it's nothing like it was downstairs. Which was rough, and fast, and desperate. Or even like it was in the bedroom. Which was a whole lot of kinky play with orgasms as the only goal.

I lose myself in the blow job. Sometimes even forgetting to fuck AJ. I close my eyes and just exist in the peaceful dream-world of slow sex.

But eventually Logan pulls his cock out of my mouth and AJ stands up, taking me with him. His large hands grip my ass as he walks forward and says, "Stand up and face Logan."

So I do that. Automatically. No questions in my head to stop me. No second thoughts. Nothing but obedience.

Because I'm tired of being in charge. I'm tired of making decisions. I'm tired of life and I need someone to step in and just… tell me what to do. Just get me through things.

And these two seem more than willing to pick up my slack.

So I turn to face Logan and find him smiling. Which is a nice look for him. Even though I have no idea who this man is, I've seen enough of him today to understand he is hard.

Not the same way AJ is, either.

AJ is clearly the muscle of this team. A huge man with cannons for arms and a wide chest that, when he wraps his arms around me, feels like protection. And AJ is a joker. A guy who likes to laugh and smile.

Logan feels like the other end of the spectrum. Hard in a different way. Hard like a man who has to make big decisions. The suit, the frown, the almost-always squinting eyes as he evaluates things and comes to conclusions.

So this smile is good. It says a lot. It says, *I'm having fun and fun isn't something I usually have.* It also says he wants more. More of me, at least.

Which I'm willing to give.

Because why not?

And let's face it, he's handsome. His hair is darker when it's wet. And his body, while also muscular, like AJ's, is different. Angular and cut like a sculpture. The low light in here catches all the lines of his body. The shape of his thighs and the hills and valleys that accentuate his six-pack abs.

I smile back at him. A real smile too.

"It's my turn, I guess," he says, grinning just a little wider.

And I know what that means. They've been fucking me different ways for hours now but Logan and I have not yet been face-to-face while he was inside me.

Fingers don't count.

But something inside me likes this. And even though I just smile at him—and am still smiling now—it changes. Not the smile, exactly. The pleasure behind it.

It morphs into something, dare I say… real?

I admit, I get a stab of guilt deep inside my heart over that realization.

Because I smile all the time. I smile to customers, and vendors who deliver my alcohol. I smile at the locals who come in to check up on me. I smile at the TV every now and then. When I find a show that can make me forget who I am and what I went through.

But they are all fake. Every single one of them for the past year has been fake until right this second. Until this hard, angular man showed me something I've missed dearly.

Logan found his own joy in me. And even though it hurts so bad—to think of another man finding that kind of joy in me—I can't afford to *not* appreciate it.

So I hope I'm forgiven for what I say next. Because I say, "It sure is your turn. I hope you make the most of it."

His wide grin goes wider. His gray eyes shine with light, even though he is a dark man and everyone in this bathroom understands that.

AJ comes around behind me, leaning his back against the shower wall. The water is still luxuriously hot—thank you, brand-new tankless water heater—and the glass walls go all the way up to the ceiling so it's literally a sauna in here. The air is thick with steam. Water beads up on our bodies, a combination of the still-raining shower head and various spray nozzles strategically positioned around the large enclosure, and the sweat that pours out of us like regrets and the repercussions of bad decisions.

Logan stays right where he is. About a foot away. Looking down at me with some emotion I don't understand in his eyes.

He's thinking about something. Me for sure. But something else too.

AJ doesn't stay still. He wraps his arms around my waist, his fingers reaching between my legs where his cock was just a couple minutes ago. His head dips into my neck and he says, "Ready for more?"

And even though I could care less about more sex at this point, I am ready for more.

More of them. That's all. Just more of them.

More touching. More soft moans and wild groans.

More connection.

So I say… "Yes."

Logan closes that small distance between us as soon as the soft, low word leaves my mouth. He reaches down to grip my ass with both hands, and lifts me up, pressing his hard chest into my soft breasts.

We kiss first while AJ repositions his hands under my thighs and spreads my legs. We kiss like lovers. Like friends, too. Maybe. Or maybe I'm imagining that. Doesn't matter. It's a very nice kiss. Slow, and tender, and passionate.

AJ chuckles behind me, his lips on my neck. Somehow we've maneuvered ourselves into the path of some random spray of water. It drips down my body as Logan fists his cock, pumping it a few times, and then aims it right at my pussy.

He enters me and I moan. The pleasure I get from this is unexpected because I've been fucked so hard, and in so many different ways already today.

But again, this is different. It's not really fucking anymore.

This time it's more like it used to be for me. Slower, for sure, than when they took me downstairs. Even slower than the way I was fucking AJ a few minutes ago.

Because it's not me setting the pace this time. It's not AJ letting me set the pace, either.

It's Logan's decision to fuck me slow.

And that is something altogether different than anything else we've done today.

AJ props me up, shifting his hands a little so he can play with my ass.

I know what's coming. Both of them inside me, but not both of them in my pussy like it was downstairs.

Just your classic double penetration.

And yet… it's not that at all. It's not the porn I've seen my ex watch back when I was still with him. Because that was always more like a gangbang.

It's the kind when three people just find themselves part of something they don't understand. It's the kind that feels like more.

And I'm stupid right now. I understand that. Because this is nothing like that.

I just need to believe it is.

So I do.

It's that simple.

AJ's finger is inside me now. Gently massaging the tight muscles that only want to say no. But he knows what he's doing. And he's being careful. He knows exactly how to talk all those tight muscles into giving in.

And they do.

They relax and his finger penetrates a little further.

I find myself moaning when that happens. Moaning things like, "Yes," and, "Do it. Just do it."

But Logan is still kissing me, so the words might get lost in his mouth. Because AJ doesn't *just do it*. He continues to take his time just as Logan begins to thrust just a little harder.

They both have thick, giant cocks. And I think to myself… like, what are the odds of that happening? Million to one? Maybe?

But then again, this day isn't just any other day. It's special. And so I talk myself into the luck.

"Look at me," Logan says, pulling away from our kiss. "Look at me, Yvette. And both of you, stop thinking so hard about this. It's just fucking, OK? That's all. Just some really nice fucking."

Which makes AJ shake his head a little. I can't see it shake because he's still kissing and nipping at my neck from behind. But I can feel it.

"Look at me, Yvette," Logan says again. "Tell me what this is."

"Fucking," I whisper.

"Yes." He smiles, placing a hand alongside my cheek.

Which makes it, once again, feel like something that is a little more than fucking.

But I give up. I have no explanation for this stupid day. I give in.

Logan bends over a little. arching his back and looking down at his cock as he slips it deep, deep inside me, then pulls it almost all the way out.

Nope. Not just fucking. Guys do that a lot. Watching themselves fuck a girl is a turn-on. But it almost always comes with hard, punishing thrusts forward. And this time it doesn't. He pushes inside me the same agonizingly slow way he pulls out. AJ has moved away from my neck and the tip of his cock is pressing against my now pliant and agreeable asshole.

But I keep my mouth shut. Willing myself not to care. Forcing myself to just feel what they are doing. Lose myself in the moment and let go.

Forget all the bad things that have happened to me.

Forget the life I used to have. Forget everything I've lost.

Forget about the love I will never find again and just…

Embrace this one last gift from these two strangers.

AJ reaches out, pulling Logan closer. They kiss like friends. Like lovers.

And I do not think about it. I do not wonder who they are. What they are to each other. Or even why they're here.

They are here for me.

They are here to give me what I need.

And this is how I accept that gift.

Logan groans as their kiss becomes more passionate, their tongues wild as AJ pushes forward and Logan pushes back. Until AJ's cock is buried deep in my asshole and they find that rhythm again. They find that perfect, rocking motion that will give me the most pleasure.

Logan growls a little, nipping at AJ's lip. And things become more intense. I can feel their muscles straining. AJ's arms, and Logan's thighs, as he balances me in the perfect position to take them both.

We are close. Even me, I realize, with some surprise. Because I'm not usually one to go all night like this.

So it's them.

They do this to me.

For me.

I reach down between my legs and begin to play with my clit.

"Yeah," Logan moans. "You're gonna come for us first this time, Yvette."

And it's dumb. I know it is. It's dumb to feel… like they care about my feelings. But I let myself live this fantasy with them.

Why not?

I vibrate my hand across my clit so fast the climax begins to build. AJ is grinding on my ass, his hips dipping under and then thrusting up while Logan eases in and out of me like we are the definition of sex.

I come.

It's not mind-blowing like last time.

It's quiet and pulsing.

AJ says, "Oh, yeah. Grip my cock with your ass, Yvette." And it's the *Yvette* part that gets me. It's something as simple as my name.

Logan leans into me, pressing his chest up against my breasts so hard, I feel like I can't breathe. And AJ pushes back, reaching around Logan to force us into this tight configuration.

"Fuck," Logan mutters. And I feel him spasm. His legs and arms as well as his cock. His hot semen fills me up inside, joining and mingling with AJ's from earlier.

AJ lets go of me and both their cocks slip out. I have no strength left so I fall to my knees and immediately turn to face AJ. He's frantically jerking on his cock, aiming it at my tits, and then white, milky come shoots out and coats my nipples.

Logan drops to the floor, sitting with his legs open and his back pressed up against the wall. He grabs me around my waist and slides me across the slick, tiled floor until my back hits his chest.

And then hugs me. Tight. With his head buried into the crook of my neck.

I don't know why. I can't possibly imagine what reason he has to hug me like this, but he does it.

And I like it.

AJ bends down on one knee and wipes the come off my breasts with one wet hand. Then he reaches for a nearby nozzle and aims the misty spray at me, like he wants to take care of me.

You are so stupid, Yvette.

They are not here to take care of you.

I know that, but the dreamy, passionate haze of sex lingers. And I don't feel like fighting it.

So I give in to it.

LOGAN

We sit in the shower like that for a few minutes, Yvette and I, my arms wrapped tightly around her.

I'm feeling… thankful.

I almost laugh at that, then chastise myself. *She is just a girl we're fucking, Logan.*

Right. Got it.

Gonna kill her in a few hours. By tomorrow night all of this will be behind me. I'll be on my way back to the city to report in to Damon. Show him proof of the job well done. Pictures of two dead bodies.

End of story.

I look up at AJ and find him washing his hair and I can't help myself. I smile.

He grins back. Shoots me with his finger. And I'm transported to another day. Another time. Back when we first met and this job was exciting and, though I hate to admit it, sometimes fun too.

AJ turns away and stands under the rain shower, talking to the wall as he rinses his hair.

"What?" I laugh.

"Clothes," he says, turning to face me. "I wish I had brought clothes. Why didn't we bring clothes?"

Uh… because we weren't supposed to be stuck in a blizzard fucking Yvette Nightingale's brains out tonight?

But I don't say it.

We both know why we don't have clothes.

"I might have clothes for you," Yvette says in a quiet voice.

AJ squints his eyes at her. An expression I know well enough to recognize as suspicion. What the hell is he suspicious about? "You have men's clothes?" he asks.

Which, I guess, now that I think about it, is weird. Since it's obvious no men live here with her.

"Lost and found," she says.

Also makes sense.

"I think someone left a hoodie last week. I could go check for you."

AJ nods. "OK." But his suspicion lingers.

Yvette either pretends not to notice or she gives no fucks. Because she unwraps my arms from around her and stands up. AJ steps aside, granting her access to the rain shower, and she steps under to rinse herself off one final time.

I just sit there, watching her, then notice AJ is watching me.

"What?" I say.

He shakes his head.

But I know what that shake means. It means, *We gotta talk about something, but not in front of her.*

"OK," I say, reaching up with a hand.

He takes it, pulls me to my feet, and then Yvette opens the shower door, steps out grabbing a towel off a rack, and says, "I'll get you towels. One second."

We watch her disappear into the bedroom, tucking the towel up under her arms and around her breasts.

"What?" I ask again.

"Hold on," he says, eyes locked on the doorway.

Yvette reappears, smiling—looking like a blonde goddess, if I'm being honest—and holds out the towels.

AJ and I take them at the same time, quickly dry ourselves off, then wrap the towels around our waists.

By the time we step back in the bedroom, Yvette is already pulling on a pair of pale yellow leggings. She's wearing a long, white shirt with long, soft ruffles on the sleeve cuffs at her wrist.

Like the outfit she was wearing earlier today— specifically the shirt that AJ ripped open—it's very feminine. Almost Victorian. Though that shirt earlier made her look more like a Renaissance princess than a vision in vintage lace.

Which is what she looks like now.

God, something is wrong with me. I don't think I've ever compared a woman to either of those things in my entire like.

"I'll be right back," Yvette says. Then she smiles. "The lost and found box is just down in a room behind the bar."

AJ says nothing. Just stares at her. So I say, "Sure. I'll go back to my duties in the kitchen."

Because I just remembered that's what I was doing before all this sex started up again.

"Oh, I guess I can open the kitchen one more time. I'll make us something."

"Cool," I say. Because AJ is still silent.

She manages one more smile, then disappears.

I wait for the tell-tale sound of an apartment door opening and closing, then turn to AJ and say, "What's going on?"

He runs his fingers through his hair, messing it up in a very sexy way. Which almost makes me laugh. Because what the fuck is wrong with me?

"So…" he starts. "You know how I went out back to turn the generator on?"

"Oh, yeah," I say. Jesus. Was that just an hour or two ago? Feels like a lifetime. "Thanks for doing that."

He holds up a finger, like he's about to start ticking things off. "One. That is some fucking building she's got out there."

"What do you mean?"

"Like, there's two cars, a car lift. You know the kind you see at a mechanic's shop? That kind. A whole fucking gym filled with equipment. And not equipment someone like Yvette would use, either. It's definitely a man's gym. I almost started doing kicks on the bag, that's how hot that gym made me."

I laugh at this. I can't help it.

"Two," he says, holding up another finger. "That generator is no joke. It's a nice fucking setup."

I shrug. "It lives in the middle of nowhere, twelve thousand feet up in the sky. Kinda typical, I think."

"Three," he says, holding up one more finger. "The snowcat and the tractor?"

"Oh, yeah," I say. "Forgot about that. OK. So what are you saying? A guy lives out there?"

He shakes his head. "No one's living out there, dude. The heat wasn't on."

"So what are you going on about?"

"There *was* a guy living here, Logan."

"When?"

"How should I fucking know? I saw the same as you these past two weeks. No dudes. But never mind that, I have one more point to make."

"OK."

He holds up a fourth finger. "She was on the terrace? In her underwear?"

"Yeah, so what?"

"She dropped that bottle of pills in the snow. Fentanyl. You know what that is?"

"Fentanyl," I say. "That's painkillers, right?"

"Not just any painkiller. It's end-of-life kind of painkiller. I know because my mom was on that shit when she was dying of cancer."

"So she's sick?"

AJ shrugs. "Or the guy who really owns this bar was, and he died."

I think about this for a second. Kinda makes sense. We never could figure out how Yvette—or Glori, since that's her real name—ended up with such a sweet deal when she left Damon with absolutely nothing.

"Why are we here?" AJ asks.

"To kill her," I say.

He laughs. "OK, so um. I'm not killing her. All right? Hear me? I'm not killing her."

"Dude," I say, laughing uncomfortably. "You know what Damon will do if we—"

"Shut up for a second. That point," he says, coming towards me so he can poke his finger into my chest as he talks, "is no longer up for negotiation. *We*," he says, stressing the word, "are not killing her. But you need to tell me why the fuck we're here. And you need to tell me now."

"We're here to kill her," I say again.

"What are we looking for?" he says. "I'm not gonna ask again."

I hold out my hands, unsure why he's so pissed off. "I mean… I'm not sure."

"How could you not be sure?"

"Because Damon just told me to call him when we found her and tell him the situation. So I told him and he said there has to be more. Stay and watch her. So we stayed."

"You have no idea why we're here?"

"You know why we're here, AJ."

He lets out a long exhale and turns away from me. But just as quick, he turns back. "Something's wrong. Something's off."

"Like what?"

"I dunno. But something's not right."

I want to say… *Yeah, no shit. Because I'm here to kill you too.*

But of course I don't say that.

"Why did she have those pills in her hand out on the terrace?"

"I dunno," I say. "She was drunk. She wanted to take a few?"

AJ laughs. But then something catches his attention. Something in the nearby nightstand.

The journal I found earlier, I realize.

He walks over to it, takes it out of the drawer and opens it up. There's a loose piece of paper in the middle of the book, which he withdraws and unfolds. Goes silent for a few moments as he reads.

Then he turns back to me, holding the paper up, and says, "Holy fucking shit."

CHAPTER THIRTEEN

I take a deep breath and hold it, unable to fully comprehend what I'm seeing on this page.

"What?" Logan asks. And when I don't answer, he says it again. "What, dammit? What's it say?"

He snatches it from my hand and begins scanning. "Oh, fuck."

I've already opened the journal to the first page. The title says *My True Confession* and it's written in a pretty handwritten script. And I'm thinking, *OK. Did she kill someone? What did she do?*

But then I turn the next page and the handwriting changes to print. To something more blocky and hard. More masculine.

The entry is dated about three and a half years ago. Everything is confusing… until I read the first sentence.

I am Damon Dell'Ariccia, and this is my true confession.

I hold it up to Logan and say, "Jackpot."

He takes the journal from me and reads the first page, then tosses it on the bed. "That's not what he was looking for."

"What do you mean? That has to be it. It's the only thing we've found."

"It's not it," he says. Then he sighs and looks down at the letter in his hand.

"But how do you know it's not it?" I ask. "It's a fucking confession."

"He's not looking for a confession, AJ. He's looking for…"

But he stops.

"He's looking for what?"

But he just shakes his head. "I don't know, but it's not a book. It's a person. That's all I know."

"The guy who so obviously lived here?"

"I don't think so."

"Logan, you're not making any fucking sense. What did he tell you? Like specifically?"

"He said… he said if I found it, I'd know it."

I shake my head. "Fuck that! Fuck that, dude! That's not a directive. 'Know it when you see it?' Well, this is it! I know it when I see it!"

"It's not it."

An angry sigh bursts out of me. He's being fucking stupid. I'm still holding the book, my thumb holding the place at the first entry, So I open it back up and read it out loud. "'I am Damon Dell'Ariccia, and this is my true confession.'" There's a page break so I flip the page and continue.

"'The first time I raped Glori Bennett she was twelve years old.'"

I am so stunned, I stop reading and just stare at those words on the page. Handwritten words. *My true confession.*

When I look up Logan is staring at me. "Still think this isn't it? We should call him."

"It's not it," Logan insists. "And we can't call him, AJ. There's no service."

Both of us look at the window. Checking to see if it's still snowing. Which it is.

"This is it," I say. "All we gotta do is take this back to him and we can let Yvette go."

Logan shakes his head. Slowly. Almost sadly.

"Yes," I say. "I'm not killing her. Not after… all this. Not after tonight. I can't do it."

In fact, a realization hits me in this moment. I'm tired of this life. I'm tired of killing. I'm tired of working for Damon. I like this place. I'm kinda jealous of whoever was living here with Yvette. I'm jealous of his gym, and his stupid shit cars, and his lift, and his tools. I'm jealous of his quaint little bar on the top of a mountain. Hell, I'm jealous of his tractor.

But most of all I'm jealous of his girl.

I'm into her, I realize.

Very fucking into her.

She is a lost, sad mystery of a woman every way you look at it.

How did she escape? I have been wondering that for weeks.

But also, in the back of my head, I have been wondering about other things too. Maybe more realizing than wondering. And this other nagging, little realization is… if she can get out *then so can I.*

I'm sick of my life. I want this one instead. Some small business with an apartment overhead. Local customers who come in for lunch just because they want to visit. Working with my wife—or whatever she was to him, since she's still married to Damon. Coming upstairs after a long day and not having to deal with traffic or loud neighbors who can't ever seem to shut the fuck up.

Eating dinner with her, and showering with her, and then taking her to bed and loving her.

I have never been in love. I have never even *pretended* to be in love.

And Logan doesn't count because he's a dude and what we have is just friends with benefits. That's it.

But I could see myself with Yvette. I could see myself up here on her mountain running this bar. Or hell, if we had to move, we'd move away. Somewhere far. Maybe another country so if Damon ever got second thoughts we'd be safe.

Maybe we'd have a kid? Change our names and be married. Open a bed-and-breakfast on a beach or something like that. Live the expat life. Raise a family that way. With a pack of little too-blonde kids with too-tanned skin running around barefoot on a beach as they grew up.

I could see that life. I could love that life.

I could *have* that life.

We could have that life.

And hell, if Logan wanted to come I wouldn't mind that either.

So I picture a whole new scenario. The three of us replacing the two of us. Everything else stays the same.

Only some of the kids would have gray eyes, like his. And some of them would have blue eyes, like mine.

But we wouldn't care.

We'd treat them all the same. We'd love them, and teach them how to surf.

I don't know how to surf. Hell, I've only seen a beach once in my life and that was in New Jersey. But I'd learn. I could learn lots of new things.

Logan sighs, pulling me out of my fantasy. "So… I don't know what to make of this."

He's holding up the letter.

I'm just gonna pretend I didn't read that letter. That's what I make of it.

"But it's starting to make sense," he continues.

"No," I say. "No, that letter is a mistake."

Logan shoots me a look I've seen hundreds of times. But it's been a while. We were a lot younger the last time he looked at me this way. It's a look that says… *You're stupid.*

"This isn't a mistake." He laughs. "You don't write a letter like this by mistake, AJ."

But it has to be a mistake. Otherwise everything we've done tonight turns into just another bad example of wrong time, wrong place.

And I refuse to believe that.

I simply refuse.

This is a really great example of right time, right place.

I feel that so completely.

"We should just do it now," Logan says. "We can still wrap her in the tarp and stuff her in the trunk. It's cold enough outside that she'll freeze and then when the storm clears we can take her to the ravine and—"

He stops talking because I punch him in the face.

"What the fuck?" he says, feeling the blood on his lip. "What the fuck are you—"

"We're. Not. Killing her."

"AJ, don't be stupid. If we go back to Damon—"

"Maybe we don't go back to Damon? Maybe we—"

"Have you lost your fucking mind? He will kill us, AJ."

"Only if he finds us," I say. "And besides. I'm not afraid of that asshole."

"You don't need to be afraid of *him*. You and I both know he doesn't kill anyone himself. He's got dozens of people like you and me to do it for him. And they will find us, AJ. We found her, didn't we?"

"That's another mystery," I say. "He knew she was here. Has been here, probably playing house with the guy who actually owns this bar. And he let her live."

"He was toying with her, don't you see that? He was biding his time and playing with her. We're living fucking proof!" I open my mouth to speak, but Logan puts up a hand to stop me. "Just… listen to me, OK? There's more going on here than you know."

"Obviously."

"He's already unhappy with you about losing that money, AJ. He's already pissed off. And he's nuts. We all know he's nuts. Always picking fights with people. Everything he does is a gut reaction. He's impulsive, and careless, and stupid. The guy has maybe five years on the job before some other boss decides to shut his stupid trap for good. All I have to do is lie low, do my job, keep my mouth shut and pretty soon someone else is gonna take over. His cousin, Joe, maybe. Or his little brother, Anthony. Damon is temporary. All I gotta do—"

"All you?" I ask.

"What?"

"You keep saying all *you* gotta do. What about me?"

He looks at me for a second, then says, "I mean *us*, AJ. I mean *we*. All we gotta do is play it smart. Then when the regime change happens, we slip away. Quietly, no drama, no debts. Just slip away."

But he did not mean us.

He very much did mean him.

"We do this job," Logan says, gripping my upper arm. "We finish it. We go home. We bide our time. And we get out."

I shake my head no. "We're not killing her."

"It's OK," Yvette says from the doorway.

We both spin around to see her standing there holding a stack of clothes that she did not just happen to find in her little lost and found.

"It's OK," she says again, sighing with a whole lot of sad resignation. "I know that's why you're here. You can kill me. I don't mind because… I don't want to live anymore."

Logan and I both look down at the note he's still holding.

Her suicide note.

Which describes, in detail, how this night would've gone if we hadn't shown up.

CHAPTER FOURTEEN

YVETTE

Did I want to get them clothes when I offered?

Most days I'd have said no. It was too painful to go down into that room. Seeing everything I lost laid out before my eyes was unbearable. Too difficult to endure.

But I liked having someone to care for. It's been so long since I had that. And so here was a chance to help in some small way. To make them more comfortable.

Even so, when the words came out of my mouth I was as surprised as they were. I count the weeks between visits. And it has been seventeen now. So the count would start over if I went down there to get them clothes.

At first, in the days following the "accident", I counted the minutes.

The bar was closed, so I didn't have to worry about customers. And I'd go upstairs, back when everything was still upstairs, and just wallow in the emptiness as I sat in the middle of all the things that used to fill me up. Then I'd go back downstairs and do something meaningless. Like wash down the already clean bar, or rearrange the whiskey bottles so all the labels were facing forward. Or play a video game.

I stayed away from the jukebox because Chris and I had a lot of fun with that machine.

Maybe that's why, when AJ held out his hand for me to dance with him, I did. I took it and I let him swing me around. Then let him fuck me with Logan.

I guess I could make an argument for that. But I'm not going to bother.

I took his hand because he offered it. I let them fuck me because they didn't ask permission.

I'd have said no if they were the timid sort. The kind of men who were not spontaneous and daring. Who were not in charge and bossy.

But they were, so I let them.

I just don't want to think anymore. I don't want to make any more decisions. I've made enough of those over the last year. Enough for an entire lifetime.

Three caskets in one year is too many to choose in ten years.

Two funerals. Three burial plots. Two times I had to fill this bar with friends and family so we could say goodbye to the people we lost.

And then… those minutes that came after the accident. After the last funeral was over. When everyone went home and all the food was put away, I just sat here. Alone.

And yes, Chris had family still. But they live hundreds of miles away down in New Mexico.

I wasn't going to go with them.

Maybe the bar was empty and l was lonely, but I didn't want to leave it behind.

So those minutes were hard. And eventually they turned into hours, and hours became days. I started sleeping on the pool table. I got pillows and blankets, stuffed them in the office, and slept on top of them at night so I didn't have to sleep in that bed alone or walk past that empty second bedroom.

I stopped eating upstairs too. Went days without cooking, just grabbing those pre-packaged cookies we sell. Or the beer nuts and pretzels we give out for free during happy hour.

But I had to do something. I had to move on. I was here, and they were not, and I had to open the bar back up. I thought I needed the money.

Of course, I didn't need the money. After Daniel—my father-in-law—died, Chris inherited his entire estate. So we were OK. It was a decent amount of money. But Chris and I never really married. Not legally. And he had brothers and sisters who I assumed would get the estate after the "accident".

But they gave it all to me.

So I didn't need the money. I just didn't know it yet. So I did open the bar, even though I wanted to just shrivel up and die like the people I lost.

But I'd find myself upstairs in those early weeks. Just sitting in our bedroom asking myself how things went so sideways.

I couldn't even open the door to baby Bonnie's room. Could barely walk past it without just dropping to the floor in sobs that felt like they'd last forever.

It was all too painful.

So I closed the bar again. Hired some construction workers, and they ripped out my cozy, middle-class two-bedroom life upstairs and replaced it with some new, one-bedroom version. Some new high-end version built for one that didn't really belong to me.

I made them erase my sadness.

And when my sisters and brothers-in-law came to visit, to check on me, they saw it and… oh, how I adore them. They said it was beautiful. And I deserved to be happy.

How? How do I deserve to be happy? When the only man I've ever loved and our baby daughter were killed in an "accident" just two months after my new, and much-loved, father-in-law died of cancer?

I didn't deserve it. Not one bit of it. I didn't deserve them, either. Those patient and supportive brothers-and-sisters-in-law.

But I didn't throw everything away when I remodeled the apartment. I took some things down to Daniel's bedroom. The room he died in. The room where cancer took everything from him. And I put some things in there. Pictures, mostly. But their clothes too. I kept Chris's clothes. And my favorite outfits that baby Bonnie never got to wear along with the one dress she wore all the time.

I didn't touch the shop, either. Never went in there again, in fact. We didn't drive those cars in there. They were just projects. The Corolla was the first car Chris ever had and the Jeep was some old clunker he bought back when he was twenty-one. To fix up and take mudding and climbing eventually. Once he fixed it up.

Which he never did. So it sits there, never used by us at all.

I never turned on the generator when Chris was alive. He took care of that stuff. So even though I have it, and the power has gone off at least a dozen times since the "accident", I never bothered to go flip that switch.

But remodeling the apartment didn't really help. Didn't fix much. Nothing, really. In fact, I think it made it worse.

But I got up every day and put on my yoga pants and my Snowbunny t-shirt. I tended bar and served lunches and sometimes dinner too, but more often than not, I never even opened the kitchen.

They say time heals things like this and I'm sure that's true for some people. It just wasn't true for me.

So two nights ago I made a decision. I went into Daniel's room—which I did not change in the remodel and which has been sitting closed up for a whole year—and found his bottle of painkillers. I filled that prescription the day he died. Drove all the way down the mountain to Pagosa Springs to get them. But he never had a chance to take them.

But I knew where they were. And I could take them.

So last night I got out a piece of paper and wrote my final words. Stuck it inside that journal for someone to find, planned an outfit to wear on my last day—I wanted one last day at the bar. One last chance to take care of people because there was no one left to take care of. And I got dressed up this morning. I did my hair, and put on makeup. I even put on some sexy lingerie.

And I got drunk as the snow rolled in.

It felt fitting to go out with a storm.

It felt right.

But then, just as I was about to go upstairs and take those pills, two mysterious, handsome strangers walked into my bar and all my best-laid plans were ruined.

I look up, because I'm looking at the floor, and realize I just said all that out loud. Just told AJ and Logan my whole story.

Well, not the whole story. Just the parts that count.

I stare at them and they stare at me.

AJ says, "Oh, shit, Yvette. Oh, shit."

Logan says nothing.

"I'm so sorry," AJ says, coming towards me. He takes the stack of clothes from my hands and places them on a nearby chair. I appreciate that. That he didn't just drop them on the floor. It's like he heard everything I just said and gets it. Like he knew they were precious things and not just faded and oil-stained jeans my dead husband used to wear. That they were more than just well-loved worthless t-shirts.

And then he wraps his arms around me.

Like we're not strangers who met this afternoon. But old friends. And he's been gone for a while but now he's back. Catching up. And all the news he's missed has been bad.

"I know who you are," I say, sighing. "I know why you're here."

"Why?" Logan says. "Why are we here, Yvette?"

I swallow hard and say it. "To kill me. Damon sent you. I've been waiting, actually. Before I decided to take matters into my own hands I figured I'd just wait. Wait for him to show and take my life too. He's already taken everything else."

Logan just stares at me.

AJ hugs me tighter.

"But you guys took too long so…" I shrug. "What else could I do but end it myself?"

There is a long, heavy silence in the room. Thick like the steam in the shower we just took.

Then Logan says, "You said baby, Yvette. How old was the baby?"

I shake my head.

AJ pushes back, places his hands on my shoulders and keeps me at arm's length so he can look down at my face.

I shake my head again. "She wasn't his, Logan. I gave his baby away."

"What?" AJ says.

But I'm still looking at Logan. He's the one who makes the decisions here. Not that I care what decision he makes now. I'm done. I'm over it. I want to die.

I just need him to understand this so when he goes back to Damon, he can make this perfectly clear.

"My daughter was not his baby. I gave his baby away the year before Bonnie was born. I don't know where he is, and even if I did, I'd never give you, or him, that information."

AJ turns. Whirling around, placing himself in between Logan and me. He says, "This?"

Like that's all that needs to be said.

But he says more anyway.

"This is why we're here? To get Damon's kid? And you knew? And you lied to me?"

Yeah, that sucks. I liked Logan. Not as much as I like AJ, but he was growing on me.

But I know who he is. It took me a while to place his face, but I did eventually. Somewhere between the toy fuck and the shower fuck it came to me.

Logan the Loyal.

Which is what Damon used to call him.

Except it wasn't because he was loyal. It was sarcasm, or irony, or maybe just a fuckin' joke.

Because Logan has no loyalties. None at all and everyone in the inner circle knew this. Damon, especially, knew this.

But apparently AJ didn't.

So I say, to him, "I'm sorry."

Which makes him turn—because I gripped his arm when I said this—to look down at me again. And he says, "What?"

So I say it again. Because it's gotta hurt and it might take a while to sink in, but eventually it will. "I'm sorry."

"What are you sorry for?"

I shrug. "That this is happening to you, I guess."

"What? Nothing's happening to me, Yvette." But then the look on his face changes. And for a second I think he gets it. That he understands. He says, "Oh. You mean, this decision that has to be made?"

But that's not what I mean, and Logan knows it. Because he opens his mouth to say something, but loses his nerve and shuts up.

"Don't worry, Yvette," AJ says, shaking his head. "We're not going through with it."

He hugs me and I let him. He holds me close and in such a way that Logan disappears from view.

"I want you to go through with it, AJ. I want you to kill me."

CHAPTER FIFTEEN

LOGAN

AJ is going to lose his mind, so I make a decision. "No one's killing anyone tonight."

"Tonight?" AJ says. "We're not killing her tomorrow, either."

"AJ—" Yvette says.

But he cups a hand over her mouth to shut her up and repeats himself. "We're not killing her."

"She'll just kill herself when we leave, AJ." I say it in a tone I don't recognize. Like… I don't think I recognize myself right now, either.

I feel disconnected. Outside of my body somehow.

But I don't have time to have an existential crisis because… the kid.

I didn't know. Not for sure. But I did suspect. I remember seeing Damon one day before Yvette—Glori—left him. They were fighting and it was loud. He was accusing her of cheating but he was always accusing her of cheating and there was no possible way she could, unless she was fucking one of his men without his permission—which he… gave. Often.

So then the fight degenerated into 'it's not mine, it's not mine, you filthy little slut.' And I made an educated guess.

But I had other business happening that day so I never thought about it again until Yvette went missing a week later.

And you'd think that your woman, who you forced to marry you as a minor and let your wedding party gang-rape on her wedding night, would be more of a priority should said wife ever just up and disappear.

But she wasn't.

I really, truly thought he killed her. And I was going on that assumption right up until he pulled me aside two weeks ago and told me to go pick up AJ and watch her until further notice.

"Watch her," he said. Never bothered to explain how she left, or why she left, or what this thing was I was looking for. He just said, "Watch her. She took something of mine when she left and I want it back. Find it."

And then, of course, he told me to take AJ out too, and dump both bodies before I came back.

But he never did say, "She took my kid."

So… I dunno.

"That journal," I say, sighing heavily. Because maybe AJ was right? Maybe that is what Damon sent me to get? "How did you get him to write that?"

Yvette huffs out something that could be a laugh or could be contempt. I'm not sure because AJ is standing between her and I like a shield. "Are you fucking crazy?" she says. "He didn't write that."

"What?" AJ asks.

"I wrote it. In his voice. It was the closest thing I'd ever get to an apology. That sick bastard was never going to say he was sorry for what he did. And I needed to move on. So I wrote that journal to acknowledge what he did and give myself closure."

Several moments of silence as AJ and I take this in.

I can almost feel his disappointment. He was hoping that was it. Was desperately hoping that journal was the magic bullet that would kill this job instead of Yvette.

But it's not.

It's the kid.

"We were, or were not, sent here to get this kid?" AJ asks.

I do a shrug, shake, nod of my head. "I don't know, AJ. I really don't know. Damon is…"

"A certified psychopath?" Yvette is angry when she says that. And I don't blame her. Not after what he put her through. But it's just… different than how she was just a couple minutes ago.

Anger is good. Defeat and surrender, not so much. So I prefer this side of her to that one.

AJ says, "Don't worry, Yvette. I'm not gonna let him hurt you."

And now I have to wonder… is it *me* he's protecting her from? Or Damon?

Could go either way.

"Why don't we eat dinner?" I ask. "It's getting late, we're all tired, and—"

"Dinner?" AJ says, like this is the dumbest thing he's ever heard.

God, he is just not gonna play ball tonight, is he?

"Yeah, OK," Yvette says. "I could use some dinner. I drank way too much today and I haven't eaten since yesterday. Didn't think I'd need it."

"Yvette," AJ says, a little bit of frustration and anger in his tone. "Stop talking like that. You're not killing yourself. So fine," he says, looking at me. "We'll eat. She needs to eat."

I nod and walk over to the clothes on the chair. The ones Yvette brought up with her. I hold up the jeans, decide they'll fit, and start slipping them on without underwear.

She didn't bring any, but even if she did, I'm not wearing another man's underwear.

AJ comes up next to me, picking up the other pair of jeans, then tosses them aside, deciding they won't fit. Too short. He's a huge guy. Two inches taller than me, at least.

Plus, he was already wearing comfortable jeans, so he just puts those back on.

I don't bother with a shirt and neither does AJ. This place feels hot now. Wood stove and central heat, probably overkill.

When we turn to face Yvette she's biting her lip. Frowning too.

I guess seeing me wearing her dead husband's clothes has stirred up feelings.

I shrug and sigh. Such a fucked-up situation.

But I didn't ask to be here. I didn't kill her husband or her baby. I didn't make her run, or marry that asshole. I didn't do any of that. None of this is my fault.

Still, I feel the need to whisper, "I'm sorry," just before I push past AJ and walk out the bedroom door.

Whispers follow me out, but fade soon enough. Because I pull open the apartment door and head downstairs to lose myself in her industrial kitchen.

AJ joins me a few minutes later. By this time I have found bread, lunch meat, condiments, and bags of single-serving potato chips.

"Turkey or roast beef?" I ask AJ when he enters the kitchen.

"I don't care," he says.

"Where's Yvette?"

"Getting drinks."

I shoot him a raised eyebrow.

"Not alcohol. Some special sparkling cider she bought at Christmas but never opened."

"And she wants to open it with us? AJ, look—"

"No, you look. I'm not discussing this any further, but I'm not killing her. So if you want to kill her, you're gonna have kill me first."

Irony, I guess. Or maybe just a really bad joke.

"Fine," I say. "We can't even leave this place until the snow stops and they clear the roads. So no more talk about that stuff. Just… eat your fucking sandwich and chill."

That's when I notice he brought the journal down here with him. "What's with that?" I ask, nodding my head to the book.

"I think you should read it. Because I only skimmed about ten pages and I'm ready to kill Damon myself. Did you know this was happening to her?"

My mind blanks out for a second, some long-forgotten memory bubbling up to the surface of being in their house one night. Unexpected and unwanted. A meeting, I think it was. Something went wrong with some other thing and I had to go there in the middle of the night. And I saw her. Just a flash of white running across the expansive back lawn, her nightgown trailing behind her like she was a comet.

She was running away.

I knew back then. I knew what he was doing to her.

"Some of it," I admit.

AJ takes a bite of his sandwich and glares at me.

"I knew he was an asshole. I knew he passed her around. But it was mostly rumors, AJ."

Mostly. Except for that night when his personal guards tackled her to the ground and she disappeared from view. Just... screams after that.

I was there long enough that I saw her being led back in after the men were done with her on the lawn. Her hair was a rat's nest filled with grass clippings and twigs. And she was filthy. Dirt on her nightgown, which was ripped down the middle. Her face, her legs, her arms. All stained with dirt and grass.

"It was mostly rumors," I say again. Because I felt... shame that night. Watching them rape her, then lead her back inside to her pretty prison. It stayed with me for a long time. And I've seen a lot of shit over the past several years. Almost all of it worthy of shame.

But none of that other shit ever touched me. Not the way that night did.

Yvette pushes her way through the swinging kitchen door holding a bottle that looks like champagne, but when she sets it down on the large stainless-steel table Aje and I are sitting at, I see that it's sparkling cider, just like he said.

She's also got three fluted glasses in her hand, which she sets down next to the bottle. She smiles.

Which is not right. Why the fuck is she smiling?

"We're celebrating," she says, reading my mind. She finds a bottle opener, pops the top off the cider, and then pours us each a glass.

This whole time AJ is watching her with a heavy frown on his face. She pushes one glass over to me, one to AJ, and then picks hers up like she's about to make a toast.

AJ shakes his head. *Not gonna do it,* that shake says.

"Look." She sighs. "I'm done here, OK? I'm done. I don't want to live anymore. This is my choice."

"You don't get to quit the game just because you're losing," AJ growls.

"Fuck you," she says. "Just fuck you." Her voice cracks a little. "You have no idea what this"—she pans her arms wide—"feels like. OK? But I do and I don't want to feel this way anymore. I lost everything. And when the day comes—God forbid—that you lose as much as I have, well, then you can have an opinion. Then you can judge me and call me a quitter. But until then, you get no say in my decisions. I don't know you," she says, her voice taking on a tone of anger. "I have no clue who you are. I know how big your cock is and that's about it. And to be honest, that's all I want to know about you."

AJ shakes his head again. "Won't work."

"What won't work?" she asks.

"You can't change my mind and your insults are just a provocation. So I'm not gonna react."

I just watch them. Kinda weirdly… maybe sickly… fascinated.

Because she's right. We don't know her. She doesn't know us.

We're nothing to each other but three people who got stuck in a blizzard and decided to pass the time by fucking.

But I do have something to say. And against my better judgment, I say it. "So why not just take the pills now?"

"Logan," AJ cautions me.

I hold up a hand. "No, listen. If you want to die so bad, why didn't you grab that pill bottle and take those pills? Do it without telling us."

"Maybe I did." She smirks.

But AJ pulls the bottle of pills out of his pants pocket and holds them up, smiling.

"Take them back," I say. "If you want to die so bad."

AJ says nothing.

Yvette fumes. "Why? So you don't have to do your job? Maybe I want to *make you* do your job?"

"Yeah," I say, ready to push back. "You'd like that, wouldn't you? Put it all on me. Play the victim. Again," I add. Just to push her button a little harder.

"*Play* the victim?" She huffs out a sarcastic laugh. "Wow."

I shrug. "Hey, you're the one who wants to die. Do I look like I give a fuck, Yvette? Do I look like a guy who goes out of his way to do *anything*? Because if I gave you that impression, I'm sorry. I'm not that guy. If you run, I'll chase you. The way Damon's men used to chase you across the lawn."

It's a low blow, but I don't care.

"I'll chase you, knock you down, shove your face into the snow, and then bring you back to hell with me."

"Nice," AJ says. "God, you're a dick, Logan. He's not gonna do that."

"No, maybe not. But only because if she runs it'll be to make me take the responsibility off herself. Why did you wait so long? If you want to die? Why today, of all days?"

"Are you trying to talk her into this?" AJ asks.

Maybe I am. Maybe I'm the coward, not her. But I don't say that. I say, "Hey, if it makes my life easier, why not? Just go die somewhere then. No one wants to be around a pathetic victim, Yvette. The world loves a winner. And you are so clearly a loser—"

She throws her cider into my face. "Fuck you."

And then she walks out.

"What the fuck are you doing?" AJ asks.

I walk over to the sink, grab a paper towel, and wipe off my face before I turn to look at him. Then I shrug. "Being the monster," I say.

"Why?"

"Because someone has to play that part."

And I walk out too.

By the time I follow them out of the kitchen Logan is behind the bar pouring two glasses of whiskey and Yvette is standing in front of the jukebox. Leaning forward a little, her long, blonde, still mostly wet hair hanging over her face, as she stares at the list of songs.

Logan comes out from behind the bar holding two glasses. I'm not really in the mood to drink, but I take it anyway.

He stares at me as he sips. No shirt. The muscles of his bare chest looking cut and contoured in the dim glow of yellow sconce lights. I don't know the last time I've seen him in such casual clothes.

His feet are bare, like mine. And his jeans are well-worn and faded. Like mine. Usually Logan is a suit guy. And that look fits him, I guess. I'm used to it. So I don't bother checking him out much, but I can't help myself now.

He does the same to me. Even though he sees me casual all the time. I don't really do suits. Not my style.

He smiles a little. And even though I'm having a hard time finding something to smile about, I smile back.

I think he's provoking her to try to change her mind. Which doesn't make much sense. We are here to kill her. There's no getting around that order without completely upending our worlds. But I really do believe he's just playing devil's advocate.

Good cop. Bad cop.

OK. I'll play.

I take myself and my drink over to the jukebox. It's at the end of the bar, near the front window—which is high up on the wall so you can't really see out of it. But it's iced over with snow anyway, so makes no difference. I take a seat on the barstool closest to Yvette and lean back on the bar to watch her pretend to be interested in songs.

"I lost my mom to cancer," I say.

She turns her head to the side just enough to peek out at me through her hanging hair.

"I was about…" I look over at Logan. "What? Fifteen?"

He nods. Not that Yvette notices. She's turned back to the songs.

"So I know how bad that sucks. She went pretty fast too. It wasn't one of those long, drawn-out processes. So it was weird, ya know?"

Yvette straightens up. Looks at me. Nods.

"It felt like one day everything was cool. Then she got diagnosed and just like that"—I snap my fingers— "shit changed. It sucked too."

"What did you do?" Yvette asks. "Did you have a father to help you?"

"No," I say, shaking my head. "He died couple years earlier. Actually," I say, correcting myself, "he killed himself."

Yvette's mouth forms into a tiny o shape.

I nod. "Yeah. Blew his brains out in our basement."

She looks over her shoulder at Logan, who is leaning against the bar a little farther down the room.

He says, "No. I didn't know him then." Like she asked a question, when she didn't. "So I wasn't there for that one."

Yvette looks at me again and I continue. "So, yeah. No. I don't know you. I just know me. I know how it felt both ways. To watch someone die of disease and to be told someone was dead due to suicide. And I don't know much about your life, but I do know this, Yvette. You have one. Here. Up on this mountain with all the weirdos who live up here with you. So even though you think you're alone, you're not. You'll be gone, but everyone who comes in here will hear about you and what you did. And every one of them will hurt because of it."

She sucks in a deep, deep breath through her nose. Grimaces. Probably picturing these tangential people who pass in and out of her bar and her life. And how she does the same for them.

"You're a fixture. I think that's something people who want to give up don't realize. You're a fixture in this world. And maybe that's not the best thing to be, but it's more than nothing. Very, very few people are nobodies. Very, very few people can take their own life and not leave destruction in their wake. And sometimes I think… you know what? Why should I care? Why should I care when there's no point to any of it anyway? Life has no point, ya know?"

She just stares at me.

"We're born. We live. We die. That's all there is to it."

She exhales out a long breath. Like she's been holding it in for a while. "So who cares?" she says. "If there's no point then it doesn't matter."

I shrug. "The point is to have experiences, Yvette. To learn things. To explore, to need, to love, to hate, to win. To lose," I add. "It's just about experiences. That's it. And some of them are good. And some of them are bad. But all of them add up to just one thing in the end."

"What?" she whispers. "What do they add up to? Disappointment and regrets? Because that's all I've gotten so far."

I stand up, cross the small distance between us, and tap her on the head. "No. They add up to *you*, Yvette."

"What?" she asks, making a face.

"You," I say. "There is only one you. So the only point of life is to be you. That's it. Whatever that is. Whatever that means. Nothing more. Nothing less. It's just… a ride, ya know? There's no winners. We're all losers in the end. We're all gonna die. So what's the point in quitting the game early when we already know how it ends?"

She shakes her head. Lets out half a laugh. "That doesn't make me feel better."

"Yeah, because your life sucks right now. Well, it did. Then Logan and I walked into your bar and the fucking sun came out."

She smiles for real now. "You're stupid, AJ."

"So I've been told. Many times, believe me. But I'm also right."

I take the pill bottle out of my pocket and place it on top of the jukebox.

Yvette looks at it, then at me.

But I just shrug. "Fuck it. You wanna quit early? Go ahead. But I'd just like to say… you're not *you* yet." I tap her on the head again. "You're still baking, cookie. You're still doughy inside. You can come out of the oven now and the world won't end. Hell, I love me a half-baked cookie. But if you just give it a few more minutes you'll cook all the way through."

She looks at Logan.

"Don't look at him," I say, tipping her chin back in my direction. "He's not in charge of you. Only *you* are in charge of you. What he does is his business. He's playing his game. He's gathering up all his experiences, just like the rest of us. And we have nothing to do with his decisions."

"He wants to kill me. You came here to kill me."

"Well, I changed my mind."

She looks at Logan again. "He hasn't."

"No. He hasn't," I say. "And he can do whatever he wants." And now I look at Logan. "But he's done a pretty shitty job at playing the game of life so far, so I wouldn't worry too hard about it."

We're all silent for a few minutes. Long, agonizing, awkward minutes.

So I get up off my stool and stand next to her, choose a song and say, "Play that one."

She looks up at me, then back down at the machine. Punches in a code that gives her free access, and plays the song.

I Wanna Make You Close Your Eyes comes on and I offer her my hand. "Would you like to dance?"

She frowns so deep for a second I think she might cry. But then she sucks in a deep breath of air and nods her head.

I fold her into my arms and she sinks. Her cheek resting right up against my shoulder as we begin to sway.

I look down at her as she looks up at me.

And then she closes her eyes.

We dance like that. Barely moving. Just a little shuffle of bare feet. Her warming me up in the cold room. The storm still raging outside.

And then Logan is next to us. Pulling us apart.

He says, "Come on. Let's go to bed. This day is done."

CHAPTER SEVENTEEN

YVETTE

One day. A single day, out of all the days I've lived.

One day can change everything.

I should know that by now. It's happened enough before. The day I met Damon, for example. The day I married him. The day I left.

All single days that changed my life. The first two made it worse but the last one definitely made it better.

I met Chris and we fell in love. I met his father and they gave me a new home. I gave birth. That was a good day.

But then I left the baby behind and that was bad.

Still, life went on. Just like AJ said. And more good things happened. I got pregnant again. Had another baby and this time I got to keep her.

But then Daniel got sick and died.

But still there were Chris and Bonnie. We raised Bonnie for almost two years before the "accident". We had two glorious years as a real family.

The thing that scares me the most about this game of life is that you're never safe. Like AJ said, you never win. We all know we're going to lose.

I understood this before AJ gave me his pep talk. Instincts, I guess. But no one has ever spelled it out like that before. I guess anyone who doesn't figure this out is just in denial. Or dumb. But everyone plays the game at their own pace.

So he's right. It's the experiences that count. The memories. The time we get.

This is just life.

And even though it feels like we're all playing by different rules because there are men out there like Damon and women out there like me, and some people are born rich and some are born super poor, and some are smart, and some are not, and some get more chances, more lucky breaks, we're still playing by the same rules.

We're born. We live. We die.

That's it.

What we do with the live part is up to us.

So I could take those pills and end the game early. But what will I miss? What experiences are waiting for me if I don't check out early? What could I learn that I haven't yet learned? Where could I go? Who could I meet?

If you had asked me the day before I escaped from Damon if I would ever be happy again I'd have said no.

Never. Ever. Life sucks. Kill me now. I'm done.

But I'd have missed out on so, so much. All the best days of my life came after that one day.

Maybe Logan will kill me tomorrow and it's over. Just like that.

Or maybe he won't and I try something new?

Maybe I give AJ a try?

And maybe Logan does too?

I don't know. It's all too much to think about right now. I'm tired. And I drank too much today. And I didn't eat.

But I have no energy left to deal.

Logan takes my hand just as we get to the stairs and leads me up to the apartment door. Inside it's chillier than it was earlier. The fire in the wood stove is just glowing embers now.

Logan doesn't let go of my hand as he leads me down the hallway to the bedroom. Not until we reach the bed and he tosses all the throw pillows off—something we didn't even take time to do earlier—and pulls the comforter back.

I sigh at the bed. It's not the bed I shared with Chris. So that's not why I'm suddenly too tired to climb in.

I just… can't see past this day. No matter how hard I try, I can't find a future.

"Tomorrow," Logan says. "We can think about it tomorrow."

Which is a concession of sorts. Because he was still hell-bent on killing me just thirty minutes ago.

AJ drops his pants to the floor and walks around to the other side of the bed, gets in and then extends his hand to me. "Come on," he says. "Just sleep. I'm too tired to think."

So I get in as Logan takes off his pants too. And then he gets in and flicks off the bedside table lamp.

I lie there between them, my fully-clothed body between their naked ones, and wonder how the hell I got here.

AJ slips his arm underneath me, pulling me into his chest like we're lovers, when we're not. I don't know. That makes me sad for some reason. This all feels very… pretend.

But he doesn't seem to care. Because he hugs me tight and leans his head against mine.

I look over at Logan, who I can't really see. He's just a faint outline of shadow from a bit of light filtering in from the window. But I think his eyes are open. I think he's staring at me.

"I'm sorry," he says. Kinda out of nowhere.

"For what?"

"For not helping you. Back when you were with Damon. I should've… I dunno. Done something, I guess."

"Like what? Save me?" It comes out snarky, which I didn't intend. Which means it's real snark and not me being a bitch. Which is worse. Because he's trying, I guess. I don't know at what. But still, he's trying.

"No," he says, sighing. "I had no power to save you back then, Yvette."

"And you do now?"

He doesn't say anything but I know he's shaking his head no.

"Don't listen to him," AJ whispers into my ear. "He has no clue what he can and cannot do yet. He has no idea how powerful he is because he's never tested it. He's never rocked the boat. Have you, Logan?"

Puzzles and codes. That's what AJ gives me. And it's too complicated. I thought he was the simple one but I guess I was wrong.

Logan sighs and turns over. Turns his back to me as he hugs the pillow. "See ya in the morning."

We're all silent for a while. My eyes close and begin to get heavy. My mind's eye swirls with weird geometric patterns as sleep creeps over me like a spider. And that weird sensation of falling I have just before I drift off takes over.

But AJ brings me back with a soft kiss to my cheek.

Why is he acting this way? What am I to him? Why does he care?

"Ya know," he whispers softly, "I didn't think there was anything left for me either. I hide it better than most. Better than you, for sure. Maybe not as well as Logan. But I've been there too. And I'm really happy I finally got to meet you today."

I squirm in his embrace. Turn over so we're face to face. Place my palm on his cheek and whisper, "Thank you."

He nods his head and closes his eyes. "Any time, cookie. Glad to help."

CHAPTER EIGHTEEN

LOGAN

It's not like I don't want out. It's not like I don't wish for more. It's not like I haven't fantasized about having my own family. A wife, kids, minivan—well, not a minivan. Not even for my wife.

But a… a Suburban. Or a Tahoe. Some too-big SUV that's actually necessary because I have shit to haul around, and kids to cart to classes, and maybe, every now and then, we buy a piece of furniture and I'm glad I have all that cargo space because I can stuff a couch or an armchair back there and don't have to pay for delivery.

It's just… I have forged a path and there's no fork in the road. There's no way out that I can see.

I mean, come on. My best-laid plan is to wait for some random second cousin to get sick of Damon's shit and blow his head off.

That's not a plan.

So what the fuck can I do?

If I kill her, I lose AJ. I see that now. He's gone round some bend and he's not coming back.

Which is fine for him. Hell, I was supposed to kill him too. So there's no life waiting for him back home.

But if I kill them, and go home, and wait things out—there's a chance. A small one, but still, a chance that I might find another path to travel in some unknown future.

If I don't kill them… there's no way I can't kill them. There is no possible scenario where I don't do my job because then we'd *all* be alive. And worse yet, Damon would know we're all together. He's got resources. He's waited this long to send us after Yvette, he'll wait forever to get revenge on Aje and me if that's what it takes.

I think I've figured out why he sent me to do this too. Why he told me to get rid of AJ. It's not that he hates AJ. It's not even that AJ is incompetent, because he's not. Losing the money wasn't his fault. It was just someone else's fuck-up that got pinned on him.

Damon sent me here and told me to kill AJ because he wanted to see if I'd do it. He's testing me.

I know what they call me. Logan the Loyal. And I know it's sarcasm because I truly do not have loyalty to anyone. That's God's honest truth. So if I fail I'd be proving him right. He'd just shoot the minute I stepped through the door.

But if I succeed, if I follow through and obey orders, well, that changes everything for me. That puts me in a position to rise. Gives me more freedom. More options for later. More ways to get out.

But then I have to ask myself… how long can I keep doing this? And I have to ask myself… what will be there on the other side of waiting? When I finally do make it out?

Nothing.

So I totally understand Yvette's defeatist attitude.

Maybe I should be the one taking those fucking pills?

"Stop it," AJ murmurs. "You're starting to piss me off."

"What?" I say, turning over on my back so I can stare up at the ceiling.

"Thinking," he says. "I'm tired of it."

I'm tired of it too. I'm tired of all this shit. And the worst part is… I want something else. Something more. And I'm stuck.

There's no way out.

"Dude," AJ says.

"I'm not thinking, dammit. Just shut up and let me sleep."

I wait a few minutes. Until AJ's breathing slows down and I'm pretty sure he's out. Then go back to my thoughts. Trying to keep them quiet from my mind-reading best friend.

There has to be a way out.

And did I just call AJ my best friend?

That's great. Just great.

I can't kill my best friend. That's some fucked-up psycho shit right there.

Still, there has to be a way out. Something I'm missing. Some evil part of my diabolical brain must have an answer I never thought of before.

It doesn't come to me. Nothing comes to me except sleep.

But I do dream. I find myself in a world with beaches, and sun, and an ocean. It's a nice place. A foreign place, but not too foreign. Friendly, easy-going locals and a harbor filled with tourist yachts and fishing boats. There's a bustling market with rows and rows of vendors selling everything you need in life.

It's a place I've been before. Back when I was a child, and then once again just a couple years back.

I'd like to live there, I decide in my dream.

One day. If I manage to live through the other side of this job.

When I wake up AJ is breathing lightly and Yvette's got her face pressed up into my back.

Immediately my thoughts from last night resurface. My little problem.

Yvette moans a little and that small noise is enough to kickstart the morning wood.

I should not fuck this girl again. In fact, I should get up, find my gun, shoot her in the head, shoot AJ while I'm at it, and then drag their bodies out into the woods and dump them both over that ravine.

Sensible, logical, Logan the Loyal is back.

Except he's not. Because AJ reaches out, snatches Yvette, and tugs her away from me and into him.

I turn my head, barely able to open my eyes. The dark night has given way to a too-bright morning and it hurts. So I squint.

"I'm awake," AJ says. "Been awake for a while now."

"Creep," I mumble. "What time is it?" He turns, taking Yvette with him, which makes her moan again, only this time it resembles words.

"What…" she croaks. "What's going on?"

"It's ten thirty," AJ says.

Fuck. Been a very long time since I slept this late.

AJ reaches his hand over to me. Feels my cock.

I push him away. "No," I say. "We gotta be serious today. The storm is probably over. Last night never happened."

AJ grunts. "Suit yourself. Looks like you're all mine today, cookie."

"Stop calling her that," I growl. He's irritating me. Him and his carefree attitude. His stupid words of wisdom.

"No," AJ says, rolling over once again so Yvette is pinned beneath his chest. I turn my head to look at them. Find them both smiling. Yvette with her eyes closed. Apparently having the same difficulty I am with the bright snow outside. AJ with his open. Gazing down at this girl like she's his wife instead of his mark.

He glances at me. "Last chance."

I reach down and grip my cock. Willing it to shrink.

Just gets harder.

I want to give in. I totally do. But I can't erase the fact that I have to kill these people. Today. Probably in the next few hours.

"Logan," AJ says.

"What?" I mumble, looking up at the ceiling.

"Just relax, man. Forget about later and just be here now."

I don't know how he does that. Just pushes his problems away until later. I've always been a worrier myself. Always got a future problem running through my brain.

He slides off to the side of Yvette and reaches over her to feel for my cock again.

This time I don't push him away. Because maybe that's the answer? Maybe that's how you stop worrying about the future?

Just be here now.

He starts kissing Yvette's neck and she bucks her back a little. Inhaling deeply like she's very relaxed. At the same time he plays with my cock. It's mostly hard already but his hand feels good. His grip is firm on my shaft and when he reaches down to cup my balls I turn over towards Yvette and reach between her legs. I find myself smiling.

"How shall we fuck you today?" I ask.

"Mmmmm…" She giggles a little. She looks a lot better than she did last night. Rested, some color back in her cheeks. Eyes still closed like she's having a good dream.

"Hmmm?" I ask again. AJ has let go of my dick and is working her shirt up her body. She maneuvers, helping him get it over her head, and her firm, round breasts and large peaked nipples capture my full attention.

I lean over, cupping one as AJ works on getting her leggings off. My mouth covers her nipple and I suck on it, then pull back and nip it gently with my teeth.

She moans, lifting her butt up so AJ can slip her pants over her hips and drag them down her legs. He throws them over his shoulder and ducks his head under the covers, easing his way in between her legs.

I pull the covers back because I want to watch.

But Yvette says, "I'm cold."

So I throw the covers over all three of us and the sweet scent of her wet pussy almost drives me mad.

AJ parts her legs and I place one hand on her inner thigh, spreading her open wider for him as he licks the length of her opening. She's not shaved and even though I prefer shaved women and manscape myself, I like it on her. Fits her rustic personality but also gives me an idea for later.

AJ is eating her out so hard now, she grabs his head with one hand. Fisting his hair as she wriggles and writhes. Her other hand finds my cock and I lie back a little, giving her access. I reach over and slip my fingers between her legs. AJ licks them, sucking on them.

I respond by pushing them inside her to get them slick and feed him her juices.

I moan too. Because his mouth wrapped around my finger makes me want it on my cock.

What are we doing?

But it's like AJ is reading my mind because he leans over Yvette's open leg and does it. His hand joins hers and they pump me together and then… there it is.

His lips seal over the top of my head, his tongue flattens out along my shaft, and he goes down.

I don't want to kill him, I decide.

Suddenly Yvette's mouth is on mine. Her soft lips kissing me, her soft hand rubbing my scratchy jaw.

I open my mouth for her just as my cock slips down into AJ's throat. Our tongues twist together. Mingle and slide in and out as AJ blows me and I finger her pussy. Her fingers join mine and she plays with herself. We play with her pussy together as we kiss.

It's intimate and sexy and when she withdraws her fingers I miss them. I miss our connection. But then they're in my mouth. Taking the place of our kiss and our tongues.

AJ is licking my balls as I suck on her fingers and imagine it's AJ's cock. I want to fuck her right now. I might want to fuck her together.

Shit. I like this. I like them. And I don't want to kill her either.

AJ pulls back and my hand immediately goes to his head to make him continue. "Don't stop," I say.

"Then quit thinking so hard." He laughs, throwing the covers off us. "You're starting to piss me off."

Yvette doesn't complain that she's cold. No one is cold. We are so hot for each other right now, we could heat this whole apartment.

"How should we fuck her?" I ask him.

"Any way we want," AJ responds. But then he winks at me and adds, "But I have an idea."

"What's that?" I ask, licking Yvette's fingers. She's turned over on her side so our eyes meet as I do this. She pumps them in and out of my mouth.

AJ sits up, turns his body around, scoots his ass up to mine until our balls are touching and our rock-hard cocks are sticking straight up in the air. And then he says, "Together."

I don't know if Yvette is just a kinky bitch who's done this before or she just has a very sexy imagination, but she understands before I do. Because she swings her legs over AJ's stomach, positions her pussy right over the top of both our cocks, fists them at the same time with her hand, and then presses them up to her wet opening.

I know we'll fit. We fucked her like this yesterday down on the dance floor. And I still remember how that felt. But nothing prepares me for this. Nothing prepares me for the experience of having one girl sink her full weight down onto the top of our two cocks and force us both inside her.

She's facing me, not AJ. His hands go to her hips to help. But mine go to her large, heavy breasts. I squeeze them and make her moan and then… we're both there. Inside her. And AJ's hips begin to rock. His balls moving against mine.

He lifts her up with those large hands of his. Bouncing her. Bouncing her tits too. She flattens her hands down onto my stomach, pressing and gripping a little with her fingernails, grimacing as we fill her completely up.

AJ bounces her harder now. With more urgency. And then she takes over and begins fucking us for real. Leaning down onto my chest as her ass slides and grinds. Her hips moving up and down in short, quick movements.

A hard fuck, I decide. She wants a hard fuck.

AJ sits up, pulling his cock out of her. She moans at his withdrawal. But it only lasts a moment because he repositions, sitting up on his knees, and pushes her all the way down onto my chest.

Our lips find each other again. Kiss. Just as AJ covers her back with his body and slips his cock back in.

It's like nothing else I can describe. This feeling of his dick sliding along mine. Nothing else.

And then he pounds her. Pounds me too. So hard Yvette and I slip up to the top of the bed and our heads hit the headboard with each forward thrust.

He slaps her ass and a loud crack echoes through the room. Yvette squeals in pain or maybe pleasure. Or probably both. And he does it again.

I want to close my eyes and just… experience it. Just enjoy it.

But AJ has other plans. Because he yanks her up off my chest by her hair. Wraps it tightly around his fist like it's a rope. This makes her sit up straight and arch her back and she says, "Choke me."

I blink my eyes at her. Almost ask her to repeat that.

But I heard her. So I do it.

I wrap both my hands around her throat and squeeze. Not too hard, but not too light either.

Her eyes flutter and close and she flops forward as she blacks out.

I release the pressure and a few seconds later she opens them again, smiling. "Do it again," she says, sitting up.

All the while AJ is fucking us like a maniac. Thrusting forward with wild abandon.

I hesitate, caught up in the experience.

Yvette slaps me. Hard. Right across my face, and says, "Do it again!"

So I do. I squeeze until she passes out and flops forward.

She takes a few more seconds to come back this time, but she demands, "Again," the minute she's fully conscious.

I shake my head no and she raises her hand to slap me, but AJ catches her by the wrist and says, "Be good, Yvette," in his low, throaty, killing voice. "Be a good girl and come." And then he pushes her forward onto my chest and pounds her hard.

Unrelentingly hard.

I wrap my arms around her shoulders when she resists and tries to sit up. Force her to stay put as we fuck.

She struggles and says, "Do it again! Do it again!"

But AJ has other things in mind. Because he withdraws, backs up, pulling Yvette by her hair as he swings her small body around. My cock slips out and by the time I sit up to see what he's doing, he's got her laid out flat on the bed, face up. Her head dangling over the side of the mattress.

He points to me and says, "Fuck her pussy while I ram my cock down her throat."

I look at Yvette and find her laughing.

"Do it," AJ says.

I open her legs, lift her knees up to her breasts, and slip my dick inside her just as AJ enters her throat.

She gags, still laughing, her hands wrapped around his shaft.

I grip her hips and fuck her hard, just like AJ was doing moments before. And then his cock disappears inside her throat and her hands reach back until they find his thighs. She tries to make him back off, but he doesn't.

She wants it hard? She wants it dirty?

OK. That's what we give her.

AJ leans forward, holding her head tight until her whole face is pressed up against his stomach. I watch, and then he looks up at me and smiles.

Leans forward and kisses me on the mouth. Whispers… "You're welcome," as his tongue plays with mine.

Yvette gags and AJ leans back, breaking our kiss. Pulling his cock out of Yvette's mouth. It's dripping with her saliva and I can't stop looking at it.

So hard, so long, so thick.

And then he grabs my head, brings my face towards him, shoves it down my throat, and says… "Come. Right now."

And we do. Yvette's pussy clamps around my dick as her body goes limp

AJ's cock shudders inside my mouth as he groans and fists my hair.

My cock stiffens and my balls go tight.

And we come.

CHAPTER NINETEEN

Logan pushes me away, my come spilling out of his mouth. I wonder what he's gonna do about that? Will he hit me?

I don't really care.

I'm fucking smiling so big.

"You dick," he says, wiping his mouth. "What the fuck?"

I grab Yvette by the shoulders and sit her up. Her body is soft and compliant and doesn't resist. I pick her up and throw her down on the bed, making her squeal.

I slap the top of her thigh and say, "Move over." And she does. So I get in beside her. "Just come here," I tell Logan, who is still kneeling near the end of the bed, wiping his face.

He takes a deep breath and turns around, flopping back into the mess of covers and pillows.

"That was fun," I say, still grinning.

I chance a look over at Logan. Find him smiling. "I'm gonna get you back for that."

"Fuck you," I say. "You loved it." And then I twist one of Yvette's nipples, making her squeal again. "And you," I say.

"What?" she hums, eyes closed.

"Don't do that again."

"Do what?"

"You know what," I say. "'Choke me,'" I mimic her in a fake feminine voice.

"What can I say? I like it."

But that's not what it was. *Choke me*. It felt like…

"Stop thinking so hard," she says, mimicking my masculine voice.

"I won't be so nice next time," I warn her.

"That was you being nice?"

"Yeah," I say. And it comes out hard and harsh. "It was."

"OK, kids," Logan says. "Don't make me pull this car over."

We're silent for a few minutes. Kinda awkward, long minutes. So I reach over and pull her close. "I don't like it," I say. "Don't do it again."

She rests her head on my chest and sighs.

"Did it stop snowing?" Logan asks.

Yvette doesn't move so I look over at the window to check, but it's impossible to tell because they're iced over. The wind is howling. No change from yesterday. So I say, "I don't think so."

"The highway is probably still closed," Yvette says, not bothering to open her eyes. "But it's Monday. So no matter what the plows will be out, even if it's just for the locals who live past the stop gates. They'll open the whole thing by tonight if the snow lets up. Tomorrow morning at the latest."

So. One more day. That's all we get.

I have a sudden urge to get off this mountain. Damon hasn't heard from us in almost twenty-four hours. He's gonna get suspicious. Gonna be wondering if we got the job done.

"Can anyone get past those gates?" I ask.

"No," Yvette mumbles, almost sleepily. "No. They keep a sheriff on each side, both ways, because people are stupid and you always get some newbie trucker on speed who thinks he's God's gift to eighteen-wheelers. So when they close shit down they take it pretty serious. It's a very dangerous pass even in the summer. And the last thing our little county needs is a rescue and recovery mission for the dumbasses who don't listen and go over the side."

I kinda wish Damon would go over the side.

"Well, I'm gonna need a shower," Logan says. "Someone spewed come all over my face."

I laugh. Can't help it. "Swallow next time, dude."

"Fuck you. There's not gonna be a next time."

Oh, but there is, Logan. There is. He just doesn't realize that yet.

Maybe I should help him out?

"You wanna know how I met Logan?" I'm looking at her when I say it so I see her eyes open.

"How?" she asks.

"Oh, God," Logan moans. "Don't tell that story."

"I really want to hear it now." Yvette giggles.

"It was in a bowling alley." I laugh.

"Shut up," Logan says. But he's laughing too.

"We were like… what? Fifteen? Fourteen?"

"Fourteen," Logan says.

"And he had decided he wanted to get drunk."

"No," Logan protests. "I was trying to get Jamie Fellows drunk so she'd have sex with me."

"Oh, that's horrible!" Yvette says.

"I was fourteen," Logan protests. "And it didn't work anyway. She was faking it."

"What do you mean?" Yvette asks.

"We thought we were all stealth. Had McDonald's cups with wine in them that we kept refilling. And she was pouring her drinks into some planter in the arcade so Logan was the only one drinking."

"I kept thinking, damn, this chick can fucking handle her shit! I gotta keep up."

All of us laugh.

"He was wasted by the time nine o'clock rolled around. And a group of us were all going to see a movie that night."

"*Austin fuckin' Powers.*" Logan laughs.

"Oh, shit. That's right. I laughed so hard in that movie. But Logan didn't. Did ya, Logan?"

"I was so sick," Logan says. "We were drinking Mad Dog 20/20. Jesus Christ. Just thinking about it makes me want to throw up. And Jamie Fellows looked at me, put her hand out and asked me if I was OK—"

"And he puked in her fucking hand!" I guffaw up at the ceiling.

"Gross." Yvette giggles.

"Needless to say, I never did get in her pants."

"We called him Mad Dog for like six years." I laugh.

"Yeah, that's right," Logan says. Like he'd forgotten that part. "That's what I was called when we met Damon. I think that's why he wanted to be friends, now that I think about it. He thought I got the nick because I was some crazy brawler."

"Well, you were that too. He didn't wear suits back then. We were the same, remember?"

He doesn't say anything. Just nods his head.

"I always liked you," I say, my voice low now. Kinda serious.

"I always liked you too," Logan says.

"No… I mean *liked* you."

"Oh," Logan says. "Oh. I didn't know that."

"So…" Yvette props herself up on an elbow to look at me. "Have you done this before? You know. The stuff you do with me?"

I nod my head. "Lots of times."

"But not in a long time," Logan adds.

"Truth."

"Why not?" Yvette asks.

"We kinda drifted apart," Logan says.

"But you've been friends forever, it seems."

"Pretty long time," I add.

"Do you love each other?" she asks.

"Sure," I say.

"You love me?" Logan laughs.

"I've loved you since that very first time we met," I say. "I just didn't realize it until last night."

He huffs out some air.

"We gotta find a way out of this," I say.

"AJ—"

"No, listen," I interrupt him. "Just… there has to be a way, ya know."

"Well, when you figure it out, let me know. Because I've got no ideas. There's no way Damon will just forget about us. So even if we take off, he'll hunt us down."

"We could kill him," I say.

Logan just laughs.

"Yeah, not gonna work," I say. "Even though everyone hates his guts they'd still want revenge for that."

"Just drop it for now," Logan says.

"For now? Dude, we've got one day to figure this shit out."

He sits up and swings his legs over the bed. Then stands up and faces me, his cock still kinda hard, swinging between his legs. I stare at it unapologetically, then let my eyes track up his body to meet his gaze. "Come take a shower with me."

And then he turns and walks into the bathroom.

Yvette and I stay put. Listen as he starts the water.

"Well?" she finally says.

"Don't worry," I say. "We'll come up with something."

"That wasn't what I was asking." She laughs. "You gonna join him?"

I nod. "Yeah. Probably. You?"

She shakes her head. "No, I'll go start breakfast. Meet me down there when you're done."

She gets up, finds her clothes, and then quickly gets dressed and disappears.

"AJ," Logan calls from the bathroom. "What the fuck are you doing?"

So I get up and join him.

"Where's Yvette?" he asks, when I step into the shower.

"Making breakfast."

He nods, staring at me. "You like her," he says. Not a question.

I nod, then step forward and reach for his cock. "I do," I say, jerking him off.

He closes his eyes and pushes me away, but not hard. Not hard enough to make me let go.

"But I like you too, Logan. We're in this together."

I place a hand on his chest and push. Forcing him to back into the wall. He just sighs.

"It's not me who's bothering you," I say, still gripping his cock. Still pumping it in my palm. "So what's up?"

He bows his head a little but looks up at me through his wet, dark hair.

I lean in and kiss him. He kisses me back and reaches for my cock.

We've never done this before. Not without a girl between us. But it feels right. Feels natural. Feels… *good.*

Our breathing becomes heavy as we press our chests together, water collecting on our skin.

"Damon," he whispers.

"No," I whisper back, tugging on his cock a little harder. "You. You're up."

He smiles and nods. "Yeah, so are you." He squeezes harder. Fisting my shaft with one hand and reaching for the bottle of soap with the other. He squeezes some onto my dick and begins to wash me with both hands.

I close my eyes and growl a little. Reach down and help him. Gathering soapy suds as we jerk me off together. My hands over his. Pulling and tugging.

It feels amazing.

But it's not all about me. So I reach out and take his cock in my hand and we jerk each other off. Washing each other's dicks as we do it.

Kissing. First lightly. Then harder as our breathing becomes heavy and quick.

"Don't leave," I say.

"Where would I go?"

"Just don't go back, Logan. Just—"

"Shut up and make me come."

"I know what you're doing."

"I'm jerking you off, asshole. And you don't seem to be enjoying it, so—"

I kiss him again. To make sure he understands. I am enjoying it—it's just… I want more. I want out. And I want him to come with me. "We could really have something, you know. We could take Yvette with us. Go down to Mexico—"

He laughs.

"What? What's so funny?"

"I think I had a dream about that. That we were in Mexico. I went to this island a couple years ago. Some place my mom and dad took me before things fell apart. That's the only good memory I have of them. Us, as a family, ya know. So I went down there a couple years ago and I was gonna disappear. Just me. I was just tired of Damon's bullshit. So I took off to Isla Holbox. Fucking perfect place, man. Just fucking perfect. White beaches, surreal lagoon, fucking sunrise that makes you want to get up early. No stress. Just… like you said last night. Just *living*."

He jerks my dick a little harder when I seem to get lost in his description. So I jerk him back. Not hard or fast, but kinda slow.

"Let's go," I say. "Let's just go there. Right now."

He sighs. "I want to, I really do, AJ. It's just… you know we can't do it."

"We can do whatever we want, Logan."

"He'll look for us."

"Down on buttfuck-nowhere Isla Holbox?" I laugh. "Come on."

"He knows I went there. I told him about it afterward. He'd look."

"So we can go somewhere else."

"It won't work."

"Fuck you," I say, pushing him back against the wall. "I'm tired of you saying that. We can make it work. You just don't want to."

"I do want to," he says. "I just think ahead, AJ. And I don't want to get us all killed."

"We're already dead." I laugh, walking out of the shower. "We're already fucking dead. Yvette wants to die and you and I hate who we are."

"Speak for yourself."

I just look at him for a second.

Then shake my head and walk out of the bathroom.

CHAPTER TWENTY

YVETTE

Yesterday morning I came downstairs dressed to die.

Don't get me wrong. I like that outfit I wore yesterday. Before AJ ripped my shirt up the front it was very nice. But I didn't wear it to make myself feel good or because I had someone to wear it for.

I wore it so when they found my body I wouldn't look like shit.

What's that old saying? Make sure you wear clean underwear in case you're hit by a car?

I don't know why people would say that to their kids, but I'm pretty sure it's a thing.

The point is… yesterday I came downstairs to die and today I'm still alive. Looking like complete crap wearing yoga pants and an old t-shirt, but still alive nonetheless.

Also… I have two sexy, dangerous strangers up in my bedroom.

AJ's right. You don't know when you're half-baked. Still gooey on the inside. Because honestly I'm having a pretty good time with them.

Except for the part where they can't leave here without killing me because Damon will just kill them when they get back. That part sucks.

I grab all the ingredients to make French toast and begin cracking eggs into a small stainless-steel bowl, musing about my current situation.

Do I feel different? Aside from fun, would I change my mind and want to live just because I had an incredible one-night stand?

I heat up the griddle while I think about that. Get the bread ready. Pour the syrup into a little ceramic pitcher and place it into a pan of hot water so I can warm it up. Put a small scoop of powdered sugar into three little condiment dishes. Peel a little fancy curl of skin off an orange to make the plates look pretty. Then grate some zest and add it to the sugar.

I'm kinda going all out for this breakfast.

Or maybe I'm just avoiding my question.

Do I want to live?

"Hey," AJ says, pushing his way through the swinging metal door. "What's cookin', cookie?"

"Cookie," I say, dipping bread into the eggs, then placing it onto the hot griddle. Repeating that process until the whole grill is full.

"Coffee?" he asks.

I point him to the single-serving machine that I use for myself and not the industrial version I use for customers. "Help yourself."

He does. Finds what he needs without asking. Which I appreciate. There's nothing worse than a helpless monster of a man.

AJ doesn't come off that way, so I'm not surprised he can fend for himself in the kitchen. He comes off very competent, in fact. More competent than Logan.

I think Logan wears those suits because he knows he's got weaknesses and that projects an image of strength and control.

While AJ wears jeans and cowboy boots because he knows he's strong and doesn't care what people think about him.

They are a nice dichotomy, I realize. Little bit of yin and yang going on. Which makes for a good team.

Or the perfect set of partners.

Which is stupid. Just plain stupid. You don't pledge your undying love to a woman you've known one day. That's dumb. Not even fairy-tale believable.

And still… I'm alive. They're here. We're gonna have breakfast. Spend the day together.

But is all that only because of the storm?

Do I want to live another day?

"What are you thinking about?"

Logan is standing in the doorway wearing my dead husband's jeans and I get a really sick, *sick* feeling in my gut.

He enters, letting the door swing closed behind him.

"I'm thinking about… how I think you should kill me."

"Stop it," AJ says.

"I think we should fuck again, but this time"—I look at AJ—"don't stop when I tell you to choke me."

He narrows his eyes at me and I suddenly know what men see when they look at him.

Dangerous. Mean. Evil. Ruthless. Threatening. Dark.

He is all those things for about three whole seconds.

And then I say, "It's my choice, AJ. You don't get a say. I'm done here. My time is up, my game over, my cookie… is baked."

Logan walks over to the coffee machine and starts making a cup.

AJ renews his badass glare. Staring me down like a wolf looking at prey.

I shrug. "That's just how I feel." And then I frown. Because I realize it's true. I'm not just saying that to argue, or be right, or any of those things. I'm saying it because I feel it.

He frowns with me. Closes his eyes. Sighs.

Logan turns around, his coffee cup in hand. Takes a sip. Then says, "So go swallow all those pills. They're still sitting on top of the jukebox."

This time AJ doesn't tell him to stop.

I turn back to the French toast, flip each piece one by one, and say, "I used to make breakfast like this for my family. Every single day I'd come down here and open up the kitchen. Sometimes it was French toast. Sometimes it was pancakes. Or eggs. Bacon occasionally. Bonnie just started eating finger foods a few months before the 'accident.' She liked pancakes."

Every time I say the word 'accident' it comes with quotes. Even when I'm not talking about the non-accident that ruined my life. It's just habit now.

I turn to face them, spatula in hand. And sigh. "It's too much, ya know? It's just too much. I can't stay here. I have nowhere else to go. Damon wants me dead. You have to kill me or he'll kill you. And I can't be responsible for any more death. I just can't."

Logan puts his coffee cup down and walks towards me. He smiles. Just a small one. And says, "You let us worry about us, Yvette." Then he leans down and kisses me on the top of the head. "But I'm not gonna talk you out of killing yourself."

I look at AJ to see if he's gonna say something. But he doesn't.

So Logan continues. "I'm not gonna do that. If it's that bad, then check out. But don't do it because you think you're saving us." He hardens his face into an expression I haven't seen before.

This is his dangerous look as well. The one men see right before he kills them. Or beats them up. Or threatens them with such things if they don't do what he says.

"We're perfectly able to save ourselves."

CHAPTER TWENTY-ONE

LOGAN

I say it because it's true. AJ and I aren't looking for someone to rescue us and even if we were, we wouldn't call Yvette Nightingale. She's a fucking mess.

"So…" AJ says, breaking the tense silence I created. "French toast." He smiles.

You gotta give that guy credit. I mean, Aje is a wall of muscle. Tattoos, scars, bad attitude, will kill you dead if you look at him wrong on a bad day… and still, when he smiles, the world wants to stop to witness it.

"What can I do to help?" he adds.

Sometimes I want to punch him, he's so damn charming. Or maybe it's the rest of the world I want to punch? The people who fall for it.

And why does everyone fall for it, anyway? Why am I the mean one when he's the actual killer in this operation?

I'm the money launderer, for fuck's sake.

Not entirely true, my little inner voice says.

But true enough.

AJ is staring at me. He says, "I make an effort."

"What?" I ask.

"I see you looking at me. I know that look, Logan. You've been giving me that look since we were fourteen."

"Is that right?"

He nods. "That look says, *Why you?*"

I roll my eyes.

"It says, *Why not me?*"

"Fuck off."

AJ directs his attention to Yvette. "He secretly hates me." And he says this the way he says everything. The way he says, "I'm gonna kill you now," just before he crashes a baseball bat into someone's face. "He's always hated me because I'm *likable*."

Yvette looks at me.

"Oh, it's nothing personal," AJ continues, walking over to Yvette. He takes the spatula from her hand and begins lifting the French toast off the grill. Places them on a nearby platter one at a time. Then looks over his shoulder at me. "He hates all likable people. So I'm no one special. Right, Logan?"

I shake my head a little. "I don't hate you."

"No," AJ agrees, even though he just said I did. "Not any more than you do anyone else. That was my point."

"I don't hate you like that either."

"Hey," he says, flashing that smile again. "I don't take it personally. These are just your demons to deal with, Logan."

"When did you become such a fucking philosopher?" It comes out angrier than I intended. "When did you come up with this bullshit? 'You're a half-baked cookie, Yvette,'" I mock him. "'Just stay in the oven a little longer.' What the fuck are you doing?"

AJ stares at me. Still smiling. "I just happen to think it's true."

"Well, it's fucking annoying. So knock it off."

"Why are you in charge?" Yvette asks me.

"What?"

"You," she says. "Why would he put you in charge?"

For a second I think she's talking about AJ, but then I get it. "Damon, you mean?"

"Yeah," she says, getting out plates and placing them on the large stainless-steel table in front of me. "He never liked you, ya know."

"He doesn't like anyone," AJ says. "Fucker is paranoid."

"Yeah, I know that," Yvette snaps, grabbing a wire basket filled with silverware and placing it next to the plates. "I lived with him, remember?"

AJ puts up a hand. "Hey, I'm on your side."

"No," Yvette says, shaking her head. "Neither of you are on my side. You're here to kill me."

"We're not gonna kill you," AJ says.

"Maybe not. But your intention was to kill me. And none of that matters anyway. I just want to know how you got to be in charge, Logan. Because I remember them talking about you and you were always a joke to them."

"Whoa." AJ laughs. "Just… relax, Yvette. We don't need to—"

"It's fine," I say, cutting him off. "I know," I say, locking eyes with Yvette. "I know what they think of me. They might not like me—and I certainly don't like them, so who cares. But I do my job. It's such a simple thing, you know? Doing one's job? But almost no one actually shows up and does what they're supposed to on a consistent basis. Being reliable is the easiest thing in the world. There are no feelings attached. There's no emotion. You just do what you're told. So no, I'm not gonna step out in front of a bullet for anyone. Least of all Damon. But if I'm told to make sure that no one's in front of that asshole pointing a gun at his face, you can bet your fucking ass ain't nobody gonna be there because I took care of it."

They both stare at me. I feel like I just made a speech and speeches aren't my thing, so the ensuing silence becomes uncomfortable and I feel the need to say more.

"You don't have to like me the way you like him," I say, nodding at Aje. "You don't even have to trust me. Hell, anyone who trusts me is a dumbass. Because everything I do, I do for me. But if you want to find a way out of this, then you need to fucking help me do my job."

"Help you kill me?" Yvette laughs. "Should I make it easy for you, Logan? And just take those pills?"

I shrug. "Up to you. I'm not here to save you, Yvette. I'm here to save me." And then I sigh and look at AJ. "And him, if I can manage it."

Which makes AJ squint his eyes in confusion. "I don't need saving."

He does. For sure. Because if I do my job he'll be dead too. But I'm not gonna argue with him about it.

"So what do you want from me?" Yvette asks. "How can I possibly help you with this little dilemma?"

"Well…" I say, thinking it over for a second. Because I *don't* want to kill her. I don't want to kill anyone. I don't want to launder money. I don't want to work for Damon. I want to go to that fucking island, live in a goddamned beach house, and start over as someone else. Live the rest of my days bumming around on the beach with a metal detector, or collecting rocks, or painting mountain lakes while watching Bob Ross reruns. Or some other stupid hobby boring people do. That's what I want. But there isn't a single person on this planet who gives a fuck about my dreams. And there's no possible way to get out of this situation unless these two people in this kitchen end up dead.

So I say… "You can start by telling me how the fuck you got away. How the hell did you escape? How did you fly under Damon's radar for so many years and why is he fucking with you now? Because it doesn't make sense. Not even if you add in the kid."

Both of them look at me. Just stare at me for a few seconds.

Then AJ clears his throat and says, "Uh… OK. Let's eat before it gets cold."

I let out a long, tired breath. Because I'm sick of this shit. I'm sick of this fucking life I'm living. I'm sick of being the monster, and I don't want to fuck over the only guy I actually consider a friend.

I just don't see any way around it.

Yvette uses tongs to lift a small pitcher of syrup out of a pan of boiling water, and places it on the table next to small bowls of powdered sugar. And then she pulls out a tall stool hiding underneath the large, commercial table, as AJ picks up a fork and begins doling out slices of French toast.

"Sit down, Logan," Yvette says. I look at her. She looks at me. Then she offers me a small smile that comes with a shrug. "You said you follow orders, right? I'm just helping you out."

AJ drags a stool across the floor, making a loud scraping sound, then sits next to her and starts helping himself to syrup and powdered sugar.

I am hungry. Fucking starving actually. So I pull out a stool across from them, and sit. "You gonna explain?" I ask, pouring syrup over my breakfast. "Or you gonna just let us all die up here on this mountain?"

"Dramatic, dude," AJ says, stuffing a healthy portion of French toast in his mouth.

"If I tell you," Yvette says, "you need to make me a promise."

"What's that?" I ask.

"That you will not tell Damon anything I say."

I shrug. "Done," I agree, not because I'm particularly invested in her secrets, I just figure he knows all this already. He's known she was up here for a long time before he sent us.

"OK," Yvette says. "Then… OK." She looks worried. Bites her lip, looks down at her plate. Cuts a piece of French toast with her fork. Eats it. Then sighs. "Damon's father got me out."

"Oh." AJ laughs. "Didn't see that one coming."

"Explain," I say. "Tell me exactly what happened."

She frowns. Stays silent for almost a minute as she stares down at her plate.

AJ and I look at each other. I shake my head at him, a warning that he should not try to make this easier by cracking jokes or being charming.

"He raped me," she finally says. Then she looks up and locks eyes with me. "Damon. His cousins. His little brother. His inner circle. All of them. His father too," she adds quietly.

"Oh, fuck," AJ says.

"His father was kinda infatuated with me. He tried to make our encounters more like... dates." She stops again, probably remembering some specific time, probably wishing she could forget it. "We'd play cards. Poker, mostly. Which I sucked at. And he'd make the stakes sexual. You win this hand, I'll do this to you. I win this hand, you do this to me. I always lost. I didn't even know how to play and he never took the time to explain it after that first night. He would just laugh at me when I made a mistake. So of course I always did things to him."

"Fuck, I'm sorry," AJ says.

She shrugs. "Whatever. I did it for the same reasons you do it, Logan. To survive. You're right, it's easy to do what you're told. To be reliable, as you put it. So I did everything he asked. And when I got pregnant I told Damon's father first. I mean"—she laughs here—"no one knew whose baby it was. I was just a *thing* to them. And they were never careful."

"Didn't he have you on the pill?" I ask.

She nods. "He did. But I decided not to take it."

"Why?" I ask.

"Because something had to change. You know?" She frowns and her face is suddenly very sad. "I get you, Logan. Because when I made the decision to change something—anything—I knew that the baby would be born into this terrible, evil family and I'd be responsible for it. But I could tell Damon's father liked me. He's evil, don't get me wrong, but I think he made Damon marry me because he wanted me."

She stops. For a long time there's silence. No one is eating.

"Go on," I say. "Because so far none of this is helpful."

"I told Damon's father first because I was hoping he'd… I don't know. Be happy? Or at least feel… proud? Or maybe possessive? And he'd put a stop to the others coming into my room at night. Not Damon, but the others."

"Did he?" AJ asks.

"Yeah," she says. "He did. But he told Damon to leave me alone too."

"How did that go over?" I ask.

She shakes her head. "Not well, as you can imagine. I tried to run away a bunch of times but they always caught me. And after each time Damon's father would come to me and say things like, 'Why do you do that? Why do you run?' Like… he's such an idiot. Ya know?"

AJ and I both nod our heads.

"So after I tell him I'm pregnant I say… I say… 'Damon wants to kill you and take over.' I tell him the things I've heard the others say."

"So it was true?" I ask.

"It was true. They really did want to kill him. I wasn't going to leave or get away, but I was hoping he'd kill Damon first and at least, if I had to be stuck in this awful nightmare of a life, at least Damon wouldn't be there anymore."

"Good plan," AJ says.

"Yeah," I have to agree. "But you do know that Damon actually did kill his father a few years ago, right?"

She nods her head. "I know. He came up here to tell me in person."

"Damon did?" I ask.

"Yup. But I'm getting ahead of myself. Let me finish."

AJ encourages her to keep going with a roll of his hand.

"So Damon's father says, 'I can get you out of here. Put you and the baby somewhere safe. I have friends out west who will take care of you. I can get you a new identity. You can start over.' Of course, he would be coming to visit me and the baby regularly. But I said yes and less than twenty-four hours later I was on an Indian reservation in New Mexico. That's how I met Daniel Nightingale. I was staying with his aunt. And Chris used to come over every now and then. We were close in age, and we became friends. So after the baby was born we got common-law married and I got pregnant again and… well, you know the rest."

"Hold up," I say. "What happened to the first baby?"

"He's safe somewhere. He was adopted through an agency."

"How did you get that past Damon's old man?" AJ asks.

"I didn't tell him until after it was done. I had the medical center on the reservation induce my labor five days early, had the baby, signed him over to a private adoption agency, and that was that."

"Holy shit," AJ says. "What did you say to the old man?"

"I told him the truth. That they were all a bunch of evil motherfuckers and I was done. The tribe took care of me. And when Damon's father came to visit on the day he thought the baby was due, they met him at the entrance to the reservation with lots and lots of guns. Whatever happened after that, I don't know. I didn't actually see it. I never talked to him again, in fact. I stayed there for a couple months and then I moved up here on the mountain with Chris and Daniel."

"So when did Damon find you?"

"About…" She thinks for a moment. "Eighteen months ago, I guess?"

"Right about the time the old man died," I say.

She nods. "His father told him, I guess. I've imagined that conversation a million times in my head. But however it happened, Damon came up here one day, walked through the door, took a seat at the bar, and ordered a drink from Chris. I was standing there, holding our baby, watching the whole thing happen like it was a bad dream."

"What did he do?" I ask.

She shakes her head. "Nothing. Not one goddamned thing. Just drank his drink, waited for Chris to go in the back to get something and then slid a piece of paper over to me."

"What'd it say?" AJ asks.

"It said, *I'll be back when you least expect it. And I will rip your world apart the way you did mine.* And then he left. Daniel was already dead from cancer by that time. But six months later Chris and Bonnie were dead. Slipped off the side of the road and hit a tree, they said. But it's not true. It was no accident. Damon killed them and left me up here to rot alone."

"He didn't ask you about the baby?"

"Not that time. But he sent a huge flower arrangement to the funeral with a note to call him. Which I did. And he said if I gave the baby back to him, he'd leave me alone."

"You didn't, of course," AJ says.

"I don't even know where he is. I told the adoption agency to hide him. To never let anyone find out his real name. And they can't find him because there's no record of me giving birth. The tribal medical center faked everything the day my son was born. Some young teenager's name is on his original birth certificate. No one can find him now, not even me."

CHAPTER TWENTY-TWO

The three of us sit in silence for a long time. Just eating our food. More out of habit and necessity than hunger or appetite. Because that was some fucking story.

When we're done Yvette gets up and says, "I'm going to take a shower and put on something pretty. Just leave the dishes here and I'll take care of them later."

And then she disappears through the swinging kitchen door.

Logan and I just stare at each other. Finally, he says, "She's lying."

And I nod my head. Reluctantly. Because I don't want it to be a lie, but it is. I've dealt with all kinds of desperate people. I mean, dudes will say anything when they think you're about to bash their head in with a bat. Anything. I've learned to spot the desperation. Learned to filter the truth from the fantasy.

And this story Yvette Nightingale just told reeks of desperation. It's overflowing with fantasy. The only difference is she's not desperate to save her own life. She gives no fucks at all about her own life.

"She doesn't want us to know where the kid is," Logan says.

I nod my head again. Because he's right. "Which part do you think is true?" I ask.

"You tell me," Logan says. "I feel very… cynical right now."

"Damon's father. I think that's true. There's really no other explanation for how she got away." Logan nods his head. "And the tribe stuff. This bar, those people. Her second baby. All that stuff is true. But the adoption?"

Logan is shaking his head nope.

"Why lie about that?" I ask. "Why just that part?"

"Because she doesn't trust me," Logan says. "She thinks even if she takes those pills or we kill her, I'll go back to Damon and tell him where the kid is."

I just… glare at him. "And you'd do it, wouldn't you? You'd tell him."

Logan shrugs. "What's the point, AJ? I mean, we're so fucking stuck here. I've been trying my hardest to find a solution, I swear to God, I have. But I can't see any other way."

"We could run," I say. "Just get in the truck, take her with us, and go to your stupid island. I've got money stashed away. I've got a lot of it, actually."

"It's not about money. I've got way more money than I need too. He'd find us, AJ. I already told you that."

"So we'll go somewhere else. There's a million places to hide on this earth. Millions of places to get lost. We can't kill her, Logan. I won't kill her so you'll have to kill me too. And *I know you won't do that* so yeah, you're stuck." Then I force a smile and waggle my eyebrows at him. "You're stuck with us."

He doesn't smile. Not even a hint of a smile. Just says, "We need to convince her to trust us. Come up with a reasonable plan."

"Like… *run*," I say. "The only other way is to kill Damon and that just brings a whole bunch of headaches along with it."

"No," Logan agrees. "We can't kill Damon. He's got too many cousins and his stupid little brother watching his back. And even though they all want him dead, no one's got the balls to actually do it because none of them could take over the business the way he did. None of them are strong enough to hold shit together afterward, so what's the point? They won't do it just to get Yvette and her baby out of danger, that's for damn sure."

"Look," I say, pushing my stool back from the table. It makes a sickening scraping sound on the tiled floor. I put both hands on the table and lean over, staring into Logan's eyes. "Running is the only plausible option. It's either complete the job or don't complete the job. And I've already decided we're not completing the job. So you've got two options here, OK? Kill her *and me*, and go back to Damon. Or leave with us. Which is it?"

He looks at me and he looks tired. He looks like he needs a nice, long island vacation. One that lasts a lifetime.

"Are you gonna kill me?" I ask.

He hesitates. And I swear to God, I get a vision of Logan pointing a gun to my head and pulling the trigger. Because that's what Logan does. He follows orders. That's who Logan is. No loyalty to anyone but himself.

But finally, he says, "No, AJ. I'm not gonna kill you."

"Then it's settled. We run."

I turn away and walk towards the door.

"Where are you going?"

"To check on the fucking weather and see if the highway's open yet."

I go upstairs to get dressed. Yvette is in the shower, so I don't bother her, just get what I need and go downstairs to find my coat.

The highway is not open. It's still fucking snowing.

Like… I've grown up in the snow. I know what a blizzard is. I've lived through many of them. But this is fucking ridiculous. And it's way too fucking cold. I'm not sure we could even get the damn truck started, even if the parking lot was plowed and the highway cleared. It's that cold.

There's at least three feet of snow in every direction. I trudge through it—and believe me, I'm a tall man. Three feet is less than half my height, but it's hard as fuck to make my way out to the road and stand there, desperate to see if anything is happening. If anyone is coming.

But we're literally on the top of the mountain in the middle of a long switchback. So my line of sight is only about fifty yards in each direction. And even if it wasn't still snowing and I could see past the wall of falling flakes, I still wouldn't be able to see any farther than a hundred yards.

If the trucks are out plowing they're starting from the bottom on each side and going up until they meet in the middle. Which is pretty damn close to where we are. So that means we'll be the very last part of road to be cleared.

But that doesn't mean we can't be ready for that.

I have a sick feeling that Damon is starting to get very nervous about this job. A sick, sick feeling that he's on his way here right now to check up on us. Which means the second they clear this highway, we need to go.

So I trudge back to the bar, make my way around the side of the building and head into the shop to get that tractor started.

Because I'm gonna plow the fuck out of this parking lot.

CHAPTER TWENTY-THREE

YVETTE

The shower feels good. Even though I've taken three showers in the past twenty-four hours, this one feels better because I linger. I enjoy it more. Yesterday I was preparing for death and today… well, I still don't much care about that. But I have a new mission now.

Keep these men from learning my secrets.

I feel confident too. Even though Logan is still the wild card. AJ is on board. Whether he believed the lies I told downstairs or not, I get the feeling he's done with Damon. Whatever it is he did for the organization, that part of his life is over.

It's Logan who still needs convincing.

And the thing about him is… he's all about self-preservation. If he can find a way to save his own ass, he will do it.

That's the hard part here.

Damon sent them, which means Damon was expecting a progress report yesterday. We are on borrowed time right now. The blizzard was a stroke of luck or maybe a twist of fate, but it'll be over soon.

That's all people were talking about yesterday on the news. Snow through Monday afternoon.

And it's almost lunchtime now.

I get a sick feeling in my stomach at the thought of Damon walking through the door of my bar. I have a sudden urge to go lock it. Get one of the shotguns, load it up, and sit at a table in front of the door with a box of shells next to me.

Shoot that asshole the second he walks through.

Because he's coming. One way or another, he's coming for me. I can feel it in my soul.

"Hey," Logan says.

I spin around, still jumpy from my thoughts of Damon, and see Logan poking his head through the doorway to the bathroom.

"Hey," I say. "You coming in for a shower?" I ask. Even though I want to be alone. I don't want to make him any more suspicious of me than he already is.

"No, I'm good. Just… checking to make sure you are."

"I am," I say. Smiling. "I'm fine."

He stares at me for a second, then nods. "OK." And disappears.

Yeah. He knows. He's probably got some fancy bullshit detector up in that head of his by now. Dealing with all those shady people in Damon's organization.

"OK, get your shit together," I mumble. "Time to put on your game face."

I rinse off the rest of the soap on my body, turn the water off, and wrap myself up in a towel.

When I walk into the bedroom Logan is sitting on a chair in the corner, looking pretty casual. One ankle propped up on one knee. He's wearing the t-shirt I gave him yesterday. Black. Says 'Metallica' in faded letters across the chest. Bare feet. Bare arms peeking through the too-tight sleeves of the shirt. He's more muscular than he looks standing next to AJ, who is definitely a gym rat and it shows. So when you compare the two of them side by side Logan comes off as lean.

But he's not. Not really. He's muscular too, he just carries it different.

This is a good look for him, I decide.

"What are you doing?" I ask.

"Waiting for you," he says.

"Do you need something?" I ask, walking over to my closet and going inside.

What to wear? I thought my last outfit was pretty good. But turns out, wasn't my last outfit. So now I need to come up with something equally pretty.

"Yeah," Logan says. "The truth."

I look over my shoulder. I can see him from here. Or, rather, he can see me. Actually has a straight-on view.

So I drop my towel and step away from it.

"Well," I say, trying to be casual as I turn back to browse my rack of clothes. "Which part do you think I'm lying about? How about we start there?"

I have a few cool dresses I could wear but it's cold and I don't feel like wearing tights. So I choose my second favorite pair of jeans. This time a light wash instead of the dark ones I wore yesterday. Which implies a more casual day ahead.

That remains to be seen.

I also choose a camo-print ribbed top with a lace-up front that shows some cleavage and has sleeves that end in a bell of black lace.

Tough girl with a side of sweet.

That's me all right.

I take both those things out of the closet and drop them on the bed, then pick out a matching black bra and panty set from my dresser drawer.

Logan tracks my naked body with his eyes the entire time.

"Yvette," he says.

"Logan?" I say back.

"I can't help us if I don't know the truth."

"Us?" I ask him.

He closes his eyes. Slowly. Lazily. Like he's trying to muster up some patience with me, but having a hard time.

"If we could all get out of this—" He stops in the middle of his sentence. "I would like for all of us to get out of this alive," he says, switching tactics.

"Me too," I say, slipping on the panties.

Again, he tracks every movement with his eyes.

I reach for the bra, slip my arms into it, then reach behind my back to fasten it. Then I lean over and adjust my breasts so when I stand up again, they are spilling out over the cups just enough to be sexy.

He sighs and I almost laugh.

"Well, we can't do that if you're not honest. We know you're protecting the kid."

I shrug and start pulling on my jeans. Then slip the top over my head and adjust the laces so my bra is showing through them.

"I did what I had to, Logan. I gave him up. He was adopted—"

"Yes," he says, cutting me off. "I think that part's true. The part I think you're lying about is knowing where he is."

"Why do you need to know that?" I say, walking back into my closet to choose shoes.

"Because I need to predict what Damon might do if I don't complete this job for him, that's why. I need to understand how invested he is in this outcome."

Yesterday's boots were my absolute favorite but they don't go with these jeans. So I choose a pair of snow boots instead. White ones with fake fur lining that spills out over the top. They are for looks, mostly. Super cute. But they keep my feet warm too. And I might need that later.

If I survive this little meeting with Logan, that is.

"Where's AJ?" I ask, suddenly wondering why Logan's in here alone.

"I think he's plowing the parking lot."

"What?" I say, coming out of the closet. I throw the boots on the floor and go fishing for thick socks. Then sit on the bed in front of Logan and start pulling them on.

"I saw him go into the shop out back and start something up. He said you have a tractor in there? So I'm just assuming. But that's something AJ would do."

I picture this in my head and say, "Yeah, it kinda is."

"He's into you," Logan says.

I stare at him for a second, then nod. "OK. I can see that. And you?"

Logan shrugs. "I might be into you too."

"How far into me?" I ask.

"Far enough to help you live through this day."

I take a deep breath and let it out.

"If that's what you want," he adds.

I don't know if that's a real question or not, so I continue to say nothing.

"Is that what you want?"

"Look," I say, suddenly feeling irritated. "I don't know you. And whatever it is you think you know about me, I'm ninety-nine percent certain that it's wrong. So if you think I'm gonna spill my guts to you, you're mistaken. You don't get to know what I want, Logan. You don't get to understand what I feel. You haven't earned it. You were sent here to kill me. And you had no problem with that before we got stuck in a blizzard together. So why should I trust you? Or AJ, for that matter?"

"Fair point," he says. "All good points. But Yvette, we're the only chance you have."

"I don't need your last chance. What part of that isn't sinking in?"

"So you're gonna take the pills?"

"I don't know."

"Then you want to live?"

"I don't know! God, just shut up!"

He presses his lips together and leans back in the chair. And this casualness, combined with his new appearance… I don't know. Makes me feel like I'm overreacting. Being stupid.

I am being stupid. And it's got nothing to do with Logan or AJ. I was going to kill myself last night. And even though the sadness is still there, somehow everything feels different now.

My plan feels absurd, and simplistic, and maybe even selfish. Not that there's anyone left in my life who gives that many fucks about me. Sure, the locals would talk. Some might even be sad. My mail person, probably. She and I chat when she comes in. And there are a few truckers who drive this highway often who stop by and always seem happy to see me.

Not much left after that. Chris's family, maybe. But… by now, I'm just a loose end in their lives. Just a leftover. They're nice but… we're not friends. I don't call up and chat with them or anything like that.

Familiar strangers, that's all.

I realize that Logan did shut up and all during this introspection the room has been silent.

He's staring at me and I'm staring back.

"What?" I say. "Why are you looking at me that way?"

He says, "Do you have a picture of him?"

"Who?" I ask, thinking maybe he means Chris.

"The baby boy."

"Oh," I say, suddenly feeling heavy, and sluggish. "Yes. I have one from the day he was born. That's it."

"You never saw him again?"

I shake my head. "No. I signed the papers and that was it."

"I imagine that was hard. Maybe… the hardest thing you've ever done."

"Logan," I say. "What part of 'you don't get to know me' didn't you understand? I'm not discussing my personal life with you."

"Harder than being raped, maybe?"

"Shut the fuck up."

"Harder than being held prisoner."

"I'm warning you—"

"Harder even than running away and starting over."

I don't bother finishing my sentence.

"Because I get it, Yvette."

"Get what?"

"Why giving him up was the hardest thing, and the easiest thing, you've ever done."

I exhale. Thinking about that.

"Because it's one thing to be a girl who is raped, and beaten, and possibly killed. But it's something else altogether to be the mother of the man who does those things."

I just look at him.

"That's why you had to leave. You did it for him. You left and took all those risks so that no matter what happens to you, that baby boy wouldn't grow up to be his father."

I nod, my eyes filling with tears. "I couldn't keep him," I say. "I wasn't safe. And if I wasn't safe he'd never be safe. Kids need to feel safe, ya know? Or they start doing things that—for whatever reason—give them the illusion of safety. But really all they do is hurt others. People like Damon hurt others because they've been conditioned to feel fear and fear makes people do awful things. I was not going to turn my son into one of those fearful, unsafe people who do awful things to others in order to feel better about their shitty circumstances. So yeah… it was the hardest and easiest thing I ever did."

Logan gets up out of the chair, walks across the room, and puts his arms around me. He hugs me tight and I let him. I let myself cry too. No sobs. Just a few tears down my cheeks.

He says, "You did the right thing, Yvette."

CHAPTER TWENTY-FOUR

LOGAN

I take her and lead her out into the living room. Over to the couch where I sit, pulling her into my lap so I can hold her. I don't love her. She doesn't love me. But everyone needs to feel cared for. Even women like her who force themselves to move on, who turn themselves into silent warriors in order to protect something bigger than themselves, want to feel cared for.

For some it's an idea or a personal philosophy. A way to make the world slightly better when they leave than when they entered. For others it's just a survival skill.

I think for Yvette it's both.

And I can respect that.

I let the silence hang as I formulate a new plan of action. Let that silence surround us like a cloak. Outside there's the faint hum of a motor. AJ clearing the parking lot. They're a lot alike. Both of them are dreamers and I'm just a pragmatist. I can understand

AJ falling for her. It's easy for him to be into this woman.

It's also easy to find her vulnerable side too. And even though AJ doesn't really come off as the Prince Charming type, he's always had it in him. The potential has always been there.

Me, on the other hand, I've never been that guy. I am the most selfish, greedy, egotistical, narcissistic asshole there is. I mean, sure, there are others out there like me. Lots of us. But I'm right up there in the top ranks, I think.

I always have an ulterior motive. Always have a hidden agenda.

Except I don't even bother to hide it. That's why Damon doesn't trust me. That's why I have the ironic nickname.

"So," Yvette says, finally breaking our silence. "What do we do?"

"Do you want to live?" I ask her. "Because if not, then my job gets a lot easier."

She thinks about this for a while. So long, in fact, I start to wonder why that fucking question is so damn hard.

Then it hits me. "Did you love him?" I ask.

"Damon?" She huffs.

"No," I huff back. "That's just stupid. That guy, Chris. Was he your soulmate and shit?"

Again with the silent introspection.

"Yvette, that wasn't a trick question."

"I don't know," she says. "I loved him. And just thinking about him being gone hurts my heart." She suddenly sits up and looks at me. "But you know what hurts worse?"

"What?"

"That Damon was the one who took him away."

Yeah, I get that. "That's not love, Yvette. At least I don't think so. I'm not an expert, so take this for what it's worth. But that sounds a lot like hate to me."

"I did love Chris. But was he my soulmate?" She squints her eyes and crinkles her nose as she thinks. "I don't know."

I nod. Because that's a firm no in my book, but no one wants to admit they fell in love for safety.

And that's what she did.

Her baby girl? Well, that's a whole different story that I won't ask about. Falling in love with children is easy. Sometimes all it takes is one look.

"I can make you safe," I say. "I can protect you and your little boy too. I know you know where he's at."

She doesn't deny it this time. Doesn't confirm it, either, but that's not the important part.

"I don't trust you," she says.

"No." I sorta laugh. "No one trusts me. Well… maybe AJ. But it's misplaced."

"How can you say that?"

"Because he knows better than to trust me."

"You would fuck him over to save yourself?" she asks.

"In a heartbeat."

She wriggles in my lap, trying to get away. Probably has an instant urge to get as far away from me as she possibly can. But I don't let her go. I say, "Sit still and listen to me very carefully, OK?"

"Why? Why should I listen to anything you say? You're going to sell us out. You basically just admitted that."

"Because in case you haven't noticed, I'm all you've got. So listen."

She huffs, and frowns, and shoots me a look of disgust. But I'm used to those looks.

"If you tell me where that kid is, I'll make a promise to protect you."

"Oh." She laughs. "That's amazing. Thank you. Let me just spill all my deepest secrets to the only man I've ever met who admits he's a lowlife piece of shit. Because that makes so much sense."

I let her feel that disgust. Maybe even relish in it a little. Because I do have a plan. I do have a way out. But all the pieces have to line up just so. Which means I need her on board.

"I can get you out of this. If that's what you want."

"I just have to trust you." She laughs again.

"Look," I say. "I'm just being honest with you. And that's probably more than you ever got from most people in your life. Let's look at this logically, OK? Damon married you when you were underage, so that means your parents sold you out. Did they tell you that you'd be raped on your wedding night? No, I'm guessing not. I'm also guessing you didn't even bother telling your father that happened, did you?"

"What's that got to do with it?"

"Everything, Yvette. You said so yourself. When kids don't feel safe they grow up and do shitty things to make themselves feel better."

"I haven't treated anyone like shit. I left, that's it. I left and kept to myself."

"Did Chris know about Damon?"

"What's that supposed to mean?"

"Did you tell him, *Hey, I'm a mobster's wife on the run. And one day, just when we think we're happy and living the dream, he's gonna come back and fuck everything up for us?*"

I give her the courtesy of silence to wait for an answer, but I already know she won't answer.

So I continue. "No, you didn't tell him that. You never even told him Damon came into the bar, did you?" This time I don't wait for her answer. "You sold him out."

"Fuck you," she says. And she gets up out of my lap so quick, I can't grab her back and keep her still. "Just fuck you." She walks over to a chair and sits down, drawing her knees up to her chest.

I let her stew like that for several seconds, glaring at me with a look of pure hate.

"Yvette." I sigh. "I'm not judging you. It's called survival, *cookie*. It's nothing more than instinctual self-preservation. That's all I'm doing too. That's my only point here."

"You're going to sell me out."

"No."

"You're going to get the information you need, call up Damon, and sell me out."

"No," I say again.

"And you're going to sell out AJ too. I can feel it. I've been watching you very carefully. I've seen it."

"Seen what?"

"I don't know," she says, shaking her head. "The only thing I do know is that you're a monster."

"Again," I say, losing patience, "I'm not denying that. I'm being honest with you. I'm not going to sell you out. I'm making you a fucking offer. And it's the only offer you've got, cookie. So you should probably stop reacting to what you think you know and listen more carefully for the things you don't."

"What offer?"

I stretch out my hand and say, "Come here," motioning to her with my fingers.

She shakes her head no.

"Yvette," I say, sternly. "Come. Here."

But she shakes her head no again.

"Do you want the monster on your side? Or don't you?"

"What?"

I smile at her. "I'll be the monster. I don't mind. But I can be your monster if you let me."

"So I'm trading one for the other?"

I shrug. "Would you rather go up against the bad guy alone? Or have an equally bad one by your side?"

"Oh, my God," she says, gripping her hair up near her ears and shaking her head. Like she wants me to shut up.

"I think it's a fair offer."

"What do I have to give you in return?"

"Trust," I say. "That's it. Just trust."

"Tell you where my son is?"

I nod. "Tell me that and I can spin some gold for you."

"How?"

"Get us all out of this mess. Start a new life. AJ and I have a place in mind. A little island off the coast of Mexico. Just picture a beach house, OK? White sand, blue ocean, hot weather. No blizzards to get stuck in," I say, then wink at her. "Maybe a little business? You can open an Etsy shop and sell seashells by the seashore—"

She manages a small laugh.

"AJ can give surf lessons… shit like that."

"You're serious?"

I nod. "I'm fucking serious. We talked about it. Just ask him when he comes back in. He'll tell you the same thing I just said."

"Why?"

"Why am I helping you? Or why do I dream of a life on that island?"

"Both."

I sigh. This is the hardest part of the plan, I think. So I need to be careful. Say too much or the wrong thing and she'll figure out what I'm up to. And maybe that doesn't matter much, but I can't have AJ getting suspicious. He would never agree to my plan.

So I say, "Do I look like a happy man to you?"

"What?"

"Just answer the question."

"I don't know."

"Take a wild guess."

"No, then. I'd guess not."

"Well, you're correct. I'm not excited about life. I came up here to do a job, figured I'd do it. I'd go back. Probably earn a few points with Damon. Earn his trust for a little bit longer. Bide my time. Wait for someone to kill him. Because someone will. There are bosses people hate but respect, and those dudes take a long time to die. But then there are bosses like Damon. Bosses who force the loyalty by asking men like me to do jobs like this. And those guys never last long because we hate them, but we don't respect them.

Someone *will* kill him. Maybe not soon enough for us. But within the next few years. Still, that won't save anyone in this room, ya know?"

She must be thinking about this, because she doesn't say anything.

"That's why I'm helping you. I hate him too. There's actually nothing to like about that guy. And sure, I'm also a monster. But like I said, I could be *your* monster, Yvette."

She inhales a long breath like she's about to say something, but the apartment door opens and AJ comes in stomping his feet. He's wearing coveralls he must've found out in the workshop. They are covered in ice balls and his face is red from the cold.

But he's smiling.

"Can I get a fuck yeah?" he asks, unzipping his coveralls so he can take them off. "We are outta here as soon as the highway's cleared. The snow is just about over."

He looks at us as he peels off his clothes and boots and leaves it all in a heap at the door as he walks over to Yvette and offers her his hand.

Unlike my gesture, she accepts his immediately. He tugs her up to her feet and then leads her across the room and flops onto the couch next to me, pulling her into his lap.

"Keep me warm, cookie. I'm cold." He places her hands on his cheeks and she shivers. But she laughs too.

Fucking guy. Sometimes I hate him for being so charming.

CHAPTER TWENTY-FIVE

"What'd I miss?" I ask. Because I can tell these two have been talking about shit while I was out saving the world from snowdrifts.

"Logan wants to be my monster," Yvette says.

"Oh." I laugh. "Well, fuckin' ay. It's a nice offer. You gonna take him up on that?" I slip my hands up her shirt and this makes her squeal.

"Stop it! Stop!"

But fuck that. I've been out in the cold for more than a hour. I grab her bra under her shirt and tug it down so I can cup my freezing hands around her warm tits.

"Oh, my God." She laughs.

"I know," I say. "You gotta warm me up." I lean in to kiss her and she kisses me back. I don't know what's going on here. And I don't just mean between her and Logan, because clearly something is going on.

I mean between her and me. Because I like her. I know I like her because that whole time I was running the snowblower on the tractor I was thinking about her. Little bit about her man who died, but that was mostly out of respect for the dude's toys. I had my pick of tractor attachments out in that garage. I could've plowed. I could've used the bucket to scoop it up. But in the end I used the blower.

Never used one of those before. Might never get another chance, either. Seeing as how we're gonna be taking off for that island.

I made a decision too.

We're going.

I already decided not to kill her, regardless of what Logan thought about that. I knew he'd come around. We've been friends too long for him not to. And he wants out of this Damon bullshit just as much as I do.

I look at him now and find him… not exactly smiling, but not frowning either. "What?" I ask.

He shakes his head. "Nothing. Just… you're such an asshole."

"Why?"

"'Keep me warm, cookie,'" he sneers.

I flip Yvette over onto the other side of me, making her squeal again, then pull her legs open and lean over top of her so we can kiss. And in that kiss I say, "He's just jealous because I get all the girls, Yvette. But…" I pull back from the kiss and look over my shoulder so I can see Logan. "I'll share you with him, if that's what you want."

Logan grunts. "Somehow I don't see that happening."

"Cookie," I say, leaning into her neck so I can kiss her ear. "Do you want us both?"

She hesitates and I don't like that. I want Logan to come with us and if he feels unwanted, he won't. He'll go back to Damon and that presents all kinds of problems.

Some of them technical. Such as he'll know where we are and he could tell Damon.

But some of them are just personal.

I don't want to leave him behind. We got into this life together, we should leave together too.

"He says he'll be your monster. Don't you want your very own monster?"

"Maybe," she says. But she's smiling so I take that as a good sign.

"How can I convince you that you need us both? Hmm?"

"I don't know," she says.

But we all know the answer to that is sex. Which makes me unexpectedly laugh. Because it's dumb, but still true.

"I have an idea," I say, pushing her shirt up so I can kiss her stomach as I continue to play with her breasts. Then I get on my knees in front of the couch and start taking off her boots.

"I just got dressed," she complains.

"And it was easy, wasn't it? Which means I can get you naked and you can get dressed again later."

She huffs, but doesn't stop me. I toss her cute little snow boots over my shoulder and start unbuckling her pants, glancing over at Logan, who has situated himself in the corner of the couch so he can watch.

I shake my head at him.

"What?" he asks.

"You're not just gonna watch."

"For now I am," he replies.

"I've got plans for you," I say.

He smiles. "Is that so?"

I nod. "Yup."

"What plans?" Yvette asks.

"You'll see. Something I know he likes to do and you're a prime candidate." Then I wink at Logan, who's squinting his eyes at me, trying to parse that out.

I ignore that look and start working Yvette's pants down over her hips. She giggles and helps me by lifting up a little so I can slide them down her legs.

"You must be a sex addict. Don't you ever get enough?"

"Enough?" I ask. "Of your gooey inside? Shit. Hell, no."

"AJ," Logan protests. "I think we've all had enough."

All right. That's it. Whatever these two mood-killers were talking about before I came in, it needs be forgotten.

I stand up, reach down for Logan's shirt, and pull him to his feet.

"What the fuck—"

But I kiss him before he can say anything else. I kiss him hard. My fingers reaching for the button of his jeans. Pop it open and then slip down inside to grab his cock. He's not hard, but he begins to grow as I grip him tight.

At first he doesn't kiss me back, but it's a small hesitation. A slight pause. And then his mouth opens and his tongue reaches for mine.

He grabs my hair, tugging on it hard as I pump his cock with my fist.

His fingers are on the button of my jeans now, trying to get it open, but I push him back and he falls into the couch cushions with a laugh. "What the fuck are you doing?"

When I drop to my knees and take his cock in my hand, he knows what I'm doing.

"AJ," he says.

I just shake my head. Because I don't want to hear it anymore. I'm tired of the excuses. I'm tired of the we-can't-do-its.

We *can* do it. We can leave. We can take this girl with us, go to that island, and be together.

But I've said all that and he's still not listening.

So I do something else to make him pay attention.

I lean forward with my mouth open, and suck his dick.

CHAPTER TWENTY-SIX

YVETTE

I'm... actually speechless.

I'm not one to watch porn, per se. And when I do, I'm not one to watch men without at least one woman in the middle. But... OK. I might've been selling this whole bromance thing short.

Because I'm turned on.

Ten seconds ago it was a little flirting. I was entertaining the thought of one more round of sex. But just barely. We've had a lot of sex in the past twenty-four hours and to be honest, my pussy is sore. It could use a break.

But like I said, that was ten seconds ago.

Now... I can't take my eyes off them. And I realize, as my hand is sliding down between my legs, my jeans are still on. Stuck at my ankles because AJ never finished taking them off. So I kick them off and open my legs as I watch AJ take Logan's cock deep into his throat.

Is this how they feel when they watch me do that?

I can only imagine it is.

Their eyes are locked. Serious too. Logan reaches down and cups AJ's head with both hands, guiding him to take him deep, then pull back. AJ does this, keeping his lips tightly sealed around Logan's cock until he only has the tip in his mouth. Then his tongue darts out and flicks across it.

That motion reminds me of the way he ate me out last night and I begin to throb.

Then Logan pushes down on AJ's head and makes him take him even deeper than before. AJ halts, breathing hard, but doesn't gag.

Logan's cock is thick and long. His girth, when I hold it in my hand, so wide, my fingers barely touch. I think back on the way AJ made me suck him off yesterday. How he wanted me deep, how he counted how long I had to stay there.

He's giving Logan the blow job I gave him.

I get up, crawl over to them, and place my hand on AJ's head. Logan has him pull back, and then, together, we push AJ's head down onto Logan's thick shaft and I start to count.

"One, two, three, four—"

AJ's lips form a smile around Logan's dick.

I keep going and he takes him all the way in his throat. Until his face is pressed up against Logan's stomach and Logan repositions himself lower on the couch to give AJ better access.

"—ten, eleven, twelve…"

When I get to twenty, Logan pulls him off and AJ sucks in air, breathing hard.

AJ climbs up Logan's chest, lifting up his shirt as he goes, and kisses him on the mouth again.

I lean in, wanting to kiss them too.

Our tongues mingle together. Eager, and desperate, and willing.

AJ puts an arm around me, bringing me into an embrace. Then he stands up, pulls me with him, and whips my shirt over my head.

My bra is still under my tits from when he was trying to warm his hands.

They're warm now. His whole body is warm.

He grabs the cups with both hands and rips it open and off my body in a moment so quick and decisive, I barely have time to regret the ruined bra.

"Come with me," he says, leading me towards the bedroom. "Follow us," he calls back to Logan. "I have a surprise for you."

I don't look back to see if Logan follows. I don't have to.

There is no way he won't follow. I don't care that just ten minutes ago we were arguing.

We enter the bedroom, but he doesn't take me to the bed. He takes me into the bathroom instead, turning on the water with casual familiarity as we pass by.

"I think we've taken enough showers." I laugh.

AJ just looks at me. Then Logan, who is naked and leaning against the door.

He took his clothes off before he followed. So… I guess he's over our little fight too?

I look at him. Just… let myself look at him. No apologies. No shame. No shyness.

His cock is rock hard now. So hard it curves up towards his stomach instead of hanging down low between his legs. It's still glistening with AJ's saliva. I relive that scene in my head as I study it. Study his huge balls, tight and firm and so big they squish up against his upper thighs.

I look at AJ for a second, but he's busy fishing through my medicine cabinet, so I look back at Logan.

Steam filters out from the shower, making a mist around his body.

He mouths the words… *Let me be your monster.*

And I feel my pussy clench with desire.

Please, he continues. Not saying the word out loud.

I nod my agreement. Then say, "OK."

"OK is right," AJ says.

I turn around and find him holding a can of shaving cream.

"What?" I ask.

"Just… say yes," AJ says, setting the can down on the countertop so he can fit a new blade on the end of my pink lady razor.

I used to wax my pussy regularly. It was something I did for me, not Chris. But the last few weeks… I just lost all interest in life and I stopped. So I have a dusting of fine hair covering my entrance.

Logan comes up behind me, pressing his hard cock into my back, and begins to wiggle my panties down my legs. They drop to the floor and I step out of them.

AJ takes his shirt off and I study his chest. His tattoos. His muscles.

He is a wall of man.

And when he takes off his jeans, his cock springs out like it has a life of its own. And like Logan's, it's so hard it stands up. And it's so long, there's a little curve at the end.

I know him now. He's been inside me enough times for me to imagine that curve pressing up against my g-spot.

Wetness pools between my legs as my clit begins to thrum with anticipation.

He empties out a small bowl reserved for hand towels and fills it with hot water. Then he hands the razor to Logan, the bowl of water to me, and takes the can of shaving cream into the shower.

"Sit," he says, pointing to the stone bench. "And open your legs wide for us."

I suck in a breath of air. I'm nervous, I realize. I've never had a man shave me before. And it's not like I'm afraid they'll cut me. Hell, I don't even care if they cut me at this point.

I'm just… turned on so hard, I might come before they're done.

But I sit. And slowly, as I watch them watch me, I open my legs.

CHAPTER TWENTY-SEVEN

LOGAN

Yvette bites her lip as she opens her legs. Looking up at me, then quickly averting her eyes. It's an unconscious act of shyness that stirs up a feeling inside me I can't quite identify.

She's beautiful. No doubt. So yes, I'm attracted to her that way. I tug on my cock, an unconscious gesture on my part just like her lip-biting. But there's more to these feelings than lust. I've had her several times, several ways, since we walked into her bar yesterday afternoon. This isn't just animal instincts. It's something else. Maybe a feeling of friendship? Or a desire for more time?

Because time is running out.

I need to take action and I can't do that until she gives up the rest of her secrets about the kid. I have to know the truth about that before I can put any plans into action.

AJ sits down on the bench next to Yvette, drawing me out of my conflicting feelings, and bends one leg so he can place his foot on the bench in front of him, while leaning back into the corner.

Front-row seats, I guess.

He pulls on his cock, slowly jerking himself off as his eyes meet mine. "Well," he says. "What the fuck are you waiting for?"

I've always thought of AJ as a simple guy. He's not hard to read like me. He wears his feelings all over his face, in his posture, and mostly speaks his mind in a blunt way that often comes off as dickish.

But I know him better. It's not that he's uncaring or ambivalent. He's just practical about certain things. If someone fucks up and needs to be killed, he kills them. Problem solved. If he feels horny, he fucks someone. If he's bored, he drinks, or plays poker, or goes for a long ride on his motorcycle.

What I'm not sure of—yet—is what he does when he's *into* a girl.

Like Yvette, for instance.

Does he get possessive? I've never seen that. I'm fairly certain I'm not the only guy he shares girls with. I've never seen him with an actual girlfriend. Just a string of one-nighters.

Does it change his loyalties, I wonder? When he's into someone?

I guess I'll find out.

"Logan," he says.

"What?" I ask, stepping forward to waiting Yvette. Her breathing has picked up a little and that only distracts me further.

"Come on, we're waiting. Save your existential crisis for later."

He's joking, I know that. But he's also not joking.

How much does he suspect? Does he know I'm here to kill him? Or have all his thug instincts been dulled by the distraction of this woman spreading her legs for me?

I inhale deep, then let it out as I bend down and place my hands on her knees, opening her legs up wider as I lean my head forward and lick her pussy.

Yvette moans and places a hand on my head. Not with any kind of force, just another unconscious gesture.

It's something more than it was yesterday, I know that for sure.

But what?

Does she like me?

How could she like me? I'm here to kill her and I just offered to be her monster.

But her soft groans and the way she moves her hips forward to give me access tells me… maybe she could? One day? If I make the right decision over the next few hours.

AJ's hand on my shoulder pulls me back to the moment. God, I'm so fucking distracted. He planned this extra trip into the shower to make me happy.

No, I decide. He planned this to make me connected to her.

I do have a thing for shaving girls' pussies. He knows this. And while I'd never call it a life-altering experience, it could be. If I let it. Because it's very intimate.

My tongue swirls around Yvette's clit until she hisses and closes her legs on my head. Squirming as a soft giggle erupts. It comes from deep inside her, that giggle.

I pull back and look up. Find her looking down. We smile.

Hers is crooked and mischievous. Mine… I don't know. But it must be appropriate because she doesn't frown.

"Ready?" I ask her.

She nods. "Just be careful with me."

Be careful with her.

"I will," I say. And I mean it.

I turn to AJ and say, "Put her in your lap."

He grins at me. Imagining how this is gonna go down. Not how he planned it, but how I want it done.

If he takes that as a threat, or a expression of dominance, he either doesn't care or gives in. Because he scoots over as Yvette slides into his lap, and opens her legs up.

I stare at his dick, hard and thick, as the lips of her pussy mold around his shaft and his balls rest against the edge of the bench.

I grip his cock with one hand and spread the lips of her pussy with the other.

Mine, I decide.

They are both mine.

Monster, my inner voice echoes back at me. *You're a monster.*

I just agree and keep going.

"Here," I say, handing AJ the shaving cream. "This is your job."

He just laughs as he aims the can between her legs and squirts a healthy mountain of foam. He sets the can down beside him, then massages the puffy cream over the fuzzy area to be shaved.

I dip the razor into the bowl and smile at Yvette. "Don't move," I whisper, unsure if she can hear my words over the sound of falling water behind me.

AJ spreads her legs, smearing shaving cream all over the inside of her knee, and I begin.

It's a slow process as I carefully slide the razor over the curve of her mound. One small strip of cream disappears, leaving behind smooth skin. I do the outside first. Then, with two fingers, I part her lips and start on the folds. Every few seconds I make sure to bump her clit with my fingertips, and each time she sucks in a breath.

I look up at her. Find her staring down at me. Again, biting her lip.

"Your pussy is very pretty," I say, smiling.

But is it pretty enough to save your life?

Obviously I don't ask her that. But I think it.

When I get to a delicate, hard-to-reach spot, AJ's fingers help me out. He slides them right between her slit, entering her momentarily. She pants a little and arches her back. Like it's all too much. And then he slides them out and parts her folds to give me access.

My dick hangs between my legs, hard and ready. My balls tight and eager.

But I decide not to touch them. Not to be anything but patient. Because I have plans for these two.

I go very slow for the rest. Clipping off small, thin hairs. Taking great care to both get them all so it will be perfectly smooth the next time I enter her, and to make sure not to cut her.

I am, after all, *her* monster now. And that comes with some perks.

And I did make a promise to be careful.

I don't often keep promises but it doesn't cost me anything to do a good job. And besides, I'm the one who'll reap the benefits of my efforts.

We're doing this for me.

That thought stops me for a moment.

We're doing this for me.

I knew that going in, but somehow admitting it makes me pause.

That was AJ's objective. Make me connect with her.

Seems to be working.

For now.

When I'm satisfied the delicate skin between her legs is as smooth as I can possibly make it, I lean back and smile.

"More than pretty," I say.

Yvette has her eyes closed. Her head has fallen back onto AJ's shoulder. She is perfectly relaxed. Her body pink from the steam swirling around us.

But she smiles back.

I stand up and reach for the detachable shower head on the wall above them. Then aim it at the tiled floor as I adjust the temperature. Making it hotter than it needs to be, but not hot enough to burn.

When I aim it between her legs she gasps. I'm unsure if it's from the heat or the pressure, then decide both.

The remaining bits of shaving cream run down over the bench in a stream of water and then my masterpiece is revealed.

My cock wants to feel it right now, but my head prevails.

Patience, I tell it. *We'll get there.*

AJ is jerking off to me. Watching me watch her. His hand coming up and over the tip of his head with each upward motion, making the tip disappear from view. I watch him. Notice how plump the tip is. How swollen and ready for more.

I wish I could shave him too, but he's always manscaped. It's not perfectly smooth like Yvette's pussy, but not enough to bother with.

My own cock is about the same.

I have another idea though.

But first… I want to fuck them.

I like the way Logan concentrates. How he heeds Yvette's request to be careful with her. This was a good idea. A very good idea. He owns that pussy now. At least for a little while. He's made it his.

Which was the whole point.

"Get on your knees," Logan says.

I look up at his face, unsure who he's talking to.

"Both of you," he says, answering my unasked question.

I lift Yvette up—she is pliant and soft, all her muscles relaxed—and hold her steady until her feet find the floor, then help her to her knees in front of Logan's cock. He's gripping it tight now. Jerking on it.

He takes her hand and places it over his and they jerk him together, Yvette's head tilting up like Logan's her master and she's his little sex slave.

I'm a little unsure how I fit into this scene, but I do as he asks and kneel next to Yvette. Logan lets go of his cock, making sure Yvette takes his place and keeps tugging on his dick, and then reaches for my hand and puts it over hers.

"You're into this, aren't you?" I ask him, helping Yvette jerk him off.

"That's what you wanted, right?"

I nod. "Yup."

"Well, then. Shut the fuck up."

I laugh, glancing at Yvette, and find her squinting her eyes at Logan. "Don't worry," I tell her. "It'll be OK."

And it will.

Because I will do everything he wants. I will make him see just how good we could be if he would just leave Damon behind and commit to this new life I'm dreaming up for the three of us.

No, I don't know this girl. Not at all. I have bits and pieces of her. I know what it feels like to fuck her. I know what it feels like to be inside her. I'm familiar with her moans and squeals and the way her pussy clamps down when she comes.

And I know she's sad. I know she's played the game for a long time now and has mostly lost.

But I also know we've started to change her mind. Even though Logan isn't trying to change her mind, he's helping. Because he's here. He showed up just now. He did everything I wanted him to.

Now it's my turn.

Just as I think those words Logan's hand is on the back of my head, urging me forward.

I do it gladly, just like I did before we got into the shower. I take him in my mouth and suck. But just as I get him to the back of my throat, he grabs my hair and pulls my head back. His cock slips out between my lips and then he shoves it into Yvette's mouth.

She takes him deep, opening up wide, both her mouth and her eyes, as she stares up at Logan's face and focuses. She places both her hands flat on his thighs, prepared to push him back if she has to, but not doing that yet.

She takes it. She takes all of it.

And just as she's about to gag, he pulls out and points his cock at me.

My turn.

Ah, I get you now, Logan. You want to face-fuck me like a girl, eh? Both of us at the same time? Play a little game of who's-in-charge-here?

Sure. I'll be your bitch.

For now.

But I'll get you back too. Just wait. Because this was my plan, motherfucker. And you walked right into it.

He shoves his cock so far down my throat, I gag instantly.

Logan laughs. "What's the matter? Too big for you?"

Fuck you. But I don't say it. Can't say it. Because his cock is doing its best to choke me.

Now my hands are on his thighs. Palms flat against his thick muscles. And I'm just about to push him away when he pulls out and aims for Yvette.

She dives in, like she hasn't been face-fucked in years. And her eyes never close. She holds his stare. Tracks him like he is her god—or maybe just her monster.

He pulls out again and thrusts inside me and even though I agreed to this, I'm still getting a little pissed off at his arrogance.

So the next time he pulls out to fuck Yvette's mouth, I slip two fingers under his balls and begin to stroke the soft skin just in front of his asshole.

"Shit," he growls, gripping Yvette's hair with both fists. Leaning in to her until her face is pressed up against his stomach.

I just smile and sneak a fingertip into his ass.

He stops for a moment. Just goes still.

See? Two can play this game, I muse.

My other hand pushes back on Yvette's forehead, forcing Logan's dick to slip out of her mouth. Then I push her forward again, but aiming her at his balls. She understands what I want, because both hands cup him as her head lowers and tilts underneath to take his balls in her mouth.

I let go of her head and take his cock in my hand, tugging and jerking on the slick shaft.

Logan goes still. He's still gripping Yvette's hair but he knows he just lost because he closes his eyes and lets his head roll back.

Game over, motherfucker.

I win.

He'll come if I let him.

I'm not gonna let him. My plan has three phases and we've only covered two.

I stand up, one hand still sliding back and forth on his dick, the other playing with his ass as I lean over and kiss his mouth.

He responds, one hand letting go of Yvette so he can place it, palm-first, against my throat and choke me.

Go for it, I think. *Give it all you've got, Logan. Because I sure am.*

I almost black out, that's how serious he is about maintaining control.

But he lets go just as the sparks and stars begin to flutter in front of my eyes.

He huffs out a laugh as we continue to kiss, thinking he's won.

"You always were too sure of yourself," I mutter into his mouth.

"And you always let me be," he adds.

I reach down for Yvette's hair. Pull on it a little. She looks up and both Logan and I break apart to look down at her.

God, she's pretty. I saw it yesterday. Hell, there hasn't been a moment I wasn't admiring how beautiful she is. But right now, as she kneels at our feet gazing up at us with wide, willing, trusting eyes—it's more than that.

She's the one.

She. Is. The. One.

She gets us. And we get her.

And I mean that in two ways. She understand us and we understand her. And she literally… gets us. Gets to keep us both.

She stands up. The top of her head only comes up to about my chin, but just one tilt of her head and her lips are on Logan's.

Perfection. I step back and take a seat on the bench. Phase three starts now.

246

CHAPTER TWENTY-NINE

YVETTE

The whole experience feels a little… out-of-body.

A dream, or an illusion, or hey, maybe it just is what it is. The actualization of an erotic fantasy.

Either way… it has changed my mind about one thing.

Dying.

I don't want to die. I don't want to give in or give up. Because I'm feeling things today that felt impossible just twenty-four hours ago.

For these men. For myself. For the past. For the future.

The fact that I'm actually contemplating a future is a huge swing in a totally opposite direction.

And Logan.

Let me be your monster.

I don't know what that means, exactly. I just know it's special. Somehow.

He will kill for me? He will die for me? He will love me? Protect me? I'm not sure.

Maybe all of that.

Or maybe he's just being literal? He will be my monster. He will be my worst nightmare.

Before this moment I'd have gone with the latter. He will ruin my life. He seems capable of that.

But now I feel a change inside me. A hope, maybe. That he will unleash this monster that lives inside him on my behalf and make all the bad things disappear.

I want to believe that. I'm desperate to believe it. I just don't know if this potential conviction is faith or a false promise.

All this runs through my mind as we kiss.

I'm kissing the monster. I'm in bed with him.

So… I guess I made up my mind.

Logan turns me around and pushes me against the tiled wall. It's not cold, because the hot water has been falling down from the ceiling for a half hour or more by now. And the whole shower is filled with steam. But there is a temperature difference as my back hits the tiles. It's that uncomfortable sting of cold you sometimes feel when something aches and you put an ice pack on it.

It's not painful, not quite. But it is.

That's the sensation I get when my back hits the wall.

But then one hand is on my throat. I watched him choke AJ. It was a clear power play between them. Logan *has* to be the leader. Has to be in control. It's the way of things between these friends who are clearly way more than friends.

So I wonder, as his other hand finds my hip and slides up to my waist, is he AJ's monster too?

Is what he was offering to me? What he gives AJ? He will die for him?

It's a nice thought.

"Yvette," AJ says from across the shower.

I look over at him. Sitting on the bench, pressed into the corner. One knee bent, one foot on the stone seat. Legs open as he jerks off.

"What?" I say. Softly. Probably too softly.

But he must hear me or maybe he reads my lips. Because he says, "Just say yes."

I nod my head. Because I did say yes. I already decided. I don't want to die. I will let him be my monster. I said yes.

But I'm not sure if that's what he means.

"No," AJ says. "Say it to him."

I look up at Logan and find him frowning. "Yes, " I say quickly. Because I don't want there to be any doubts. Then I clasp my hands behind his neck, draw him down as I stand on my tiptoes, and kiss his mouth, whispering, "Be my monster," past his lips.

He lets out a breath of air that is something between a sigh and a laugh. And then his hands grip under my thighs and he lifts me up. His hard cock pressing against my lower stomach as I wrap my legs around his ass.

"You're sure?" he asks.

I'm not sure of anything except… I don't want to die now. I want to live. And I need him to do that. Because he was sent here to kill me.

So I say, "Yes. I want to live."

Logan kisses me hard. It's a desperate, hard, unyielding kiss that feels very much like a claim of ownership.

I close my eyes because as sick as it is, I want him to claim me and to own me.

I want them both.

AJ has already made his promise and now I have Logan's too.

I wonder what he'll want from me in return?

Choke me with his cock again? Stick his fist in my pussy? Some other kinky bit of fuckery that we haven't yet done?

But when he reaches down for his cock and slips it inside me, he does it slowly. Carefully. Gently.

He goes very slow.

He says, "You OK?" when he enters me.

Which makes me laugh a little, the way he just did. Something between a sigh and a huff. "Fine," I say. "Keep going."

He does—but again, it's slow. And thoughtful. And painstakingly unhurried. So that it takes many moments, maybe even an entire minute, for him to be deep inside me. Something he did quickly and with much force just this morning.

Is this what it means to be his? For him to be mine?

He is a killer. He is ruthless. He is… maybe… *evil.*

But not with me.

Not anymore.

With me he is just himself.

It's hard not to be impressed. To be swept away in the tide of his possession.

"Your pussy feels so nice," he says.

And it does, I realize. It's smooth. I've always liked the first fuck after being waxed or shaved down there.

It's so much more sensitive. Even if I was just masturbating with a toy, it always felt different.

So it should not surprise me that this time feels different. Feels like we are more connected and in tune. That there's actual emotions attached to this physical act.

But then I understand. It comes to me without effort. It's just… there. Actual, and authentic, and real.

AJ did this on purpose. He took a kink of Logan's and linked it to me—a beauty for Logan's beast.

I glance over at AJ and find him grinning.

He knows what he did. But Logan doesn't. Not yet, anyway. All Logan knows is that he wants to fuck me slow. He wants to feel that pussy he shaved. Enjoy it. Make it last.

Is that enough, I wonder? To tame him?

"Is it enough?" I ask him.

He smiles lazily. Like the way he's fucking me. Pushing in, and stopping. Then pulling out, and stopping.

It shouldn't be enough. There's not enough urgency, or friction, or blind lust to maintain the arousal. Not nearly enough to make us come.

And yet… there's more than enough at the same time.

He kisses me again. Just lips, no tongue. And still I worry it's not sufficient. There should be nipping and biting, and teeth crashing, and reckless abandon.

"Oh," he sighs. "It's enough."

So it is. Like his words are law. He says it and it's true. I should believe him because he wouldn't lie. Not to me. Not after I took ownership of his demon inside.

So—even though I shouldn't because he is who he is and that monster inside is loose, and has been loose for maybe decades—I do believe him.

And I say, "OK," as I come.

CHAPTER THIRTY

LOGAN

The moment she gives in something changes.

I don't know what it is. It could be love, I just don't think so. But whatever the emotion is that floods the blood inside my cock, it changes things.

The promise I made her becomes real.

I come too. I don't even expect it. Don't even realize it's gonna happen until it happens.

Her body goes limp. Utterly soft. Her head drops to my shoulder as her legs drop to the floor. She quivers and shakes. Like she is spent.

And she should be. I have literally lost count of the number of times we've fucked.

I pick her back up and walk over to the bench where AJ is sitting, then sit next to him. Close enough that our shoulders are pressed up against each other.

Yvette sinks into my chest like she might fall asleep, her arms around my waist, her thumbs swirling lazy circles on my wet skin.

I sigh and look at AJ, find him smiling. I glance down at his cock, still in his hand, and see that he came as well. All over his fingers. He's still massaging the tip. He's looking me in the eyes when I glance back up. "What?"

He shakes his head, stands up, steps under the shower head to rinse off, then opens the glass door and walks out.

"Where are you going?"

"Hold on," he calls, grabbing something from the medicine cabinet. When he returns to the shower he says, "OK, Logan. Your turn."

He's holding up another razor.

I look down at my dick.

"No." He laughs. "Your face. Give Logan a shave, Yvette."

"Oh," I say. "OK."

Yvette forces herself to sit up, her eyes heavy and half-closed. "Seriously?"

"Fuckin' serious," AJ says. "It's good for us, trust me."

I think about that for a second. How he wanted me to shave her to bring us closer. And how he's gonna make damn sure that the tenuous bond we've formed grows stronger.

He's really invested in this. More than I am, for sure.

Yvette takes the razor and AJ hands her the shaving cream, then settles back down in his corner to watch.

"Have you ever done this before?" I ask Yvette.

"Did I question your skills when you took a blade to my pussy?" She raises one challenging eyebrow at me.

"No." I laugh. "You didn't."

"Then shush and trust."

She squirts a large dollop of foamy cream onto the side of my face, sets the can down, and then begins to smooth it out across my jaw.

Her touch is gentle, and easy, and tender.

"But no," she says, dragging the cream over the top of my lip. "I've never done this before. I have, however, shaved other things hundreds of times." She stops, looks down at me with a serious expression, and says, "I won't hurt you."

A long exhale escapes my lips. Something that might be relief on another occasion. One where I was stressed. I didn't think I was stressed out right now. Had forgotten all about why I'm here and how this day is supposed to end. But the exhale proves otherwise.

"Hmmm," Yvette murmurs.

"What?"

"Maybe you need a cool chevron mustache?"

I laugh out, "No."

"A goatee?"

AJ laughs now too.

"No," I say. "Just color inside the lines, Yvette."

"Oh, no. Wait. I got it. Mutton chops!"

"Yvette," I say, starting to get a little worried.

"I'm kidding, you oaf. One boring shave coming your way. But a chin strap is always an option."

I can say, for sure, that I've never had a sexy, naked woman sitting in my lap talking to me about beard styles. But I might like it. And AJ's idea to do this was a good one. It is bringing us closer.

That's stupid, I realize. But then again—shaving another person involves a lot of trust and vulnerability. So maybe not.

"OK, hold still," Yvette says. "I gotta concentrate on your new gunslinger sideburns." She winks at me as she gently drags the razor down my cheek.

AJ laughs again. I glance over at him. Find him relaxing in the corner. One leg up, foot on the bench. The other on the floor. His cock is still semi-hard but he's not jerking off. I guess we're finally all satiated. "It's all fun and jokes until she's sitting in your lap with a razor," I tell him.

He rubs the ever-present stubble on his chin and grins. "She's not touching my pride and joy."

Yvette points the razor at him. "Is that a challenge? Because I can rise to the occasion."

We all laugh a little, but it's true.

She can rise to an occasion. She built this life, after all. Got away from psycho Damon, started over with strangers. Gave birth among them. Then sent her baby away to have a better life. And then, when all that was over, she squared her shoulders and moved on. Started over from nothing.

And Damon took it all away just because he could.

What a dick he is. Why hasn't anyone killed him yet?

It's a dumb question because the answer is obvious. No matter how much people dislike the guy, he's in charge. And you can't ever be sure who will remain loyal to save their own ass and who will stand up and fight for something better.

So no one tries.

I mean… I could've killed him plenty of times. AJ too. But we never have. Says a lot about us, I guess.

"Besides," AJ continues, "we bonded on the dance floor yesterday."

Yvette smiles, presumably at the memory of the dance, or maybe the first fuck that came after. But she doesn't say anything. Just concentrates on my shave. Gently dragging the razor across my jaw, then tapping it into the bowl of water, and every few strokes placing her warm palm against my cheek to check for smoothness.

"Tell me something," she says.

"Tell you what?" AJ asks.

"I dunno. Something about you guys. If we're going to run away together I should know you a little better."

Are we going to run away together? Did we actually come to this conclusion?

"OK," AJ says. "What do you want to know?"

"Have you always loved each other?"

I can't stop the laugh.

"What's so funny?" she asks.

"I mean… *love*?" I laugh again.

She stops working and looks down at me. "You don't love him?"

I glance over at AJ, looking for help. But he just shrugs. "Well… sure, I guess."

"You kiss him," she says.

"Yeah. I kiss lots of people."

"So AJ's just a one-night stand? No different than some random girl you pick up in a bar?"

And now I don't know if she's the random girl in this hypothetical, or if she's talking about other random girls. I sigh. "I like him."

"Enough to fuck a girl with him, so… *obviously*. But what else? If you don't love him, how do you feel about him?"

"Do we have to talk about feelings?" I ask.

"Yes," she says, squirting a new dollop of shaving cream on the other side of my face. "We're about to fuck up each other's lives in a major way. I think it's good to go into this knowing how we feel about each other, don't you?"

"I dunno," I say. Because I don't do feelings. And I definitely don't talk about them.

"We don't even know each other," Yvette says.

"We kinda know you," AJ replies. "We've been watching you for a while now."

"Not inside the bar. I never saw you."

"No, just following you when you go places."

"Because you wanted to see if I knew where the baby was?" she asks.

I suck in a deep breath, really uncomfortable with this conversation.

"We didn't know about the baby," AJ replies.

"Then why were you here?"

"We just…" AJ looks at me for help. Because he doesn't really know why we're here. "Uh… you gonna handle this, Logan?"

I clear my throat to give myself a second to think up some plausible answer. Then just toe the line and say the script. "He told me he was looking for something you had. And I'd know it when I saw it."

"Hmm," she says. "Sounds pretty cryptic if you ask me. Maybe almost suspiciously vague."

"Yeah," AJ says. "It does." His eyes meet mine and they're suddenly worried. "You don't think he's got other plans for us, do you?"

Shit. "What do you mean?"

"I dunno. Like… why are we here?"

Yvette stops to clean the razor in the bowl of water, then stares down at me. "Aside from killing me, that is."

"That's it," I lie.

"That can't be it," AJ says. "First of all, here's weird point number one. We haven't worked together in a long time. Like… really long time. Couple years, at least. And weird point number two—you don't even handle the hits anymore. That's my job. So why send you and me? Why not me and one of my other guys?"

"I don't know, Aje."

"Also," he continues, "you and I both know that when Damon says 'You don't need clean-up,' that's a bad sign. I've been thinking about that ever since you hung up with him yesterday. Pretty much everyone who goes into a hit without a clean-up crew gets offed in the end."

"That's not true," I say. "You did a job right before we left with no clean-up crew and you made it out alive." What I don't say is, *I sent in my own clean-up crew afterward.* Because that was before I knew he was on my hit list. Those guys he was with on that last job were probably supposed to kill him and they chickened out. It's kind of a big deal to off your boss, even when his boss tells you to. That's what I figure, anyway. "And I already told you," I add, "I got a guy on stand-by anyway."

"Yeah," AJ says, not sounding convinced.

"You got a guy on stand-by," Yvette says. "To clean up my dead body?"

OK, I need to put an end to this conversation. "No," I say. "Anyone can get rid of a dead body. It's the DNA wipe-down that gets people caught."

"Oh, right." She laughs. "I knew that." Then she rolls her eyes and turns to AJ and says, "Can you get me a hot towel, please?"

AJ nods, gets up, and walks out of the shower.

Yvette leans in and whispers, "If you want me to trust you, lying doesn't help."

I'm just about to open my mouth and deny my lies when she places two fingers across my lips and says, "Don't."

AJ comes back in with a hand towel, gets it wet under the hot shower, squeezes it out, and hands it to Yvette.

"Thank you," she says, taking the towel. She places it against my face, gently wiping away any leftover shaving cream, and then presses it one more time against my now smooth skin.

She smiles at me when she takes the towel away. "You're really handsome, you know that?"

I nod out of instinct. Then regret it and say, "I think you're very beautiful, Yvette."

This time her smile isn't as big. Almost a frown. "Thanks."

AJ can't see it though. He's behind her when it comes out because it's only meant for me.

Yvette places both hands on my cheeks, leans in, and kisses me. And through the camouflage of this kiss she whispers, "I'll let you be my monster. Just don't hurt me."

I stare at her. Our eyes locked. But then she pulls away and leans her head on my shoulder. Sighs with something that might be… relief.

God, what am I doing?

I'm making promises I can't keep, is the answer I don't want to admit.

AJ catches none of this because he's busy settling back into his corner. And once he is, he says, "So? I win, right?"

I laugh and feel Yvette laugh too, in the form of a slight shake of her body.

"Whatever," I say. But then I amend that to add… "Whatever you want, AJ."

"That's what I thought," he says, leaning back against the wall.

We're quiet for a few moments and I have a sudden urge to know what everyone is thinking. But most of all I want them to know what I'm thinking.

"Yvette," I say, shaking her a little in my lap.

"Hmmm?" she asks quietly.

"You ever been to Mexico?"

I see AJ look my direction from the corner of my eye.

"No," she murmurs. "Why?"

"Because I got a place there."

"Wait," AJ says. "You already have a place?"

"Yeah. I bought it about a year ago. Whenever I get bored I look at houses down on that island."

"Hold on." AJ laughs. "You house-hunt as a hobby?"

"I told you I wanted out, Aje. I wasn't just talking out my ass."

"Yeah… but you said we can't go there because Damon knows about it."

"Sure," I say. "I did say that. And it's still true. But when I bought it I was just thinking of myself. And now that we're all reevaluating our life choices, it's as good a place as any."

Yvette sits up in my lap and looks at me. "You're going to kill him?"

"Who?" I ask. Too quickly. Because I was thinking about AJ and how Damon wants him dead when her question comes out.

"Damon," she says. "Who else?"

"Oh. No. I'm not gonna kill Damon."

"Then what are we gonna do about him? Just pretend he's not a threat?"

"Just trust me," I say, then realize if there's one thing these two people know best about me, it's that I can't be trusted. So I add, "I'll take care of it."

They're both silent for a moment too long so I redirect their thoughts to something practical and slap Yvette's ass. "OK, let's get out of this shower before we shrivel up like prunes. Where did you get those clothes this morning?" I ask. "Got any more? I don't want to put my suit back on."

She frowns at me, but nods her head. "Yeah. In a bedroom downstairs near the bar."

I stand up, taking her with me, and then set her down next to AJ. "Mind if I go look?"

She thinks about this for a few seconds longer than I expected, but then finally shakes her head. "No, go ahead."

"Find something that'll fit me too," AJ calls as I step out of the shower and grab a towel. I wrap it around my waist, and call out, "Sure," over my shoulder as I make my way out of the bathroom.

Yvette and I leave the shower. She goes hunting for her clothes while I dry off and stare at the fogged-up mirror.

"I'll be right back," Yvette calls from the living room. "I'm gonna go help Logan find clothes."

"Sure," I say, wiping a circle of steam off the mirror so I can see my face. She called him handsome. Which he is. Otherwise I wouldn't bother with him. That's superficial at first glance, but… you know. I'm into the threesome shit. And it's a lot easier trying to talk a girl into two dudes when they're both hot with big cocks.

I chuckle in the mirror. Because sometimes I find myself ridiculous.

But then I frown and stare at my features again.

Perhaps I should've let her give me a shave? Just to make the edges of my ever-present stubble sharp. Because damn. I think my plan worked maybe a little too well.

They made a connection. Which I wanted, but only because I felt like Yvette and I were out ahead of Logan and he needed to catch up.

But now… I feel a little left behind.

How did that happen so quick?

That's why these threesome trysts we have are always temporary. It's really hard to love two people at the same time with equal measure.

I'm not worried about me. Or Logan, for that matter. We know how to share. We know how to detach from the jealousy.

But Yvette… she's not used to this the way we are.

Could she, one day, maybe… choose one of us over the other?

It's always a risk. But we're about to take so many risks that I'm not sure this is one we need at the moment.

What if we get to that island and she decides she likes Logan better? What would I do?

Or what if Logan is really into her now and she decides she likes me better? What would he do?

Would we fight over this woman? Would we erase the history we have to possess her? Would we stoop to any level to get what we want?

You don't have to look too far back into history to see that men do lots of stupid things for a woman. They ruin friendships, and families, and sometimes whole civilizations over their possessiveness. And Logan and I are already that guy to some degree. The kind who wants what he wants and does whatever it takes to get it.

That's us.

Is it stupid to think we can pull this off? Not only the part about escaping Damon. That's its own monster. But the part about taking one woman between us.

It can't ever work, can it?

Good fucking God. What did I do?

My phone rings. It's in my pants, which are on the bathroom floor.

I know who it is without looking. Only one person it could be.

I pick it up, tab accept, and say, "Damon."

"AJ," he says. "You're still alive."

"Yeah." I laugh. "Sorry about that. Fucking huge-ass blizzard came through here yesterday. We got stuck in the bar."

"Is she dead?"

"Uh…" I want to lie. But I don't know what Logan's plan is. So it's a bad idea. "No," I say. "Not yet."

"Well, that surprises me."

Here's the really creepy thing about Damon. He's an asshole to the nth degree. He loses his temper regularly. Just goes off on tantrums and rants. Like all the time. But he has this other side to him too. This side he's showing me right now. The calm, evil side that says, with a straight face, to the men in his wedding party, "Go ahead and fuck my new wife."

Anyone who thinks Logan is the world champion of zero emotions hasn't seen this side of Damon.

"We're gonna do it now," I say. "Then head out. Probably be back tonight."

"Both of you?" he asks.

Which puzzles me. "What do you mean?"

"I mean what I said. Both of you are returning home?"

"Yeah," I say, getting a very bad feeling about this.

"Well, that's why I'm surprised."

"What?"

"Because I told Logan to kill you before he came home. And obviously he hasn't done that either."

"What?"

"You heard me, AJ."

"Why the fuck would you tell him to kill *me*?"

Damon sighs on the other end of the phone. "Because, AJ. I'm done with you. And it was a test for Logan. To see if he would. Obviously he's failed. Miserably. So I'll tell you what I'm gonna do. I'm gonna give you the chance I gave him. Kill my wife, then kill Logan, and you can come home and keep your job. Keep your life. Keep everything just like it was when you left."

I am literally speechless. There's so much to unpack in that statement.

"AJ?" Damon barks.

"Yeah. I'm here."

"Did you understand my instructions?"

"Yeah. I'll get it done."

I can almost feel his evil smile on the other end of the phone conversation. Almost see it in the mirror in front of me.

"Good. Then I'll see you tonight."

He ends the call and I'm left standing there in front of the mirror. It's fogged up again. The steam still swirling around in the bathroom.

So I can't see my face. Which is a good thing.

Because I don't know who I am right now.

CHAPTER THIRTY-TWO

LOGAN

Downstairs it's cold and it takes me a few minutes to find the bedroom she's talking about. There's a hospital bed in there. So… guess this is where her father-in-law died.

Pretty. Sad.

Choosing clothes for us yesterday must've been a thoughtful decision for her, because there's a pile of them on a chair near the window. I walk over to it, then instinctively pull the curtain open to look outside.

Upstairs I hear AJ and Yvette walking across the floor. Then some muted talking. There must be a vent in here connected to the bathroom.

Snow has stopped. There's even a hazy ray of sunshine on the trees.

And as if on cue, I hear a rumble. Like a fleet of snowplows going past the bar, clearing the highway, and just underneath that, I hear a ringing phone.

Well, I guess this little sideshow is over. Really is time to get back to business.

I hunt through the clothes, find a pair of jeans and a t-shirt for me, but nothing for AJ. And I'm just about to turn and leave when I spy a box of baby clothes on the floor.

I pick up a dress and stare at it. Peach-colored. With soft white, eyelet lace around the neck. There's a stain on the front of it. Like this dress could've been worn yesterday.

"Find anything?" Yvette says.

I drop the dress back into the box and turn around. She's put her clothes from earlier back on but her feet are bare.

"Uh, yeah." I hold up the clothes. "These OK?"

She nods. But I can tell it bothers her a little. Or maybe she's thinking about the baby.

"That was her favorite dress," she says.

Guess it's the baby that's bothering her.

And just thinking that in my head—the casual, emotionless way it comes across, even internally—makes me wonder what kind of person I am.

It's all well and good to dream, right? To say, *We're going to that island. It'll be fine. Trust me, I have a plan.*

But I'm callous. Even I know that. I'm a fucking stone when it comes to emotions. And even though I know that, and have always known that, it's disturbing to actualize it in this moment.

"It's a nice dress," I say, trying to be normal.

Yvette huffs, then holds out my phone. "A call came through," she says. "Upstairs. It was Damon."

"Oh," I say.

"Yeah. Guess the storm's over, right?"

I nod. "Yeah. I just heard the plows go by on the highway."

She bites her lip and frowns.

"Yvette," I say. "There's just one thing I need to ask you."

"What's that?"

"The other baby," I say. "Damon's—"

"It's probably not his," she says, irritation in her voice. "So I'd prefer if you didn't call him that."

"Oh, right." She's right. There's no telling who the father of that child is. "But… you know where he is, right?"

She stares at me hard for a moment. "Why?"

"Because I want to know. I don't want you to lie to me. I'm taking a huge risk here, Yvette. So I need the truth in order to make accurate decisions."

She thinks about this for several moments.

Upstairs I hear AJ walking around again.

"He didn't see the phone call come in," she says. "It was on silent. I just happened to glance over at it while I was getting dressed. It fell out of your pocket."

"OK," I say, then wait. But she doesn't answer my question. "We could go get him, " I offer.

"Who?" she asks.

"Your son, Yvette. We could go get him."

"He's not mine. Not anymore. He has a family. I won't steal him away from that normal life I risked everything to provide just to make myself feel better."

"Right," I say. "Never mind."

I drop the towel and start pulling on the jeans. She watches me. Thoughtfully now. Then says, "But I did lie. I do know where he is."

I hold my breath. Say nothing.

"He's in New Mexico living on an Indian reservation. With the Nightingale people."

I nod. "Well… good," I say. "Good. I'm glad you figured it all out and…" I don't finish. Because it's stupid.

"I thought about it though," she adds. "After Chris and Bonnie died. I thought… he's mine. I should go get him. It would've helped? Maybe?"

She looks at me like she needs this idea to be validated. So I say, "He is yours. You're his mother. And at least if he was with you, you'd have more than nothing."

She swallows hard and nods. "Yeah."

"So why didn't you?"

She shrugs. "I was too sad to start the fight, ya know?"

"Yeah, I get that."

"Because there would've been a fight. If there wasn't, if they didn't fight for him, well, then I made a mistake when I signed him over for adoption. And I can't live with that. So there *would* have been a fight."

"I'm sure they would've fought hard."

We stare at each other for a moment. Then, just as I'm about to say some other stupid, off-the-cuff thing that will make her feel worse, my phone lights up.

I'm holding it in my hand so Damon's name shows up on the screen.

"I'll let you take care of that," Yvette says, then turns away and disappears.

I sigh at the phone, then tab accept and say, "Yeah."

I listen as Damon talks on the other end.

I nod my head as he goes on and on about us disappearing. Say things in between his rants. Things like, "Blizzard." And, "No cell service," and, "Not yet.

But soon." And "Yup." And, "You got it." And, "Call you when I'm done." And then, finally, "See you tonight."

And then I end the call.

Because I have a job to do.

CHAPTER THIRTY-THREE

YVETTE

When I walk back into the bar AJ is just coming down the back stairs from the apartment. He's dressed, but no shoes.

"My boots are still wet from clearing the snow," he says, noticing my gaze down at his feet. "Any chance you've got a size twelve and a half shoe in your treasure chest of clothes?"

I smile at him. Because even though I shouldn't trust him, or like him, or want him… I do. All three of those things. "No," I say. "Chris wore an eleven."

"Well, shit," he says, walking towards me. "Guess I'll have to make do."

He opens his arms as he approaches and that fills me with a warm feeling. Something like acceptance. Or maybe gratitude. Or possibly just lust.

"Why are you smiling?" he asks, taking my hand and wrapping his arm around my waist like we're about to dance.

"Oh, I dunno. Maybe because this time yesterday I was about to kill myself. I was thinking there was nothing left for me in this life."

"And now?" he asks, twirling me a little. Like we really are dancing.

"And now… I guess I can see past it, ya know?" I sigh. "Depression sucks. Like… really sucks. Because I was so sure I was done. I woke up every day with this weight on my chest. Like I was suffocating. Or just dying of a broken heart. And then two hitmen walk into a bar—"

He laughs.

"—and one dazzles me with his charm and dancing. And the other one makes me feel like maybe there's a way to get past this ache and loss. So…" I sigh. "I don't know. I'm just gonna stay on the ride, I guess. Does any of this make sense?"

He nods. And both of us look over at the jukebox where the bottle of pills is still waiting. Right where Logan left them. "You wanna dance?" he asks, pulling me back into his embrace.

"I think we are dancing," I say, gazing up at him.

"Yeah, but like… really dance."

"OK," I say.

He unwraps his arm from my waist and leads me over to the jukebox. "We gotta choose a song," he says. "One last song on this jukebox, Yvette Nightingale. Better think hard about that."

"Hmmm," I say. "Maybe we can have two?"

"Or three," Logan says.

Both AJ and I turn to look at him. And God, it hurts my heart a little to see him dressed up in Chris's clothes. Makes me feel like a traitor for some reason. But if Chris were here, and AJ and Logan weren't here to kill me, he'd have given them the shirt off his back.

He was that kind of guy. He didn't deserve the shit I brought with me when I came into his life.

Logan was right after all. I'm not innocent in this. I could've told Chris what he was getting into. Let him make a decisions based on facts. He might still be alive if I'd done that.

I probably wouldn't be here right now. Don't know where I'd be if Chris didn't bring me home with him and his father after the baby was born. But at least I'd have a clear conscience.

"What's the rush?" Logan asks. "I mean, shit. You have to pack, right, Yvette?"

Do I have to pack? Do I want to take things from this place? Since it wasn't even mine to begin with?

"Are you and I gonna dance while she does that?" AJ asks. And for some reason it comes off like a challenge.

Are we gonna dance?

Meaning… are we gonna fight?

"No," Logan says. "We're not."

"Good," AJ says. "I don't want to dance with you."

"Likewise," Logan says. Then he smiles and says, "So choose a song, Yvette. I think I'll get us a drink. One last toast, huh? To the bar? To your life?"

"And one for the new life," AJ says. "Coming up."

Logan nods. "I guess everything comes in threes today."

"Good thing too," AJ says. "Because we come in threes as well."

"What the hell is going on here?" I ask.

"What do you mean?" AJ says.

"You two are talking in some secret code."

"Are we talking in code?" AJ asks Logan.

"Nope."

AJ shrugs and smiles at me. "See? No code. Pick a song, Yvette."

I look down at the song list. I know it by heart, don't even have to look to find the number. Just punch in my code for free songs and the code for my choice. Then I look up at AJ and say, *"Perfect Duet."*

He chuckles just a little, his smile wide and real. "Can't go wrong with Sheeran and Beyoncé." Then the song comes on and he takes my hand and leads me away to the middle of the floor, twirling me once, then bringing me back into his arms.

We settle like that. My face against his shoulder, my hands up around his neck. His hands on my hips as we sway.

"You're a nice surprise," I say.

"You as well, cookie."

Cookie. He turns me around and I see Logan at the other end of the bar opening a bottle of champagne. The cork pops off and some spills out, but he catches most of it in a glass. Then AJ turns me, and I lose sight of him.

"This dance is better than the one we had yesterday," AJ says.

"How come?" I ask.

"Because I know you now. And I really like what I see."

Logan comes closer to us. Leans against the bar. "What song do you want, AJ? I'll put it in for you."

AJ thinks as we dance, his eyes closed. And I doubt many people get to see him like this. So easygoing. So calm. So comfortable.

I'm lucky, I realize. That I'm one of them.

"*Give Me Love*," AJ finally says. "Sheeran for the win. I saw that in there yesterday and thought, *Well, shit. I could use me some love.*"

"Me too," I say.

Logan puts money in for the song. I guess he didn't want to ask me for the code and break my moment with AJ.

Which is… very mature of him. They don't seem to have a problem sharing. Which gets me curious. "When did you guys start doing this? You know. Having sex together with the same girl. Or—" I realize maybe I assumed wrong. Maybe they have sex without a girl. "Or do you have sex a lot? Together. Alone, I mean."

AJ laughs. "We don't. Have sex alone together. But we started this maybe… what? Fuckin' more than ten years ago, right?"

Logan has returned to his place by the champagne. He's leaning against the bar again, all casual. "Yeah, I think the first time we were just really fucked up and on drugs."

I laugh. "So you didn't plan it?"

"No," AJ says.

"You didn't like… make up rules, or anything?"

"It was just one night," Logan explains. "Nothing more than that."

"Hmmm," I say. "Have you ever shared a girl long-term before?"

"No," Logan says.

AJ is just swaying me to the music. Maybe ignoring this conversation.

"So how do you know it's going to work?" I ask.

"How do you ever know something's gonna work?" Logan replies. "Everything's a risk, Yvette. How did you know leaving Damon would work?"

"I just didn't care," I say. "I had no choice. I just needed to get out of there or I was going to kill myself."

"Well," Logan says. "We're kinda in the same situation, right, AJ?"

"Pretty much," AJ says.

I look up at AJ. Because this is code talk again. I don't know how I know, I just do. They're discussing something between the lines. "What are you guys not telling me?"

"Nothing," AJ says. "I think we've been pretty honest with you. Damon wants you dead. We don't. So what else can we do but make a go of it?"

"Right," I say. "I see that part. But the part I'm confused about is… how do you guys know you'll still want to do this in say… a week?"

"Jesus, Yvette." AJ laughs. "Give us a little more credit than that."

"But—" I stammer. "But don't you think we should have rules? Or come to some sort of agreement?"

"About you?" AJ says, sincerely surprised about this new line of questioning. "Are you asking me if one day I might wake up and be like… 'I'm done sharing and now I have kill Logan?'"

"Um… no. No. That wasn't quite what I was thinking."

"Let me explain," Logan says.

AJ and I both turn to face him. He's holding two champagne flutes in his hand. AJ and I take one each, automatically. Then Logan goes back to get his glass, comes back to us and takes a seat at the table nearby.

"First," he says, "Cheers. To our new beginning. May it be filled with everything we ever dreamed of."

"Cheers to that," AJ says, downing his drink.

I do the same, but only drink half, then walk over to the table and take a seat next to Logan.

"We're not done dancing," AJ says.

"I think this is important," I say. "I don't want to come between you two. And I don't want to get to that island and figure out that one of you can't live with our decision."

Logan sighs as AJ comes over and sits down next to him. "I can live with it. Can you, Aje?"

AJ nods. "I can too."

"Listen carefully, OK?" Logan says, directing his words to me. "You can't come between us. Understand? It simply cannot happen."

"So you two don't have normal feelings like jealousy or greed?"

AJ laughs. "Oh, fuck, yeah, we do. But…" He stops to look at Logan. "But we're loyal to each other. Maybe we're not loyal to anyone else. Fine. That's probably true. But we're loyal to each other."

I look at Logan because he doesn't say anything. They're locked in a heated stare that makes me uncomfortable and I'm not even participating in this exchange.

"Isn't that right?" AJ asks Logan.

It takes several more seconds but Logan finally responds with a nod. "Yeah. That's right."

But in my head I hear that name they call him. Logan the Loyal. And they call him that because it's a joke.

He's not loyal. Never has been.

So how can he be loyal now?

CHAPTER THIRTY-FOUR

LOGAN

I know what they're both thinking, but it doesn't matter anymore. What's done is done.

"Do you have any idea how pissed off Damon is gonna be when he finds out we're all still alive but not under his control anymore?"

I'm talking to AJ, but looking at Yvette. Because I can't meet his eyes right now. If I do, I won't be able to tell the lie.

"I have an idea," Yvette says.

"Yeah," I say. "I'm sure you do. You could probably write a whole book about your experience with Damon."

Which is unfair and maybe a little mean. Because she did write a whole book about it. It's up in her journal. The rapes. The beatings. The verbal abuse. It's all in there.

But she needs to think about this. They *both* need to think about this. Because that's who that guy is. He will never stop. He killed her husband and their infant daughter just to get revenge. Just because she didn't want to be raped, and beaten, and verbally abused anymore and took it upon herself to leave.

Not kill him. Not hurt him. Not even spit threats and insults at him.

Just leave. Just walk away with nothing.

And even if you add in the fact that she was pregnant, he has to know that the baby probably isn't his. That's how many times he let his inner circle rape her.

Doesn't matter though. Not in Damon's mind.

She committed the ultimate sin. She turned him into something *meaningless*.

And he can't stand that. He'd rather be killed than forgotten.

So he bided his time. He planned this whole thing so carefully just so he could maximize the depth of his retribution over her betrayal. Take away all her hard-won happiness.

"He is going to hunt us down, Yvette." But again, I'm really talking to AJ. He's the one who needs to hear this from me. I just can't tell him that yet. "There is no limit to the resources he will spend in order to find us. There is no line he won't cross, there is no wait that is too long, there is no way out. Do you understand this?"

She swallows hard and nods. "I do," she whispers.

"We're all we have left."

I let that hang there. Staring at her. She stares back and then I switch my gaze to AJ and say it again, just for his benefit. "If we do this… we're all we have left."

AJ's gaze can't meet mine. It hurts to see it. I want to tell him that. I really do.

I want to say, *I'm sorry. I had to do it.*

I want to tell him I love him. And if we did this I'm sure I'd love Yvette too. I'm sure we, of all people, could make this fucked-up threesome work.

I want to tell him thank you. For being my friend. For always having my back. For trusting me today.

Because he did trust me. I heard his phone ring upstairs. I knew who it was. I knew what he said. And I also knew, with my whole heart, that AJ would never do it. He would never betray me the way I would him.

And that's why I knew I'd win out in the end.

AJ sways a little in his chair, almost falls over.

Yvette puts a hand to her head, eyes heavy and closing. "I feel… funny," she says.

"I know," I whisper, sadness in my voice. "I'm sorry about that, cookie. I really am. But it couldn't be helped. I'm the monster here, not AJ. And that means I'm the only one who can finish this job."

And then I get out my phone, call up Manny, and say, "We're ready for the clean-up."

We're ready for clean-up.

The pills.

That's all I think about as I sway to the side and then fall out of my chair.

The pills. I can't focus my eyes. But I try. I desperately try to find the pill bottle on top of the jukebox. Hoping it's still there.

It isn't.

He drugged us with the fentanyl.

Isn't it ironic that Yvette will die the way she planned after all?

There was never going to be a fight. Not Logan's style, is it? Why should he bother? Why should he risk it? When he can just dump those pills into some champagne and have us drink it?

We trusted him. *I* trusted him.

There wasn't even a single moment when Damon called that I considered following through with his request. Not a single moment.

But Logan has never been loyal.

Not to me, not Yvette, not to anyone. Not even to Damon. He's just… doing his job. That's all this is to him. That's all *we* are to him.

A *job*.

I don't want to believe it. I want to pretend this is all a mistake. I lie there for an eternity dwelling on my own misplaced faith, still willing it to be a misunderstanding.

But Yvette is on the floor beside me. We are face to face, her eyes mostly closed. Heavy and unable to focus.

"Yvette," I say. Except it doesn't even come out as a word. Just a mumbled, garbled pathetic string of sounds.

I want to tell her things. So many things. Like… we could've made it. We could've fixed things. Started over. I could've given her the life she deserved. Maybe eventually, we'd fall in love.

The island could've been our paradise. The beach Logan told her about. The sand, and the house, and the fresh start.

How could he do this to her? How? After all she's been through. After all her loss…

And how could he do this to me?

Logan the Loyal.

I should've known better.

I really should've known better.

My world darkens to the last song on the jukebox. Logan's pick.

Time to Pretend.

No, I think. *You've been pretending this whole time.*

This is reality.

This is who you always were, Logan.

A traitor to the core.

Someone is wrapping me up in a tarp.

Voices.

Logan saying, "He's waking up. Give him more."

Another voice. One I don't recognize.

The cleaner.

Then a sharp pain in my arm. And heat, as drugs are pushed into my vein. The warmth overtakes me and I start to fade again, just as someone grabs my feet and pulls me across the floor.

I force myself to stay semi-conscious as I'm dragged outside into the cold, bitter wind, and snow.

I plowed this parking lot. I cleared the way so they could slide my body across the ice.

I made it easy for them.

My eyes are heavy and they resist, but I am strong, so I force them open one more time as I'm lifted up and dragged across the floor of an empty cargo van.

No, I realize.

Not empty.

Because Yvette is beside me. Blood all over her neck like it was sliced open.

I'm sorry, I try to say. *I failed you and I'm sorry. I trusted him and that was a mistake.*

But it's just meaningless thoughts. No words.

I fade to black…

The next time I wake to the sound of Yvette moaning and the first thing I think is… she's still alive. All that blood and she's still alive.

I don't try to talk this time, just wait for the inevitable push of drugs into my veins. We are still in a van. Or some other moving vehicle. Because my body, still limp and weak, rolls from side to side as we take corners. Yvette's body bumps into mine and she moans again.

"AJ," she whimpers.

I try to talk but I can't. So I think.

I think… *I'm here. You're not going to die alone.*

I can give her that. One last gift. I can be there with her when we die.

The next time I come up from the blackness I don't fall back into the stupor and hazy dream world, but begin to wake up.

"Yvette," I manage to croak. My throat dry like sandpaper.

No response.

We are still moving.

He's taking us back, I realize.

Back to that beast Damon. Where Damon will torture us, and rape her, and—

The van stops. The brakes squeaking.

Then voices speaking Spanish along with the unmistakable *click-clack* sound of a shotgun loading.

Minutes pass, the driver quiet. And I open my eyes and sit up.

Look around. Groggy, but finally awake.

Realize four things.

I am not wrapped in a tarp, but a thick blanket. Like the kind movers use to protect furniture.

My hands are bound in front of me, not behind me.

The blood on Yvette's neck is not from a wound. Because it's dried up and flaking and there is no cut slicing across her throat.

We are still alive and if we do die today, it will not happen quickly.

CHAPTER THIRTY-SIX

YVETTE

When the dizziness hit me I thought it was just… hunger, maybe. Just… I was in need of food. Low blood sugar.

But then AJ slumped to the floor and Logan didn't move to help him. Just stared at me.

"What?" I managed to mumble as I began to slump over. Then the real question. "Why?" As he caught me before I hit the floor and dragged me over to AJ.

"Shhh," he said. "Just sleep, Yvette."

So I did. I couldn't help it.

But not completely. It was a hazy, half-drugged dream-sleep. Filled with bad memories and the feeling of being out of control.

A nightmare, really.

I opened my eyes to find Logan and another man standing over me. Blood dripping from Logan's hand. Blood that lands on my neck. Then his fingers. Gently smearing it around.

I can smell it. Copper with a hint of iron.

I try to ask him what's going on, but they are just jumbled thoughts. No chance of ever turning into words.

They speak but I can't understand them so I stop trying.

The next time I wake up to a sharp pain in my arm as drugs flood my body again. Logan says, "He's waking up. Give him more."

And I want to scream at him. Scream about my misplaced trust. Hate myself for falling for it. Hate him for lying to me. For making me think he cared.

Let me be your monster.

Hate that I agreed.

Because this is what monster Logan looks like.

I don't know what happens next. I just know I'm in a vehicle and we are moving. I feel like this goes on for a long time. I feel like I'm about to wake up, but then I sleep again. I start to think that there's no such thing as time. It's an illusion. This isn't real, just a nightmare, and if I could only wake up, everything will be fine. None of this really happened.

But I'm wrong.

Because I do, eventually, begin to wake.

And it's one hundred percent real.

"Yvette," AJ says. He sounds very far away, but I can feel his body next to mine. Just pressure and warmth.

Then the sound of a shotgun loading.

AJ moves. Maybe even sits up.

Why are we still alive?

But I know why.

Logan's taking us back. He's delivering us to Damon. He told us, over and over again… there is no escape. The island was a lie to make us compliant. To make us cooperate. Just a lie.

"Yvette," AJ says again. "Are you awake?"

I don't want to be awake. I'd rather die than go back to Damon. Rather die than let him rape me and beat me again.

And oh, God… I start to cry.

"Shhh," AJ says. "Don't, please. Don't cry."

"I told him," I say. And to my surprise, my thoughts come out as words.

"What?" AJ whispers. "Told him what?"

I sob.

"Yvette!" AJ whispers, more urgency this time. "You told him what?"

"I told him where the baby is," I wail.

"Shhh," he says again. "Please. Don't cry. And be quiet."

"What's the point?" I ask, rolling over. But I'm wrapped up in a blanket and I'm stuck. Which makes me panic.

"Yvette," AJ says again. "Sit up. Just… sit up and calm down."

"I can't," I say. "I'm tied up."

"You're not," he says, his tone very firm. "You're not tied up, Yvette. You're just tangled in the blanket. Now try, OK? They're outside and pretty soon they're going to open that door and that's our last chance, do you hear me? That's our only chance. If we want to escape—"

"Weren't you paying attention?" I laugh. "We can't escape!"

Shouting outside. They're speaking Spanish. That's why I couldn't understand earlier.

"Sit up!" AJ hisses in a low whisper. "Now!"

So I pull up my knees, roll over, and kick my way free of the thick blanket. It's freezing once it's off. So cold. And it's dark. Just blackness.

"They're going to dump us," I say.

"I don't think so," AJ says. "We drove for a long time. Maybe days. We're not in Colorado, Yvette. We're far, far away."

"Why is it so cold?"

"It's not. That's just the drugs. It's warm in here. Just… wake up and you'll see. I can't do this without you, Yvette. I need your help."

He's right. I'm not tied up. Not even my hands. I push the blanket aside and reach out. Find his arm and grip it tight.

"There you go," he says in a calm tone. "See. You're not tied up. Now listen. They're gonna open the door, and when they do, I need you to stay behind me and—"

But before he can finish the doors open and light floods in. Flashlights blinding us in the eyes.

AJ rushes forward, yelling at the top of his lungs. Lunging at them. Diving headfirst into the body that appears as a black silhouette against a streetlight.

They hit him with the butt of a shotgun.

They yell in Spanish.

They push him back.

They point their fingers and make wild gestures with their hands.

But they do not shoot.

And when AJ finally stops fighting, one says…

"Welcome to Mexico. If you behave, we will untie you now."

CHAPTER THIRTY-SEVEN

Yvette is sweaty and flushed when they pull her out of the van. She stumbles into the night but three men hold her up by her arms. Steady her as she tries to get her bearings.

It's not hot, but it's not cold either.

We *are* in Mexico. I don't know how I can tell, I just can. I don't see any street signs. It's just an empty parking lot lit up by a single street lamp. But we're somewhere on the coast because I can smell the ocean and off the distance there is the call of seagulls rising with the sun.

Three more men point guns at me. The one in front says, "AJ," in a thick Spanish accent.

I just glare at him. I want to kill him.

"Just… be good," he says. "And we will free you."

"Who the fuck are you?" I growl.

The one to his left aims his gun at my head with a little more intent.

"Do not attack us," the leader says. "We're here to help you. And we don't have much time. So please, forgive and forget so we can make the boat."

"What fucking boat?"

"Questions are for later," he says. "Now is for… gentleness."

Gentleness? I screw up my face, not understanding. My mind still foggy with drugs. "What the fuck are you talking about!"

"*Cállate!*" he hisses. "Shut up! Do you want everyone to know you are here?"

"Maybe," I say, but with less venom. Because… I start to understand. And then… no. No. He didn't do that. Please tell me this is not—

"Well, we like to live, friend. We like to keep secrets too. But we will shoot you if you make that impossible. So choose carefully, AJ." He says my initials with an oddly American accent. "Choose carefully."

When I stay silent he smiles.

Then waves his hand in a gesture that says, *Please get out of the van.*

I do. With some difficulty. Because unlike Yvette, I am tied up. But only my hands, not my feet. So I scramble to the edge of the van and cautiously step out, still a little unsteady from being drugged.

"Good," the leader says. "*Muy bien.* And *gracias.* Now come with us."

"Untie me," I say. But they don't. His two henchmen grab me by the upper arms and pull me along while the leader walks behind me, gun pressed into my back. Yvette walks in front, supported by two other men and another out in front of her. "Where are we going?"

He ignores that too.

Great escape plan, AJ. You really took control of this situation.

But… I don't feel too bad about my failure. Because I'm starting to understand that this *is* my escape.

Our escape.

Logan. What did you do?

We walk across the parking lot to the docks. It's mostly empty. I'd guess… maybe four AM? They lead us out to a fishing boat. The guy in front stops, points at the ramp, indicating Yvette should board, then helps her with a shove when she hesitates.

"It's OK," I say. "Get on the boat, Yvette."

"Where are we going?" she asks. "What's going on?"

"Just get on the boat," I say.

She shoots me a worried glance over her shoulder, but by then the men in charge of her have had enough and are pulling her along.

I go willingly, but stop to turn once I get to the top of the ramp. "Thanks," I say to the leader. He has put his gun away and he smiles.

"*De nada,*" he says. "I owed him, now I do not."

I smile, getting it, then turn my back to him and follow Yvette into the cabin and down a narrow, steep flight of stairs. We stop in front of a door and wait for the three men to open it.

We go inside, but we're not done. Because one of the men opens a hatch and points for Yvette to climb in.

"No," she says, looking back at me. "No."

"Yvette," I say. "Just get in. It'll be OK."

I don't know that for sure. And when I follow her down into the hidey hole, I feel her unease. Because it's dark, and cramped, and it smells like fish.

One man hands us a battery-powered lantern and says, "Stay in here. And do not come out no matter what." He points to two cots, then a small fridge, then a bucket that is probably our toilet. "Sleep, food, water, shit," he says. "Someone will come and let you out when it's time. Be quiet. No talking."

"How long?" Yvette asks. But he closes the hatch. Sealing us up in the darkness. And there is the unmistakable sound of a padlock being fastened on the door.

Yvette begins to hyperventilate.

I hold her, saying, "It's OK," over and over again.

But all she does is shake her head.

Her trust is gone.

Have we been kidnapped? Have we been sold? Or is this all part of some genius plan cooked up by Logan?

We have no idea.

All we know is that we are locked in a hot, cramped hole that reeks of dead fish for what seems like years.

We say nothing.

Not one word.

There's a whole crew on board and I'm pretty sure none of them know we're down here. They could be taking us anywhere. At one point we stop moving, the boat rocking wildly, wind beating against the hull.

We stay like that forever.

Then we motor on again.

They are fishing, I realize. Just doing their jobs. Probably a dozen or more people on this boat with us.

Eventually we hear the unmistakable sounds of a harbor. For all we know we're back where we started. Damon coming to meet us when they open that hatch.

But it's just the fear taking over.

I think we both know where we're going.

The air is so sweet when we're finally let out of the hatch, I inhale it like water. It's hot, and humid, and clean.

Only one man appears at the top of the hatch when it opens. He has no gun, just a frown. Like we're putting him out. Or hell, maybe he didn't even know we were here until ten minutes ago when someone called him up and said, "Oh, hey. Don't forget about the stowaways down in your secret hidey hole."

But he helps Yvette out, then me, and leads us up to the deck.

There's another man waiting on the dock. And when we disembark, he points to the shore, smiling and urging us forward.

It's the middle of the night again. So it's hard to tell where we are until we're on land, in a beat-up old car, heading into town.

There is a sign that says, *Bienvenido a la Isla Holbox.*

I think Yvette starts to cry.

It's been so long since we talked, we don't do it now. Just stay silent as we pass through the town and head across the island to the opposite shore.

"Oh," Yvette says. Her first word in… days? I don't even know how long we were on that fishing boat so my internal clock is all fucked up. It feels like lunchtime, but the sun is just barely up over the horizon to the east, so it's obviously not.

She's looking out the window as we pull into a long driveway that leads to a house.

"Oh," she says again. Like she's figured something out.

"Oh," I say, coming to the same conclusion.

"He's here," she says. "This is his house and he's here."

I think I smile. It just feels so weird after all that's happened, it takes me a minute to realize it.

The car stops and the driver gets out. He opens the driver's side passenger door for Yvette and she gets out, facing into the wind as it blows her long, blonde hair away from her face.

I get out my side and join them to take in the house.

It's big, but not massive. Contemporary Spanish style with a stucco exterior and red-tiled roof. It, and the dense shrubs on either side of two groupings of massive palm trees, block the ocean view from here. But there's no mistaking that's what's on the other side.

The blue ocean, the white sands, the perfect paradise.

The driver says a long string of words in Spanish, which nether of us understand. But he points to the house and we get it.

Then he leaves.

Yvette takes my hand and smiles. She's filthy dirty. We both smell like fish. But this smile turns her instantly beautiful.

"We should go in," she says. And she can't contain the excitement in her voice.

We know what happened. Sort of.

Logan smuggled us out of the country and brought us here.

Just like we planned.

We walk forward, find the front door open, and walk inside.

There's a breeze blowing through the open patio doors on the back side of the house and there it is.

Paradise.

"Logan?" I call.

No answer.

"Logan?" I yell louder. "Where are you?"

Silence.

"There's an envelope," Yvette says, walking into the large open kitchen where the patio doors are.

And yup. Sitting on the long dining room table there is, in fact, a very thick yellow envelope.

"What's in it?" I ask.

She picks it up, opens the flap, and peeks inside. She frowns. Then dumps the contents out on the table.

Two passports slide out.

That's my first clue that we don't, in fact, have any idea of what's happening here.

Because there should be three passports. Not two.

The second thing that comes out is a stack of photographs held together by a thick rubber band.

"What the fuck?" Yvette says. Then she holds them up for me to see and says it again. "What the fuck is this?"

I know what it is. I can see what it is.

It just doesn't make sense.

Suddenly… none of this makes sense.

Because that top photograph is a picture of Yvette.

Tied up in a tarp, only her head visible.

Her neck slit and bloody. Her eyes black and closed.

And she is dead.

Except she's not dead. She's standing here right in front of me.

I take the stack of photos from her hand and look at the next one.

Me.

Bloody, bruised, and dead as well.

"What the fuck?" Yvette says, for the third time.

"Oh, shit," I say. Because there's a letter too.

A letter from Logan.

And suddenly everything makes sense.

She hands it to me, shaking her head. "I don't want to read it."

So I read it instead.

Dear cookies…

I'm sorry for the long trip. I'm sorry for the drugs. It was a shitty move, I know that. But it was the only move I had left. If I had my way I'd have put you on a yacht. I'd have given you a stateroom with an ocean view. I'd have a private chef, and there would've been snorkeling, and sightseeing, and dolphin-watching as we made our way to paradise.

But then I wouldn't be sure that you'd be safe. And there's no point in going to all this trouble and having you end up dead. So I'm sorry for that. I hope the house makes up for it. I hope you can put all the ugliness it took to get here out of your mind and just concentrate on your future.

"No," I say, shaking my head and putting the letter down. I don't want to read the rest. I can't read the rest. Because I know what he did and I won't accept it.

But Yvette doesn't feel the same. Because she picks the letter up and begins to read out loud.

"'Someone has to go back and face Damon. Someone has to show up with proof that you two are dead. Someone has to obey his order.'"

"No," I say.

"'Someone has to be the monster.'"

"Fuck you, Logan. Just fuck you."

"'And that someone is me.'"

"He's not coming," I say. "He's not fucking coming. He did all this and he's not even coming!"

Yvette just looks at me. Unable to find the right words to help me process what just happened.

But it doesn't matter. Because there is only one way to process it.

He went back to die so we could live.

I don't know the last time I cried. I really, honestly do not remember that's how long it's been. But right now, that's the only thing I want to do.

CHAPTER THIRTY-EIGHT

LOGAN

Life is shitty, and dark, and filled with assholes like Damon who have more power than they deserve and more money than they'll ever need.

Basically, life is just unfair.

Just how it is.

But every once in a while a chance comes along to even the odds. Or make up for past transgressions. Or just... be the good guy for once.

I guess that's why I did it.

I am, after all, nothing but a self-absorbed narcissist.

So there. I did it for me, not them.

Someone had to go back. There was no way Damon would ever believe we were all dead without proof. There was no way all three of us could ever get out.

And like I said, I am the monster. It's practically my job title.

So I went back with the proof.

Big thanks to Manny for not only helping me clean up afterward, but also arranging the bodies to make them both look really dead. I guess he's seen enough of them to know what they look like. He stopped at a drug store down in Durango before he came up the mountain to get some supplies.

We used baby powder over a foundation of makeup for the blue-gray skin.

I cut my hand open and trickled blood all over Yvette's neck and even traced it across her throat with the edge of a knife.

We wrapped AJ and Yvette up in tarps, heads sticking out, and took photos. Then we took them out, put them in the van, and I packed the dummy tarps with clothes and blankets and tossed them over the ravine, just like AJ and I planned.

Took a picture of that too.

Damon actually smiled like the evil motherfucker he is when he looked at that photo.

I'm sure some hapless hiker is gonna find those bundles in the summer and think… what the fuck?

But who cares. Damon won't find them and that's all that matters.

So here I am. Back in the org, my loyalty proven, and hell, I even got a promotion.

A fat bonus in the form of cash I don't need, girls I won't fuck, and drugs I don't use.

Lucky me.

In my letter I spelled all this out. I told them the house was owned by my shell corporation, which they now officially owned. I told them to never come back, never call me—the number's been changed anyway because I know you, AJ. I knew you'd try, you loyal motherfucker, you—and I'd never see them again.

Would I have liked it to turn out different?

Sure.

Sure, I would've like to end up on that beach with them. Live in that house with them. Fuck them silly every night and then again every morning.

But someone has to be their monster.

And that someone is me.

It's enough, I decide. To do this good deed. It's enough for me. It gets me through all the ugly things I have to do to live until the day Damon falls. And he will fall.

When? Who knows.

I'm going to die in this life. I'm one hundred percent certain that Damon will take me with him when someone finally comes for him.

And that's OK too.

Because they are safe.

If Yvette could walk away from her son to keep him safe—and stay away, even when she had nothing left but the child she gave up—then I could walk away from her. And AJ too.

If she is that strong, I can be stronger.

If she is that selfless, then I can be too.

"I still miss you," I say, looking out over the city from my new penthouse apartment. "I still miss you. But I can live with it."

Because sometimes love means walking away.

So that's what I did.

This is how I love you both now.

From far, far away.

CHAPTER THIRTY-NINE

YVETTE

Dear Logan,

It has been one week since we arrived at your beautiful house and every day when I get up I look around, hoping that you came in the night and didn't want to wake us.

I hope you're sleeping on the couch, or sitting out on the beach watching the sun rise, counting the minutes until we wake up and realize you're home. That our little team is now complete.

But every day, for the last seven days, I've been disappointed.

I have begged AJ to let me call you or send you a letter but he says we can't. That you sacrificed too much to get us here safely and we owe it to you not to ruin that.

So I'm writing this letter so that when you finally do come, you'll know how grateful we are. And how much we miss you. And what you mean to us.

In the meantime I beg AJ for stories instead. I want to know everything about you. And AJ is happy to tell me. He smiles every time he says your name. Every time he revisits some adventure the two of you had. Even the times you fought.

And I want to tell you that you are brave, and strong, and so much more than anyone ever thought you were. I hope you know that. I hope you believe it. Because you gave up your own happiness for us.

We love you for that.

I want to know what you're doing. I want to know how you spend your days. I want to know where you live, and what you eat, and who your friends are. And AJ won't tell me those things. He says you wouldn't want me to know you that way. He says I should think of you as the man you were when you saved us, and not the man you were before.

So I have made up my own world for you. I gave you a new job—saving homeless puppies, obviously. ;) And you're really good at that, just FYI. You've already been nominated for the Puppy-Saver of the Year Award and I know you'll win.

I gave you a new house. Even though I didn't know where you lived before all this happened, I figured new everything was in order. So you've moved to the country and have a million puppies because you can't bear to part with them. Kittens too. It's peaceful out there. Like it is here. You deserve that. You deserve a quiet life like we now have because of your selflessness.

For the past few nights AJ and I have been playing a game called "What did Logan do today?"

And he answers, or I answer.

You have pretty exciting days saving puppies.

But it makes me sad to play the game and imagine this new life for you, Logan. Because I know your reality is hell. I know you're still stuck and we're free. I know you want more and you can't have it.

Sometimes I think… I should've never told you about how I wanted a better life for my baby boy. Because I fear that was the moment you decided to be my monster for real. To fight all my battles for me, even though we were almost strangers.

If I could, I'd take that back. I'd be selfish and tell you I was going to go get him. Take him with me. Think only of myself.

Because maybe, if I had said that, you would have come with us? You would be in paradise with us right now and not a slave to the devil called Damon.

I've been thinking about how I could repay you and so far the only thing I've come up with is to keep you alive in my heart. In both our hearts. That's why we talk about you. We need to keep you alive so when you do come, you'll fill that empty space up like you were always there to begin with.

I know you will come. One day you'll be here with us.

We will wait for you.

Love, Yvette and AJ

CHAPTER FORTY

Dear Logan,

Dude. What the fuck are you doing? Jesus fucking Christ man, it's been more than a month! If I have to listen to one more story about you saving puppies I'm going to puke! You need to be here. You need to drop everything and get your ass down to Holbox, OK?

We miss you. And nothing is the same without you. I know it's dumb because the three of us were only together for twenty-four hours, but something happened in that one day. Something big. Something important. Something we all needed.

And yeah, don't get me wrong. I'm so fucking grateful for what you did. I love this life but it's not complete, OK? We need you in our bed. We need you.

But don't worry, I've been saving your spot. Yvette and I went shopping online for some sex toys and we got a fat dildo. We named it Logan. You bring us both lots of pleasure, just FYI.

But for real, dude. It's not the same. And I have news. Big news that I really want to tell you in person. I almost called you on the phone. Actually, I did call you. But you changed your fucking number. Not even an old voicemail to leave a message.

Which is so you, ya dick. You knew I'd try, didn't you?

But see, that's why you should be here. You know me better than anyone. And like I said, I have news.

Yvette is pregnant. She threw up this morning so we walked into town and bought a pregnancy test. She peed on that stick in the drugstore bathroom. I'm pretty sure the whole fucking town knows by now because Rosie, the cashier, lives to gossip. You gotta meet Rosie. And her husband, Loco. I don't know his real name, but everyone calls him Loco. They've tried to explain the story to me like seven times but the only words I understand are 'robar' and 'zapatos.' So I think someone tried to steal his shoes and he went loco? Maybe?

See, if you were here you could translate. Your Spanish was always better than mine.

Plus, you deserve all the props for that plan. Such a crazy plan. Hey, maybe you're Loco? lol You're gonna have to fight Loco One for the name, but don't worry, you'll win. He's like four feet tall and fifty years old. Plus, I got your back.

I hope you know that. I will always have your back.

So just come, OK? Or call. Or hell, send me a postcard. Just say the word and I'll come back and help you leave. I'll kill Damon myself if I have to. Just… come back to us.

I don't know why I'm writing this since we can't send it. Yvette writes you every night. Every single night. She tells you what we did and she makes up a story about your day. But tonight I wanted to write because dude… we're having a baby!

We're having a fucking baby! And you need to be here for that. You need to be here to watch Yvette get chubby and round. And hold her hair when she pukes. And go to the doctor appointments with us to hear the heartbeat.

And be there for the birth.

You have to be here for the birth, OK?

Promise me you'll be here.

OK. I guess that's it for now. We're writing all these letters in a journal so you can catch up once you do come. We haven't forgotten you. We will never forget you so please, don't forget about us.

I will always be here for you. All you gotta do is let me know you need me and I'm there. I will drop everything to come help you.

Please… let me have your back the way you had mine.

Love you, man.

For real. We love you.

AJ and Yvette

CHAPTER FORTY-ONE

YVETTE

Dear Logan,

I told you the baby was gonna be huge! I told you! Almost ten pounds! He's perfect, by the way. And he has your eyes. I just knew immediately those were your eyes because when I looked into them I saw you. I saw so much of you.

I really thought you'd be here for the birth but I understand why you couldn't come. It makes me sad. But don't worry, every time I feel sad because you're not here I just remind myself of what you gave up so AJ and I could start over.

It's just not the same without you.

OK, enough sadness. I bet you want to hear all about the baby, right?

Well, we named him Lucas because it goes good with Logan. And we already showed him a picture of you that AJ had on his phone from ages ago.

I know new babies can't smile, but I think he smiled when we showed him your picture. I think he knows you're one of his daddies. But if not, we will make sure he understands. So that when you come home he'll already know you.

His hair is dark and thick and his eyes are gray. Not blue, Logan. Gray.

He's yours, we know he's yours. We had the DNA test done by mail and just got the results today, that's why I didn't write you as soon as he was born. Sorry about that. I was tired, too. I'm sure you understand.

But don't worry. I have lots of help. AJ is fantastic. He's been getting up with me to feed. Every three hours. Crazy, right?

Oh, I've missed this so much. It made me sad for a few days after Lucas was born because I thought of Bonnie and how much I missed her and Chris. I had a little postpartum depression but I'm getting better now.

Writing you about this now feels good. I should've done it sooner. I'm sorry you had to wait to hear all the big news. It was just… hard not having you here.

I try not to think about my old life but that makes me sad too. Because you're a part of that old life. And Chris and Bonnie and my baby boy.

And I feel so guilty for living on sometimes. So fucking guilty.

Writing you used to make me so happy every time, and so hopeful, but I'm not so sure it does that anymore. AJ thinks I should stop pretending. You're not coming. He thinks I should face that fact.

But I can't give up hope. He doesn't want to either, he just worries about me. He worries that I will get depressed again and not be able to pull myself out of it. He thinks about that pill bottle. Sometimes I look at those pictures of us you left. And I relive that one day we spent with you.

One day.

How can one day feel like forever? How can I miss you so much? Love you so much? After knowing you only one day?

I don't know. I don't understand it. I just know we still feel that way about you and we still want you. And if you come here, Logan, we will bring you into our family. We promise. We will.

We will never forget you, or what you did, or that you're Lucas's real father.

You will always have a place in our hearts.

We love you.

Yvette and AJ

Dear Logan,

This is a hard letter to write but I feel like it's time. It's been three and a half years, dude. Such a short time in the grand scheme of things, I know. But it feels so long since you were with us. You feel so far away.

Yvette had our second baby. I made her stop writing you when we found out she was pregnant again, so… sorry you didn't know that until now.

Gabriella. A little girl this time. My blue eyes and Yvette's very blonde hair.

Rosie's daughter—remember Rosie? The drugstore cashier?—well, her daughter Yalesia helps us out now. So Yvette isn't overwhelmed. She's doing great actually. Didn't get depressed after giving birth and I hate to say this, but I think it's because I've kept her from you.

We still have your picture up on the wall in the kitchen and Lucas, oh, man, dude. You're really missing out. This little boy is so you. So rowdy, but sweet. So rough, but gentle. But Lucas walks by your picture every day and says, "Hi, Daddy." Except he mostly says it in Spanish.

He loves the ocean. We spend a lot of time on the beach just hanging out.

I started a little kayak business taking people on tours of the mangroves and in the summer we have a bioluminescence tour at night. Lucas loves to see the plankton glow at night. He's something, man. Really something.

And I know you're probably thinking he doesn't need you. He has me, and that's enough. But Logan, dude. We *still* need you. So please, get your shit together and come back to us.

Because I can't write these letters anymore. It hurts and I just don't think you're coming. I know you're alive because we heard through various sources that you've been sending the Nightingale people money for Yvette's son. We finally made contact with them about two years ago. Yvette needed to know everything was OK. And it was. Still is.

So we know you're alive… just… what are you doing? Why aren't you here?

Did you forget about us?

I figured you had shit to take care of. I get that, I do. You risked everything. You sacrificed your own happiness to save us. But it's time, man. It's time to save yourself.

Did you fall out of love with us? Or find someone new?

It's cool, if you did. We'd be heartbroken, but we'd be able to move on if you just told us to stop waiting.

I'm not gonna lie, I want to give up. I want to stop hoping. Because I don't think you're coming.

But I can't. I can't just forget about you. Who you are to me, what you mean to me, what you did for me.

I can't ever forget how you gave us everything and kept nothing for yourself.

So I won't.

I refuse to give up on you.

I will wait for as long as it takes. I will wait. But we're not going to write any more letters in this book.

So… goodbye, I guess. For now. Maybe forever. But I hope not. I really hope it's not forever.

I wish I could save you like you saved me. I wish you would give me that chance.

We will always love you.

AJ, Yvette, Lucas, and Gabriella

LOGAN

I am a hard man to love.

I get that. I have an awful job working for an awful man. I risk prison and death pretty much every day. And when I got back after the blizzard and showed Damon the proof that AJ and Yvette were dead, he was happy with me and my place in the org.

For a while.

But then one of his cousins betrayed him and he called on me to step in since AJ was gone.

And I killed him.

That's what I do now. Not money laundering

I have killed dozens of people over the past five and a half years since AJ and Yvette escaped to the island.

But three days ago something changed.

Damon is dead.

Not by my hand, even though I've gone to bed every night and woke up every morning wanting to kill him so I could leave and be free.

It was his little brother.

Oh, I helped, of course. I set it all up. But I made a deal with the little brother. He gets power, I get to leave.

So my apartment is empty. Sold it two weeks ago and I'm on my way to sign the closing papers now. And I have no job. Not that I need one, I have plenty of money. And I have no friends, because all of the people I call friends would kill me just as quick as I'd kill them. And no family, because that shit was over back in my teens.

I just have them.

Except… I'm not sure I do, actually.

There's a part of me that still thinks I have a chance with AJ and Yvette down on Holbox Island. But it's a very small part of me.

I know they've moved on. I've had someone watching them this whole time. Making sure no one got suspicious. Making sure Damon didn't go looking. Making sure they were safe.

So I know they have children and one of them could be mine.

I know they are happy and complete too.

I know they don't need me.

Showing up now, after all these years, would just rip their world apart. But still, I have a small glimmer of hope that it could still happen. Even after five and a half years, it could happen.

The airline app on my phone has two flights. One to New Zealand where I will start over fresh. And one to Mexico where I will interrupt their lives.

Which choice is the right one?

I don't know.

The problem is… I'm not the same man they used to know. The problem is they're not the same either.

But the real issue has to do with how this whole thing started.

One day.

Just one day.

That's all we ever had together.

And there's no possible way this is real. There is no possible way to fall in love in one day. It just can't happen.

Except it did.

Maybe I'm just imagining it because my life has been a nightmare since I left them? Or maybe I'm just crazy? Fucking delusional and I'm living this fantasy life in my head because I needed something to hold on to.

Or maybe I'm just afraid.

They only had one day too, the logical part of my brain says. They got to that island with the exact same history as I have now. They started from nothing and they made it work.

They're happy, they're in love, they've started a family.

All of that without me there to complicate things.

You will fuck it all up, Logan. Because you fuck everything up.

That's my real fear, I guess.

Not that it wasn't real, but that it was, and my part in it is over. Has been over since they got to the island.

I leave the apartment and take a car to the closing office. It takes me exactly ten minutes to sign the papers and then I'm on my way to the airport with a single carry-on bag of possessions.

When I get there I stare at the departures board. Weighing my options.

New Zealand? Or Mexico?

New Zealand feels safe. It feels far, far away. It feels like I could become someone new. Start over for real. No one would know me any other way.

Mexico feels like the past. Mexico feels like I would have to accept who I am. Embrace it. Live with it.

Mexico makes me afraid.

Will they reject me? Do they hate me? Do they secretly fear that one day I will show up and ruin everything?

Do they wake up each morning praying I stay away and go to sleep at night thanking God for answering their prayers?

My heart hurts just thinking about that.

It aches in such an overwhelming way I tab the little button on my phone app and complete the check-in.

And that's it.

My decision has been made.

When I arrive at the beach I pick them out immediately. There's not a lot of people on the sand, only about two dozen. And they have their backs to me.

But still, I would know them anywhere. I could be blind and still pick them out in a crowd.

They're sitting on a blanket, the little girl in Yvette's lap, the little boy holding a kite as he runs back and forth trying to make it fly.

AJ calls out to him in Spanish, "*Ven a comer ahora, Lucas. Entonces volaremos la cometa.*"

Come and eat, Lucas. Then we'll fly the kite.

His name is Lucas and I love him immediately because kids are like that, aren't they? Easy to love.

But fear grips me as the little boy turns to his father. His gray eyes meet mine from a dozen yards away. Lock on. He picks me out immediately.

Squinting his eyes, he marks me as a stranger. Someone who does not belong.

And I want to run. Because I know how this will end. I know I have no place here.

But I don't run. I don't want to alarm him. I turn, very slowly, and walk back the way I came.

Then his little-boy voice calls out, "*Hola, papi!*"

And I turn back.

Yvette and AJ slowly turn their heads.

And they are smiling.

END OF BOOK SHIT

Welcome to the End of Book Shit where I get to say anything I want about the book even if it makes no sense. It's a little bit like the "author's note" you see at the end of some books except I write them the day I upload, don't ever edit it, swear a lot, and give no fucks about what people think of me when I'm done.

It's kinda like drunk-Julie.

So this book has a little story behind it because back in May of 2014, during the week that BEND released (and got banned) I had planned a little trip down to Mesa Verde. If you're not from around here Mesa Verde is an archeological site in the southwest corner of Colorado where an ancient native tribe, for whatever reason, decided to build their homes into the side of these cliffs.

And I figured that hey, Mesa Verde is in Colorado… I live in Colorado… how far away could it be? And also, Hey! I should go see that shit like right now, because it's kinda cool. So this week that BEND released and got banned I ended up on this road trip down to Mesa Verde.

I was wrong, by the way. It's not close at all. Like anyone with a phone, even back in 2014, could figure that out pretty quick. But when I plugged in the hotel address it was on Main Street and who knew that like… every town in the fucking world had Main Street, right?

So the app told me it was like three hours away but it wasn't taking me to Mesa Verde, it was talking me to Main Street in Alamosa and actually said, "You have arrived at your destination," when I stopped to pee at a McDonalds.

Fucking Mesa Verde was seven hours away, you guys. SEVEN. I had no clue. I could've gotten to Mount Rushmore quicker and that shit is like two states away. (Welcome to the Rocky Mountains, people. Land of no direct access to anything).

So anyway, to get to Mesa Verde you have to go way the fuck past Alamosa and drive through the Rio Grande National Forest and go through Wolf Creek Pass. I had never been down to this part of Colorado so I had no idea that this actual highway was a total fucking death trap. However, on the other side of that goddamned mountain your reward was this amazing overlook area called "Scenic Overlook in Mineral County". Not an exciting name but it was a totally amazing view.

And normally I'm not a "scenic overlook" kinda road tripper because I'm anxious to get where I'm going, but after climbing that fucking mountain and totally thinking I was gonna go over a cliff seventeen different time and thanking my lucky stars seventy-three times that I had this stupid idea in May and not January, I needed a break.

So I pulled over and took a picture.

As did every other person who made it over that mountain alive. And here's where the relevant part comes in…

So I was standing there are the guard rail minding my own business and next to me are these three people. Two guys and a girl. And they were all laughing and taking selfies and group pictures and there were kinda hands-y with each other.

So of course, my dirty book author mind goes right to the logical conclusion that these people are in a committed threesome. I come up with this whole story about them Where they're from, where they're going, what they're gonna be doing tonight. And this was back before I wrote 321 but I was kinda plotting it in my mind. And I kept thinking, holy shit. My book ideas are totally real. I'm not crazy, this shit happens.

So I make up this whole story about this thriple, including all the dirty parts, all in the span of five minutes. And I'm totally thinking this is gonna make a good book when the second guy's wife comes over to join them and I realize they are actually family.

My book idea was shattered. Those people. If they only knew what was going on in my head.

But FIVE YEARS later Julie is writing another menage book and this whole scene pops into my head and I figure, hell. It's my imagination. I'm just gonna use that idea anyway.

So that's how we got Logan, AJ, and Yvette. A banned book that turned into a badly-planned road trip, that turned into Julie's sick imagination.

Anyway. I loved Logan. He was my favorite and I know what y'all are thinking—there should've been a bonus epilogue, but you know what? I think another epilogue would've ruined it, so I decided not to go there. And I've heard a lot of grumbling lately about authors doing bonus scenes and making readers sign up for their newsletters to get them, and I just wasn't in the mood to deal with that shit. Because this ending is an ending and the extra epilogue would've been a bonus in my mind. And I don't really see anything wrong with asking people to sign-up for your newsletter to get it, but if that's not a "thing" anymore, I'm cool with just leaving things as they are.

So that's it. Logan's kid recognized him because AJ and Yvette made sure he would, and then they smiled when they saw he finally made it "home". If you want to imagine them fighting over the kid and Logan threatening to take them to court, be my guest. But that's not how I imagine it.

The beauty of books, right? Everyone gets to have their own interpretation.

I have a lot a NEW THINGS coming up very soon. The next book will be out the last week of March (yes, March, just a few weeks away) and I haven't announced it yet or revealed a cover or a title or anything. In fact I have three books written at the moment just waiting to be released. You'll be seeing A LOT from me from March through the end of the year so I hope you're ready for some smut and a few surprises, because that's all coming up quick.

As always, THANK YOU for reading, THANK YOU for reviewing, and I'll see you in the next book.

Your servant in smut-dom forever,

Julie
AKA, JA Huss

ABOUT THE AUTHOR

JA Huss never wanted to be a writer and she still dreams of that elusive career as an astronaut. She originally went to school to become an equine veterinarian but soon figured out they keep horrible hours and decided to go to grad school instead. That Ph.D wasn't all it was cracked up to be (and she really sucked at the whole scientist thing), so she dropped out and got a M.S. in forensic toxicology just to get the whole thing over with as soon as possible.

After graduation she got a job with the state of Colorado as their one and only hog farm inspector and spent her days wandering the Eastern Plains shooting the shit with farmers.

After a few years of that, she got bored. And since she was a homeschool mom and actually does love science, she decided to write science textbooks and make online classes for other homeschool moms.

She wrote more than two hundred of those workbooks and was the number one publisher at the online homeschool store many times, but eventually she covered every science topic she could think of and ran out of shit to say.

So in 2012 she decided to write fiction instead. That year she released her first three books and started a career that would make her a New York Times bestseller and land her on the USA Today Bestseller's List eighteen times in the next three years.

Her books have sold millions of copies all over the world, the audio version of her semi-autobiographical book, Eighteen, was nominated for a Voice Arts Award and an Audie Award in 2016 and 2017 respectively, her audiobook, Mr. Perfect, was nominated for a Voice Arts Award in 2017, and her audiobook, Taking Turns, was nominated for an Audie Award in 2018.

Johnathan McClain is her first (and only) writing partner and even though they are worlds apart in just about every way imaginable, it works.

She lives on a ranch in Central Colorado with her family.

www.ingramcontent.com/pod-product-compliance
Lightning Source LLC
Chambersburg PA
CBHW070839020826
48982CB00022B/1495/J